A PENNSYLVANIA DUTCH MYSTERY
WITH RECIPES

As the World Churns

Tamar Myers

THORNDIKE
CHIVERS

This Large Print edition is published by Thorndike Press, Waterville, Maine, USA and by BBC Audiobooks Ltd, Bath, England.

Thorndike Press, a part of Gale, Cengage Learning.

Copyright © Tamar Myers, 2008

The moral right of the author has been asserted.

The text of this Large Print edition is unabridged.

Other aspects of the book may vary from the original edition.

Set in 16 pt. Plantin.

Printed on permanent paper.

LIBRARY OF CONGRESS CATALOGING-IN-PUBLICATION DATA

Myers, Tamar.
  As the world churns : a Pennsylvania Dutch mystery with recipes / by Tamar Myers.
    p. cm. — (Thorndike Press large print mystery)
    ISBN-13: 978-1-4104-0634-7 (hardcover : alk. paper)
    ISBN-10: 1-4104-0634-2 (hardcover : alk. paper)
    1. Yoder, Magdalena (Fictitious character) — Fiction.
2. Pennsylvania Dutch Country (Pa.) — Fiction. 3. Large type books. I. Title.
  PS3563.Y475A9 2008b
  813'.54—dc22   2008002173

BRITISH LIBRARY CATALOGUING-IN-PUBLICATION DATA AVAILABLE

Published in 2008 in the U.S. by arrangement with NAL Signet, a member of Penguin Group (USA) Inc.

Published in 2008 in the U.K. by arrangement with the author.

U.K. Hardcover: 978 1 405 64560 7 (Chivers Large Print)
U.K. Softcover: 978 1 405 64561 4 (Camden Large Print)

Printed in the United States of America
1 2 3 4 5 6 7 12 11 10 09 08

For Anne Bohner

ACKNOWLEDGMENTS

I would like to thank Shelagh Caudle, editor at www.ice-cream-recipes.com, for permission to use the scrumptious ice cream recipes. I would also like to thank my husband, Jeffrey, for all his encouragement and support; my dear friend Gwen Hunter for her friendship and inspiration; and, of course, my four-legged staff of three.

1

Not all men are created equal. I learned this fact while honeymooning with my second husband, the Babester, but I will leave the particulars to your imagination. Suffice it to say, whilst showering that evening, I threw back my head and burst into joyous song. Of course, I took care not to swallow too much water and drown like a turkey in a rainstorm.

"Oh, sweet mystery of life," I trilled, *"at last I've found you!"*

"Hon, are you all right?"

"Right as rain! Never been better. Tut-tut, cheerio, and all that sort of rot."

Gabe stuck his head into the tiny bathroom. Fortunately, the shower curtain was opaque.

"I thought maybe you'd hurt yourself."

"No sirree, Bob. I am as fine as frog's hair."

"Boy, you sound happy."

"Never happier. In fact, I was just thinking —"

"Just a second, hon, the phone's ringing."

"Let it ring. Ta-ling-a-ling-ling."

"But it might be Ma."

As my sweet baboo ran off to answer that
stupid machine, my rare good mood dis-
sipated like steam from a mirror. We'd been
married for less than six hours and this was
the second time my mother-in-law had
called. Our wedding was supposed to have
cut the apron strings that tied son to
mother, but what good did that do when
the two of them were joined at the hip? It
was going to take a team of orthopedic
surgeons to separate this pair.

"Tell your mother to take a long walk off
a short pier, dear." It's all in the delivery,
you see? Had my tone been any lighter, I
might well have bumped my head on the
ceiling, thereby adding to the dent that was
already there. On the ceiling that is, not my
head.

My dearly beloved must not have heard
me. The walls of our Motel One (it charges
by the hour) were sufficiently thin for me to
hear his voice, but too thick to allow me to
hear what was being said. Since he sounded
agitated, I knew I'd been right: it was his
mother. There are only two people in this

world who can rattle my sweetykins: myself, and the woman who bore him.

I tried to dry off with the only towel, which was as thin as a facial tissue and not much larger. Finally I scooped up the bath mat, picked off a few hairs, and used that instead. After donning sensible Christian pajamas — flannel, and a good deal thicker than the towel — I slipped into my heavy terry robe and prepared to face the music.

"Okay, dear, let her rip."

Gabe was off the phone by then and sitting on the bed, his back to the bathroom. His head was bowed, his face cupped in his hands. It was a typical post–Ida Rosen pose. Try saying that correctly three times in rapid succession. But beware: the prize for getting it right is a weeklong visit from the old badger herself.

I know, Jesus commanded us to love our enemies. But with all due respect, the Lord didn't have a mother-in-law. Also in my defense, I'd like to add that I don't hate Ida Rosen as much as she hates me. In fact, she *despises* me. Not only did I take her son away from her, but I refuse to lie down and let her run over me. Literally — with her car.

My handsome groom turned slowly. "Hon, I'm afraid I have some bad news."

"But you promised," I wailed. There are those who claim that only sirens are capable of wailing, but those folks have yet to meet me. "You said that we could have the first three days of our honeymoon all to ourselves. You said —"

"Babe, I'm sorry."

I eschew cussing, but sometimes a gal has to do what a gal has to do. "Ding, dang, dong, blast it all! If you think I'm going to share our room with —"

"The call wasn't from Ma; it was the warden from the state penitentiary."

"Excuse me?"

"Sit down first."

I waved a hand dismissively. "No, no, go on. Why would the warden be calling us? How did he even know we were here?"

"You left a contact number with Chief Ackerman, remember?"

"Yes, but it was for emergencies only." Our little town has only one police officer — a young and inexperienced one at that. Since I am the mayor, we are frequently in touch.

"This is an emergency. *Please*, sit down."

"No!"

He stood. "The warden said that Melvin is — uh — ah —"

"Spit it out, dang it!"

"Melvin is missing."

"Missing how? You mean like playing hide-and-seek?"

"They don't know. No one has seen him since lockdown last night."

"*What?* That's almost twenty-four hours ago."

"The warden said he didn't want to get us worried, and then have Melvin show up in the bottom of a laundry bag like last time."

"He works in the laundry room, for crying out loud. He knows they check the outgoing bags."

"Yes, but this is the same man who once tried to milk a bull. Am I right?"

I felt my chest imploding for want of oxygen. "Does this mean what I think it might?"

Gabe nodded somberly. "That son-of-a-twitch has escaped."

The room swayed, then spun, and soon my poor brain couldn't keep up with all the motion. I have a vague recollection of Gabriel lunging for me. Then all went black.

My full name is Magdalena Portulaca Yoder. And no, I did not take Rosen as my new surname. Neither did I wish to add it with a hyphen. Why should I? Plain old Yoder has been good enough for my family for hundreds of years. Besides, if Gabe truly desired a linguistic connection, he was quite free to adopt the name Yoder — which he didn't.

At any rate, I am a simple Mennonite woman, whose ancestors were originally Amish settlers from Switzerland. The older of two children, I was born and raised in Hernia, Pennsylvania, where I still reside. My sister and I are co-owners of the PennDutch Inn, a full-board establishment that caters to well-heeled folks who want to be culturally enriched merely by soaking in the ambience. We are delighted to comply.

My waiting list is two years long, but when it's their turn, my lucky guests find that they have the privilege of signing up for ALPO, which stands for Amish Lifestyle Plan Option. In short, they can pay extra for the joy of cleaning their own rooms and helping with chores. Lately I've added Ultra-ALPO, which means they can shell out even more in order to have the full Amish experience of having their climate-control units turned off at the front desk. After all, the Amish don't use electricity, so AC is unheard of, and a proper Amish home is heated only by a stove located on the ground floor level, whereas my guest rooms are all upstairs.

I run my business with the considerable

help of my cook, Freni Hostetler, and *despite* the whining of my pseudo-stepdaughter, Alison Miller. This brings me to my sister, whom I love with all my heart. That said, Susannah is a free spirit whose work ethic is limited to putting on makeup and rearranging her CD collection. She is absolutely no help around the inn, even though she is half owner.

My baby sister might have turned out quite differently, had not our parents been squished to death between a milk tanker and a truck loaded with state-of-the-art running shoes. Yes, she was already an adult by then, but a fragile one. Sadly, Susannah coped with her loss by becoming a world-class slut, sleeping her way from Pennsylvania to Alaska and back again.

Then one day, inexplicably, Susannah fell head over heels in love with Hernia's Chief of Police, Melvin Stoltzfus. He professed to love her in return. Everyone in town was shocked, most of all me. I hadn't thought that Melvin possessed a brain, much less a heart. I know that sounds uncharitable, but only to those who have never actually met the mantis — I mean, man.

I could go on and on about Melvin's glaring faults, but in any event, I would finally have to admit that for a while he was actually good for Susannah. She settled down. True, she continued to wear her outlandish sari-like outfits — fifteen feet of filmy fuchsia fabric was her favorite — and carry her pooch, Shnookums, around in her bra. But she was *happy*. Ultimately, isn't that what we all want?

Then a year ago, Melvin, who was supposed to be our law enforcer, was convicted of murder in the first degree. Not only that, but his victim was our minister. Faced with both undeniable evidence and a confession of his guilt, Susannah fell into a deep funk, one from which she has only just begun to recover. Today, at my wedding, was the first time she'd worn anything but black since the verdict was read (although her dark gray bridesmaid dress left something to be desired).

To learn that Melvin was on the loose would be like picking a giant scab off her heart. What's more, it was bound to be utterly terrifying. I certainly was scared out of my wit (I'm down to my last). What was to stop him from returning to Hernia and killing me, the person who'd apprehended him? The answer is "nothing." Evil, such as lives in Melvin's miniscule heart, is as unstoppable as Congressional pork.

Was it any wonder then that I fainted?

16

2

"What happened?" I asked for the billionth time.

"You fainted, hon. When I told you that the warden called and said Melvin was missing, you just collapsed."

I gazed up into my Pooky Bear's big brown eyes. Or were they blue? He appeared to have two heads.

"I can't believe they let him escape. It's just so unreal."

"Here, babe, let me help you sit up."

"Mebbe she vants to stay on the floor." It was a woman's voice. A most unwelcome woman.

My blood ran cold. "No!"

"You see? She doesn't vant to sit."

I struggled, first to a sitting position, and then finally to my feet. Yes, I swayed a bit, but, like the Empire State Building, I am vertically enhanced. I read somewhere that it sways from side to side as much as several feet in high winds. I generally sway a bit less.

"Ida," I gasped through clenched teeth — not an easy feat, mind you. "What are you doing here?"

"Ma just got here, hon. She was kind enough to bring me my pajamas. I was sure I'd packed them —"

"Indeed you had, dear, but I *un*packed them."

"Oy! Married yust a few hours, and already dis von's a slut."

"Ma! Please, stay out of this."

"Yes," I agreed sweetly, "stay out of this. *Far* out of this. I hear they're having a sale on condos in Fiji. If you hurry, you can catch the slow boat to China out of New York tomorrow morning, and make connections from there."

"Gabeleh, you see how she talks to me?"

"Ma, you deserved it." He turned to me, flashing pearly whites that were the envy of dentists from Boston to San Diego. "You really unpacked my pajamas? You little minx, you."

I could feel myself blush. It started in my toes and worked itself up to the roots of my bun. At five ten, I haven't been called "little" since the third grade, and I'd never been referred to as a minx. How sinfully,

18

deliciously erotic. If it wasn't for Ida, I'd have thrown my stud muffins on the bed and shown him what puts the yo-yo in Yoder — if you know what I mean. Alas, I had to settle for giving him what I'd hope was a suggestive wink.

"Hon," he said, "is there something wrong with your eye?"

Before answering, I glared at his mother for good measure. "No, my eye is fine. Gabe, we've got to get back to Hernia immediately. Susannah, Freni, Alison — they could all be in danger. I need to call Chief Ackerman, then the county sheriff —"

"I don't think he'd hurt them: it's you he's probably after."

Ida tugged on her son's arm. Apparently she'd yet to be filled in on the prison break.

"Who vants to hurt her?" She sounded hopeful.

"Melvin Stoltzfus. Our former chief of police."

"My sister's husband," I added.

"You see, Gabeleh, vhat happens vhen you marry a shiksa? I told you it vas a terrible idea. Marry that cute little Schwartz girl, I always said. Mit hips like dat, she could give me lots of grandchildren. But no, you gotta marry dis —"

"Ma, butt out. Please."

"*Vhat?*"

"You heard me, Ma. And you're right: Magdalena is my wife. I won't have you talking about her like that."

Ida Rosen looked as if her only son had slapped her across the face. "*Nu,* so now you talk back to your mother?"

"I'm sorry, Ma, but you have to respect the woman I chose to marry."

"Respect, shmect. If dis von" — she pointed at me with her chin — "and me vere drowning, who vould you jump in to save?"

"I'd save you both. I'm a good swimmer, thanks to all those summers I spent at Camp Minimitzvah."

"Ya, but if you had to choose?"

"Then I guess I'd save Magdalena."

"For this I come to live in Hemorrhoid?" Ida Rosen stabbed repeatedly at her enormous bosom with a make-believe knife. "Oy, the pain. The pain."

"It's Hernia," I said, and grabbing her by equally ample shoulders, steered her over to the bed. "And if you insist on dying now, dear" — I gave her a gentle push — "then do it here. You'll be much more comfy."

She allowed herself to topple back onto the mattress, which was surprisingly soft, and proceeded to moan about her multiple injuries, both to body and soul. Gabe, who wasn't at all fooled, turned his full attention to me.

"What do you want to do first, hon?"

"Besides get your mother on that slow boat bound for Fiji?"

He nodded.

"I'll call Susannah and break the news to her. I'm also going to tell her to get over to the PennDutch pronto. Meanwhile you call Freni at the inn. Tell her to make sure Alison's inside, and then lock the door. Then someone needs to call Doc Shafor — Oh shoot! What about Barbara and the triplets?"

My new husband pulled me to his chest and held me tightly, seemingly oblivious to his sputtering mother on the bed. I'm only human, ergo I should not be judged too harshly if I gently maneuvered him so that Ida could see my smile. But just to be clear, we weren't dancing.

"Don't you worry about a thing, Magdalena. They'll locate Melvin any minute, and I bet dollars to doughnuts that they find him *inside* that maximum-security prison. And even if he did manage to make it outside, I won't let him hurt you."

I wiggled my way to freedom. "Me? I'm not worried about myself, dear; I'm worried about you."

■ ■ ■ ■

But two weeks had passed, and the menacing, murderous mantis had neither been seen nor heard from. It would have all seemed like a bad dream, were it not for the fact that PennDutch was filled with relatives. There was Freni and her husband, Mose, who are both some sort of cousin to me — in fact, in so many ways, it is possible that they qualify as my siblings. Then there was their son, Jonathan, and his wife, Barbara (although from Iowa, she's distantly related to all of us), plus their triplets. And of course there was Susannah, who is my sister, but given our family's convoluted relationships, probably a cousin as well. Last, and arguably least (in terms of blood shared), there was Doc Shafor, an octogenarian with the libido of a bonobo on steroids.

Oops, I forgot about Alison. She's only a pseudo-stepdaughter, but she has Miller blood trickling through her persnickety teenage veins. This means she too is my cousin, possibly even my aunt — but most probably not my mother. At any rate, such is to be expected in a community as inbred as ours.

As a matter of fact, prick anyone in Hernia whose family has local roots going back two generations, and you'll be bled on by one of my kinfolk. I advise you not to do it. But do try living with this bunch underfoot, whilst maintaining the cheerful Christian visage for which I am so well-known. It is not humanly possible.

Now throw into this chaotic mixture the smell of fear, the needs of newlyweds, and the mother-in-law from Gehenna, and what do you get? A Magdalena Yoder who wakes up screaming at the top of her lungs.

"Hon! Wake up, you're having a nightmare."

"What? What? Who's there?"

"Apparently Melvin. You've been thrashing about shouting his name."

"Oh yeah. I dreamt I had him in a headlock, but his head came off, and the inside was filled with cheese. Limburger cheese."

"Do peace-loving Mennonites often use the headlock maneuver?"

"Well — we can't be responsible for our dreams, can we?"

"Keep answering a question with a question, and you'll automatically turn Jewish. That's a proven fact."

"Says who?"

Like Solomon wooing Bathsheba, my

beloved began planting kisses on . . .

"Oh my stars!"

"Already?"

I threw off the covers. "The first Annual Hernia Holstein Competition begins next week. The first guests will be arriving today and I'm nowhere near ready." I hopped out of bed, threw on my robe, and paced the room in circles like a chicken in a crate. The bird noises I made were instinctual, but not intentional.

"Babe, calm down. You're practically hyperventilating."

"Buck, buck, buck, brack. Buck, buck, buck, brack. Buck, buck —"

"That's what I thought you said."

"— and what am I going to do about my rooms that have been taken over by family?"

"How about we put them up in my house?"

"But they're paying through their noses to stay at the infamous PennDutch. These folks have had reservations for over a year."

"No, I mean that we put the relatives up at my house, so that the guests can stay here."

"You mean that?" It was, of course, the perfect solution. Gabe still owned the house just across the road. It was empty now, because Ida hadn't wanted to be alone with a convicted murderer on the prowl, but if the whole shebang moved over there with her, she wouldn't be alone anymore, would she?

"Of course I mean it. And don't worry, I'll take good care of them, so you'll be free to look after your guests here."

Why is it that we women can read between the lines, whereas most men can't even tell when the lines have been crossed? I could see Ida's handwriting all over this page.

"You're going to be staying at your house, aren't you?"

"It's only temporary."

"So is appendicitis."

"Take it easy, hon. There's no need to get all worked up about this. I'm less than two minutes away. For all intents and purposes, it's just like being here."

"Hmm. You've got a point. Why didn't I think of that? I'll move over there too. It'll give the guests more freedom that way."

"Yes, but — I mean, there isn't enough room."

"Sure, there is. I'll be sleeping with you, silly. I know, it's hard to get used to the fact that we're married. Now we can do anything we want — except have sex standing up."

"Because it might lead to dancing?"

"Bingo. The worst of sins. Dancing, that is. Although bingo is a sin, too, if it's for money, because then it becomes a form of gambling —"

"There won't be room because Ma will be bunking with me."

I jiggled pinkies in both ears to make sure they were working properly. "*What* did you say?"

"We have to double up, hon, or there won't be space for everyone."

Is it truly just as bad to think nasty thoughts as to say them? And if that is the case, wouldn't it be healthier to say the bad thoughts aloud, thereby venting steam and lowering one's blood pressure? And since it seems unlikely that a person would be punished twice for essentially the same sin, I must conclude that giving voice to one's nasty thoughts — an action with clear health benefits — is less of a sin, and bears fewer consequences, than keeping them bottled up. That said, I chose the lesser of two evils.

"Will hedge shears be sufficient, or do you need to see a surgeon?"

"Pardon me?"

"To cut the apron strings, dear."

"I don't need this," my beloved said, and strode away.

3

The first annual Hernia Holstein Competition was Doc Shafor's idea. He'd been a veterinarian and knew something about cows, and he'd lived long enough — Doc claims to have played with Johnny Appleseed as a child — to see that our dear little town was on the verge of losing its identity.

We'd always been a farming community but, more and more it seemed, we were becoming a bedroom satellite of Bedford, just twelve miles away. Young couples were discovering that it was cheaper to buy a house in Hernia than in Bedford. Also, our school system is small and the teachers are excellent. Crime in Hernia is negligible — just as long as one doesn't count murder. (We have more than our fair share of that, but the victims are invariably adults, so it is still safe for children to play in our streets.)

At any rate, if we Hernians wished to preserve our heritage, it was incumbent on us to refocus on agriculture and animal husbandry. Doc had been to other dairy cow competitions, and seen what a boost they were to both the morale and the economy of the host community. He suggested that we concentrate on Holsteins, since that particular breed appears to do better in our microclimate than it does in just about any other. In fact, were it not for the fact that the majority of us are humble people of Mennonite and/or Amish descent, there would be a lot of bovine bragging going on in these parts.

Frankly, I thought a cow competition was a little "lame," as Alison might say, but I didn't want to hurt Doc's feelings, so I played along. Boy, was I ever surprised by the response we received with regard to our ad in *Milk Monthly,* in which we depicted "Hernia as the Holstein capital of the world" and the competition as "*the* most coveted event of the century." Calls came in from as far away as Japan. Even if we built a tent city on one of the local farms, and utilized every motel room in Bedford, our infrastructure would still not be able to handle the number of would-be participants, let alone the spectators.

The only way to deal with this problem, we quickly decided, was to set an exorbitant entrance fee for each cow, as well as charge the public an arm and a leg to watch the proceedings. We also set a cut-off date for registration that eliminated all but the wealthiest and most on-the-ball *Milk Monthly* subscribers.

Although I jacked up my room prices to even more obscene levels, they were invariably booked immediately. In defense of my greed, it must be said that I tithe my income, *and* that for the duration of the competition, my room charge included a stabling fee for cows. The latter was not something most motels in Bedford were able to offer.

Freni's husband, Mose, and son, Jonathan, built five partitions in my pasture and five in my barn. Four of these were for guests' use, and one was for my two cows, Matilda Two and Prairie Queen. Both these gals — my cows, not my guests — were Holsteins as well as very productive milkers. Matilda Two was exceptionally well equipped, with teats as long and smooth as uncooked wieners, and an enormous udder — one that was wrinkle-free where it attached to her barrel and virtually void of unsightly veins. Had I not been one of the event's organizers, I would have undoubtedly paid a king's ransom to enter her in the contest.

The guests were scheduled to arrive as much as a week in advance, in order to allow the cows sufficient time to recuperate from the stress of travel. Not surprisingly, the guest who had the farthest to drive was the first to show up. I could tell by the license plate that he was from North Dakota, which meant he had to be Mr. Dorfman.

I'd been feeling lightheaded a lot the past week, so I was not totally surprised to see *two* Mr. Dorfmans exit the truck cab, one from either side. Of course I knew that double vision should not be taken lightly, and I fully intended to hie myself off to a doctor as soon as the competition was over and I'd taken care of my personal problem — i.e., gotten her accepted as a team member on a yearlong expedition to Antarctica. In the meantime, I had a business to run.

"Welcome to the PennDutch Inn," I called out, ever the mistress of false gaiety.

"Howdy. I'm Harry Dorfman." A beefy man with very little neck and flyaway eyebrows proffered a paw as coarse as an artichoke.

"And I'm Harmon," said another beefy man with very little neck and flyaway eyebrows, but whose hand felt like a pineapple.

My sigh of relief ruffled both sets of eyebrows. "Your reservation just said 'the Dorfmans.' I was expecting a married couple, not identical twins. Or is one of you a clone?"

Harry laughed. "Yeah, we're about as identical as twins can get. Even our wives can't tell us apart."

"Except for one thing," Harmon said. "On that score we ain't identical."

"Excuse me?"

"Harry has him a birthmark in the shape of Uzbekistan on his left thigh, and I ain't married."

At least that is what I thought he said. However, my ears were ringing, the world seemed to be closing in on me, and I felt like throwing up. Harmon Dorfman might have said anything.

"Are you all right, ma'am?"

"What?"

"You look like you're about to pass out," one of the twins said. I could barely see their faces, much less focus on their lips, so identifying the identical speaker was impossible.

"You better sit down, ma'am," the other said.

"Don't be silly, dears. I'm fine as frog —"

I teetered. I tottered. I did everything but topple. Sure enough, a minute or two later I was feeling fine again, just not as fine as amphibian hair. I attempted a smile. "You see?"

"Miss Yoder," Harry said, "I'm going to call your doctor."

"You most certainly are not."

"But you're obviously not well."

"Well, shmell —" Another truck towing a trailer was about to pull into my drive. "I'll be fine. I promise. Right now I suggest that one of you run ahead and reserve the stall of your choice, and the paddock that you like best. I'm assigning them on a first-come-first-served basis."

The nature of competition being what it is, both men made a beeline for the barn.

I was feeling much better by the time the next couple finally presented themselves for introduction. The Pearlmutters had obviously been having some sort of disagreement, and had remained in the cab of their truck while attempting to wrap things up. Eventually, reconciliation gave way to embarrassment, but when I shook hands with them I could smell the lingering scent of anger.

The Pearlmutters drove an expensive new

truck and their livestock trailer was top-of-the-line. Jane Pearlmutter, however, was dressed in clothes that would have been rejected by every Goodwill store in the nation — excepting one in eastern Alabama. Her stringy, dishwater blond hair was pulled back from her face and held in place by a pair of brown plastic barrettes. Her blotchy pink skin was devoid of foundation, her pale blue eyes unadorned by mascara, and her thin lips the color of boiled liver. I live amongst plain people, and am plain myself, but one has to really work to look this bad. Based on these rather generous observations, I deduced that either she was exceptionally devout and had taken vows of both poverty and homeliness, or else was so wealthy that she could afford to have no pretensions whatsoever. Then I remembered that her tall, dark, and handsome husband, Dick, was a retired stockbroker, which answered that question for me.

"Welcome to the PennDutch," I said warily.

"I'm Dick," he said. "And this is my wife, Jane. We're here for the first annual Hernia Holstein Competition. Is this the right place?"

"Indeed it is. I'm Magdalena Portulaca Yoder, your hostess with the mostess, except that today it's closer to leastess due to unforeseen circumstances. But one thing I am *not,* is listless, so not to worry, you will have the bestest stay this side of the Poconos."

"Are you sure?" Jane asked.

"Forsooth, I tell the truth. Of course, I can't give you a written guarantee that you'll enjoy your stay, but for only one hundred dollars more a day —"

"No. What I mean is, are you sure that you're Magdalena Yoder?"

"Pretty sure. Although Papa used to joke that I was a petunia he found in the onion patch. But of course if that was true, then my parents would have named me Magdalena *Petunia* Yoder, and not Portulaca."

"Honey," Jane whispered, "the brochure said she was Mennonite. This woman is anything but."

Dick Pearlmutter, who was dressed in expensive togs and had neatly combed hair, gave me the quick once-over. "Well, she is awfully pretty."

"Not only that, but she's not dressed like that woman on the brochure."

Just a year ago I would have taken offense at the word *pretty,* believing that it had been uttered with utmost sarcasm. Then one day I ran into an old classmate of mine who'd become a plastic surgeon. To make a long story slightly shorter, I learned that for nearly half a century I'd been suffering from body dysmorphic syndrome. The ugly duckling I'd thought I was, had long since turned into a gorgeous swan — minus the feathers, of course. And the beak. And at least one of the webbed feet.

I cocked my head, which really does reside at the end of a long, graceful neck. "The woman in the brochure is Amish. She's my cook, Freni. And indeed, dears, I am a Mennonite, born and bred. Well, not bred like a dairy cow — I certainly haven't produced any calves — but you know what I mean."

Plain Jane had the chutzpah to circle me, like I was a statue in Madame Tussaud's Wax Museum. "Where's your costume?" she demanded.

"My *costume?* Halloween is still many months away. But if by costume you mean clothing that identifies me as a Mennonite, take another gander. Observe that my broadcloth dress extends below my knees and that it has sleeves which are long enough to hide unsightly underarm flab — not that I have any, mind you. A quick glance should confirm that my bosom — as fair as any fawn King Solomon ever laid eyes on — is appropriately covered. Then gaze longingly at my lovely size eleven feet, and see that they are sensibly shod in sturdy black brogans, which were machine-made from second-rate leather somewhere on the subcontinent. Now lift up your heads, O ye gates — I mean, O ye Pearlmutters — and appreciate the work that went into my two braids, which wrap around the back of my head like a pair of coiled garter snakes, although perhaps my white organza prayer cap obscures them somewhat. That said, I must impress on you that only a *small* number of Mennonites still dress the way I do. The vast majority dress like everyone else. Capiche?"

By the end of my delightful monologue, Jane Pearlmutter was shaking in her flip-flops, and had practically climbed into her husband's arms. "That woman is crazy!"

"Aren't we all, dear?"

"Dick, I want to go home."

"You do realize that you've paid in full, and that none of it is refundable — don't you?"

"I don't care!"

"And of course you would be forfeiting the competition for best Holstein, seeing as how it will be impossible to find alternative lodging for you and your cows."

"Sweetie," Dick said, his arm protectively

around his wife's shoulders, "we did read somewhere that this is poised to be the number-one event of its kind in the world."

Plain Jane wrenched herself free. "We read that in her stupid brochure!"

I gestured towards the Dorfman brothers' cattle carrier. "Before you go, take a peek in there. You're never going to see Holsteins as fine as those two."

"You wanna bet?"

"With entries like this, the Hernia Holstein Competition is destined for world-class status."

Dick gently edged his wife aside and stood facing me, nose to nose. "We have two entries as well. Both of them are from the finest bloodlines available, and conform perfectly to the standard. Miss Yoder, we're not going anywhere. Now where do we pasture our cows?"

I quickly turned my head so that my smug smile — admittedly a sin — wouldn't be seen. It was going to be a fine competition.

4

As Mama used to say, "There is no rest for the wicked." No sooner had I gotten both couples settled in, and their cows pastured, than a third truck pulled down my long gravel lane. This vehicle, however, had seen better days, as had the cattle carrier. However, the couple that emerged was quite attractive in an offbeat way.

Vance Brown — he immediately introduced himself — was approaching middle age, and short in stature, but he still had a full head of dark hair and a neatly trimmed beard and mustache. His wife, Candy Brown, was a willowy strawberry blonde whose delicate features were all but hidden by a galaxy of freckles. They both seemed as friendly as dogs at suppertime, and I looked forward to getting to know them better.

On their registration form, I had Vance down as a dairy farmer, but agreeable as she was, I just couldn't see Candy mucking out a barn or scrubbing milk vats. Since subtle interrogation appears to be one of my few God-given talents, I decided to give it a try.

"What's your shtick, Candy?"

"Pardon me?"

You see? Ida's bad habits were rubbing off on me. Where was the soft-spoken Mennonite lass from yesteryear? I tried again.

"Are you employed outside the home, dear?"

"Not anymore. We have three children, and one in the oven. Getting away for competition is a real treat for me."

I gave her a second, more careful look. Her tummy was as flat as a thin-crust pizza. If she gave birth any time soon, it would have to be to a paper doll — unless she literally meant that she had one in an oven somewhere.

"You don't say."

"Candy keeps herself in great shape," Vance said, his voice filled with pride. "Tell her what you used to do, sweetie."

Candy's deep blush appeared to connect her freckles. "I'd rather not."

"Aw, come on, sweet cakes."

"Nah."

"Oh, come on, cinnamon roll," I said. If you're going to use pastries as forms of endearment, you may as well be specific.

"All right, if you insist."

"Which I do. But just so you know, that was one of those giant cinnamon rolls with cream cheese icing on top. You know, the kind you find at airports."

Candy took a deep breath and looked away. "I was a pole-dancer."

I prayed for a gentle tongue. "You do know, don't you, that dancing is a sin? But as regards your nationality, you ought not to be embarrassed; I've known many fine Poles in my life. And a few good Lithuanians as well."

Vance suppressed a laugh, which annoyed me to no end.

"Well, I have," I snapped. "Shame on you, Mr. Brown. Your children are half Polish, so if you look down on this lovely woman —"

"Not that kind of pole!"

I clapped my hands to my face in dismay. "Oh no. Don't tell me that now there's a dance hall in Antarctica."

"Miss Yoder, you're a hoot."

"And a holler. But this isn't at all funny; sin never is. Because the Bible tells us to carry salvation to the ends of the earth, I've often wondered about sin down there. I mean, I sort of knew there had to be sin going on in Antarctica, given all the scientists working in such close quarters, but I was curious as to which kind. What would there be to steal, and how could you conceal it? Murder would be stupid, because there is nowhere to run to hide. And you couldn't very well covet your neighbor's ass down there, could you?"

The Browns looked a mite confused which, sadly, is par for the course with folks lacking a proper spiritual upbringing. I would have plunged on with my analysis of antipodean iniquity, had not a fourth truck and trailer turned into the drive.

The last guest to arrive was a Mrs. Gertrude Fuselburger, an elderly widow from western Maryland. She couldn't have been a day under eighty, and might even have played with God as a child. I have a special place in my heart for old people (perhaps because I plan to be one myself someday), but extremely old people make me nervous. After all, my tiny elevator is not entirely reliable, and the only other way to reach my guest rooms is to climb an impossibly steep stairs. It was just about all Mrs. Fuselburger could do to get down from her truck.

Fortunately, she was accompanied by two male employees, both of whom appeared to be of Latin American descent. They carried her bags into my tiny lobby, and then set about unloading her Holstein, all without saying a word. I had not been introduced to the men, both of whom managed to avoid eye contact, so you can imagine my confusion.

"Where will your employees be staying, dear?"

"I don't believe that's your concern."

"I'm just curious, dear," I assured her. "It's not that I think they're here illegally, because I don't — well, maybe I do, but as proprietress of this fine, upstanding establishment, I merely want to ascertain whether or not you plan to have them stay in your room with you."

"They most certainly will *not* be staying with me."

"But you see, dear, there are no other rooms available, anywhere in the county."

"Miss Yoder, I must insist that you mind your own business."

"Well, I never! Actually, I have, but I didn't like it much. After all, minding our own business is an unnatural act, right up there with dying one's hair black after the age of sixty." Oops. That last remark just slipped out, like a bean-salad serenade at a family picnic.

"*What* did you say?"

"I said, if the Good Lord had wanted us to mind our own business, he wouldn't have instructed us to be our brother's keeper — or innkeeper, for that matter."

"You were commenting on my hair."

"I was?" In truth, I was. I have never understood the desire of some women to hang on to the hair color of their youth, when their faces have long since moved south to join the rest of their bodies. In my humble — and not yet gray — opinion, dyed hair only accentuates wrinkles.

"Are you stupid, as well as rude?"

Now that hiked my hackles. During all those years when I'd believed myself to be as ugly as a stump full of spiders, I'd comforted myself with the fact that I have an IQ well into the triple digits. How dare she ask if I was stupid? As my hackles hiked even further, I could feel my self-esteem plummet to the floor.

"Miss Yoder, are you just going to stand there like a post, or are you going to show me to my room?"

I brushed off my bruised ego before taking the high road. "Let's take the impossibly steep stairs, dear. But not to worry. Only one person has ever fallen to her death on it, and she was pushed."

"What's wrong with your elevator?"

43

"It stopped working about six months ago, about the time that Japanese couple went missing. Funny, shortly after it stopped running, it started making these strange noises. After a week or so the noises stopped, but then there was this terrible odor — well, I've been meaning to have it fumigated, but just haven't gotten around to it. You know how busy we innkeepers are."

"The stairs will have to do."

"I'm putting you in room four. It has a *single* bed. Occupancy is *one.* You'll be pleased to know that it has a view of both Stucky Ridge and Buffalo Mountain. Although to see the former, you will have to sit on your window ledge and lean out to the left. Of course you may want to tie yourself in first. Just don't use the rope that's wrapped around the leg of the bed. Last time it didn't hold."

"Miss Yoder, either you are stark raving mad, or the most delightful person I've had the pleasure of meeting in the past half century."

"I'm nuts, dear. Nertz to Mertz. I guarantee you that after spending a week with me, you'll run screaming from the inn."

"You're delightful, just delightful. You may call me Gertie, if you wish."

"Must I?"

"We're going to be best friends, Magdalena, just you wait and see."

Seeing as how he is a dear friend of mine, Doc Shafor was never on Melvin Stoltzfus's short list of friends. When asked if he would like to stay with Gabriel and company across the road, instead of in his somewhat isolated house on the other side of town, the kind old gent immediately agreed. I had no doubt, however, that perusing me had something to do with his decision.

Doc and Ida Rosen used to have a "thing." In fact they almost married. Although they are no longer a couple — they claim to hate each other — they are still quite involved, if you get my drift. I think the young people these days call it "benefits without friends."

At any rate, Doc, who was my papa's best friend, has had at least one of his bloodshot eyes on me since the day I became legal in the eyes of the law. To be fair, this interest in me began a respectful length of time *after* the death of his beloved wife, Belinda. By then, Doc had learned to cook, and his attempts to woo me have always involved food.

Although I can usually boil water without burning it — I once prepared a delicious meal of fried ice — I have little interest in

45

cooking. For Doc, on the other hand, the preparation of calorie-laden meals has become a passion. Even when he's expecting to eat alone, he prepares a feast. I used to wonder about all that waste, but then one day, to my shame, I learned that Doc delivers his bountiful leftovers to the homeless shelter over in Bedford.

Now where was I going with all this? Oh yes. I had just gotten word that my fifth party of guests was canceling — apparently their Holstein was having a nervous breakdown from travel stress — when I saw Doc exit the Rosen house and head my way. I decided to meet him at the end of my long drive. After my encounter with Miss Fuselburger, I needed a breath of fresh air.

Doc always kisses me on both cheeks and then aims for my lips. I always evade him by snapping my head to one side, thereby making him kiss my ear. Lately he's come to enjoy this, so this time I dropped my head and made him kiss the crown.

"Mmm. Your hair smells like Midnight Pleasure."

"But I showered since then!"

"It's the same perfume my Belinda used."

"Oh." There was no point in informing him that I don't use fragrances of any kind. "Say, Doc, what brings you to this side of

46

Hertzler Road?"

"I came to see the cows — if that's all right."

"Of course. After all, the competition was your idea."

"Yeah, sorry I couldn't have been one of the official veterinarians like you asked. But at my age — well, the younger ones need the opportunity to shine."

When he's not pursuing me, Doc is a wonderful friend. Except for the crunching of gravel beneath our feet, we walked in companionable silence up the lane, and then left to the barn. About thirty yards from the barn, we both stopped suddenly and sniffed the air.

"Now *that's* perfume," we said simultaneously.

"Jinx, you owe me a Coke," I said, when we were through laughing.

"What?"

"It's something I picked up from Susannah. When two people say the same thing at the exact same time, the first one to say that phrase gets a free soft drink."

"Ah. But you have to agree, Magdalena, few things on this good earth smell better than cow dung."

I did agree. Maybe it's because I was raised on a dairy farm, or maybe it's in my

Swiss genes, but the odor of manure is indeed perfume to my nose. However, let me make it perfectly clear: my attraction to mammal emissions applies only to herbivores, and primarily cattle. Cat and dog poop need not apply.

Doc was impressed with the trouble I'd gone to in order to see that each group of entries had equal, but separate, accommodations. He was also quite impressed with the entries themselves. At each pen he paused to shake his head in appreciation. "Now that's a fine animal," he'd say.

Indeed, they were all fine animals. No doubt about it. The crème de la crème, pun quite intended. And, at the risk of sounding proud, Doc thought my two girls belonged to a guest. He told me that next year I should dissociate myself from the event and enter one of them — which, of course, I'd already considered. He was particularly taken with Matilda Two's exceptional udder.

"You don't see many that well-endowed," he said. "How many gallons?"

"Six."

"Wow. Isn't that a record?"

"Record's six point two."

"When I was a young shaver —"

"Shafor shaver —"

"But just barely shaving then. Anyway, when I was just out of vet school, we were lucky if cows gave half that much."

"The breed has evolved — well, not *evolved* evolved, since evolution doesn't exist, but — you know, changed."

"Magdalena, Magdalena, whatever am I going to do with you? Your apple not only stayed close to the tree, but it's still firmly attached."

"Meaning?"

"I am merely observing that you choose to ignore scientific evidence so that you can cling to your literal interpretation of some three-thousand-year-old documents that were meant for another people living in another time." He said it without pausing. Surely it was a remarkable feat for an octogenarian, and would have been quite impossible had he been president.

"Doc, I'm not going to argue theology with you."

"Because you'd lose?"

"Because you're wrong, and I'm right."

He grinned. "I still say we'd make a mighty fine couple. I'd be the spit, and you'd be the fire. If you ever decide to ditch that young whippersnapper of yours —"

"It's never going to happen. But anyway, Doc, you're impressed with the cows, huh?"

49

Good news can never be repeated too many times.

"They're all exceptional, but . . ." He sucked air sharply through his teeth.

"But what?"

"I've been thinking about one of them. Something's not quite right. Do you mind if I have another look?"

My cow-proud heart sank. "It isn't one of mine, is it?"

"No, of course not."

"Which one is it?"

Before Doc could answer, I heard a howl call my name.

5

Avocado Ice Cream Recipe

Ingredients:
3 ripe avocados
3/4 pint (375 ml) milk

1/2 pint (250 ml) double (heavy) cream
1 tablespoon fresh lemon juice
1/2 cup granulated sugar

Take the avocados, peel and seed them then put into a blender with the milk and make a purée. Pour the purée into a mixing bowl, add the sugar, lemon juice, and cream, and beat until creamy. Then transfer the complete mixture into an ice cream maker, and follow the manufacturer's instructions.

6

"Ma-ah-ah-ah-ah-ah-ahm!" Alison howled again.

I turned to see my pseudo-stepdaughter stomping up the driveway, her arms crossed in front of her chest, her eyes flashing.

"Later," I said to Doc. I prayed silently for patience, and if I was not to be given that, then a painless and temporary case of lockjaw. Having delivered up my requests, I braced to face her wrath. (A mother — especially a pseudo-stepmother — doesn't have to do anything wrong to be wrong.)

Alison galloped the remaining distance. They were her legs, of course, but disproportionately long like a colt's. I couldn't help but marvel at how much she'd grown in the past year.

"Mom! Where were ya?"

"Right here. Where did you look?"

"Nowhere. Didn't ya see me just come over from across the road?"

"I saw you coming up the drive. What happened?"

"*She* happened, that's what."

"She who? Your Auntie Susannah?"

"What? Nah, Auntie Susannah's cool. It's her I can't stand."

"Cousin Barbara?"

"Mom!"

I racked my brain for whoever else might be staying across the road at the family compound. The only other females were the babies — bingo! Toddlers and teenagers don't always mix, especially when the former get their sticky hands on the latter's stuff.

"Which one was it? It wasn't little Magdalena, was it? Sweetie, they're only two years —"

"I'm talking about Grandma Ida! Only she ain't my real grandma, so I ain't gonna call her that no more. Even if ya try and make me. You ain't gonna, are ya?"

Oh, what music to my sinful ears. Much to my annoyance, Alison had taken to Gabriel's mother like ticks to a deer. You would have thought that interfering little woman had hung the moon, for crying out loud. Of course it wasn't Alison's fault, seeing as how she was starved for affection; so it was clearly Ida's fault. And how terribly selfish

53

it was for Ida to encourage this behavior, because she already had a child and —

"Mom, are ya even listening?"

"Of course I am, dear. Prattle on."

"So then she says that I gotta brush my teeth *three* times a day, instead of the two times ya make me do it, and that if I don't, I can't watch no TV."

"She lets you watch *TV?*" I don't even own a set, much less allow Alison to watch it — although I'm not so stupid as to think that Alison doesn't watch it when she's on sleepovers, wherever they might take place. From a practical standpoint, I know that Alison is growing up in a world dominated by television, and that there is nothing I can do to change this. I do not, however, have to be part of the problem.

"Mom, I wanna move back in here."

"But then you won't get to watch *any* television."

"That's okay. I'd rather read anyway."

I clasped the child of my heart to my heart. "I love you," I whispered into her hair.

"Yuck, Mom, don't get gross."

I'd seldom been happier.

Freni outdid herself in the kitchen that night: roast beef, mashed potatoes, pan gravy, green beans with bacon, baby peas with pearl onions, buttered corn, wilted endive salad, Jell-O salad with canned fruit, watermelon pickles, homemade chow-chow, homemade rolls, butter and homemade gooseberry jam, and, for dessert, freshly churned vanilla ice cream served with warm peach cobbler.

Human nature being what it is, it never surprises me when guests don't appreciate Freni's culinary skills, or lack even the manners of a drunken orangutan. But whether they're crude, or just plain rude, the one thing my guests must do is dress neatly for dinner and sit at their assigned places around my massive table. This table, by the way, was made by my ancestor Jacob the Strong, and it is the only thing to survive when my inn was demolished by a tornado some years back. At any rate, my place is at the head of the table, facing the kitchen, where I preside like a benevolent dictator — unless my guests misbehave. When that happens, my goodwill can dissolve just as quickly as a campaign promise.

Because this is my establishment, I insist on saying grace before meals. Lately, however, in an effort to be inclusive, I have asked for volunteers — just as long as their version of grace is directed to the one true God, and doesn't involve statues of any kind. I must admit that I am particularly pleased when Episcopalians and Roman Catholics volunteer to pray, since I know that their efforts will be brief, and thus the food will not get cold.

There are times when I can't get volunteers, but on this occasion, no sooner had I made the offer than Harmon Dorfman plunged right in. While it was immediately apparent that the beefy farmer from North Dakota was a Protestant of some sort, it eventually became clear that he didn't know when to quit. After thanking the Good Lord for the food, he went on to ask for fair weather during the forthcoming competition, rain for the crops back home, peace and prosperity for those countries that deserved it (he named fourteen), cures for every disease imaginable (I lost count after twenty-six), immediate relief for Aunt Harriet's lumbago and Uncle Marty's shingles, funds for a new irrigation system . . .

"Amen," I said gently.

". . . and Thou knowest Stanley Dillbaker needs a new combine . . ."

"Amen."

". . . and we just thank you Lord for your tender mercies . . ."

"Let's hope the roast is still tender. Amen."

". . . and soften the hearts, Lord, of those who wouldst . . ."

"Amen," I growled. "Oops — sorry, Lord."

There was a smattering of applause, mostly from Alison. Vance Brown immediately lunged for the mashed potatoes, while Harry Dorfman practically threw himself on the meat. You would have thought Harry would be used to long prayers — then again, maybe he was.

"Miss Yoder," Jane Pearlmutter muttered, "you don't have to be so mean."

"What was that, dear?"

"If you didn't want him to take forever, you shouldn't have asked him in the first place."

"Point well taken." I turned to her handsome husband, Dick, whom I'd seated beside me on the left. "Tell me, how did you get interested in dairy cows?"

"I love milk."

I smiled pleasantly. "Yes, but weren't you a New York stockbroker?"

"The stress got to be too much. My doctor said either I had to quit or risk a heart attack. I was kicking around for something else to do — I can't just do nothing — when I remembered that my grandparents used to own a farm. I was just a little kid then, but even just thinking about it made me feel calm and peaceful. Then the more I thought about it, the more obsessed I became with the idea. To make a long story short, we bought a hundred and twenty acres about an hour outside the city, and I've never looked back. The hard part was convincing Jane to leave the rat race behind."

"You were a schoolteacher, right?" Despite her attitude, I was as sweet as a piece of brown sugar pie.

"No."

"But I'm sure that was on your application."

"You must have me confused with someone else. Miss Yoder, I was — *am* — a board-certified plastic surgeon."

"And a very successful one too," Vance said, the pride in his voice unmistakable. "She had a lot of celebrity patients. Go ahead, Jane, tell them who some of your patients were."

"You know I can't do that," she snapped.

He grinned sheepishly. "But if she could tell you, you'd be amazed. Jane perfected a facelift technique that leaves virtually no scars."

"You must be referring to laser resurfacing," Gertie said. "I've had some of that myself." The poor thing seemed blissfully unaware that any resurfacing she'd had done, had long since reverted to potholes.

I smiled charitably. "Isn't that interesting, dear."

"It certainly wasn't that," Jane snapped. "My specialty is cutting, not lasers. In this technique I make small incisions at the *back* of the scalp, not just above the hairline, as is usually done. Then I thread ultrafine filaments —"

"Yuck," Alison said. "Can we talk about something else?"

"What a capital idea," I cried gaily. It was forced gaiety, of course. "Knock, knock, who's there?"

Alison groaned. "No, Mom. You don't say 'who's there'; I do."

"No, really. Did any of you just hear a knock?"

I heard it again. But it wasn't so much a knock, as it was a thud. Nevertheless, didn't the irritating interloper — it was the dinner hour, after all — see my lit doorbell? Even the Amish knew to use it, for heaven's sake. As for my kin across the road, they don't even knock before barging into my private bath.

I smiled to hide my irritation. Although my facial muscles were getting an extraordinary workout, a good hostess must always exude a calm, collected air — right up until the moment she explodes.

"Excuse me."

Being vertically enhanced, as I am, it didn't take but a second or two to reach the foyer. Doc Shafor must have been still in the process of slumping, because when I opened the front door, he fell right in.

Mere words cannot describe my horror when I saw Doc lying there. For one thing, his face was covered with blood. Atop his head was a bump larger than any goose egg I'd ever seen. Then there was the matter of his left arm, which appeared to have been taken off, and then reattached facing the wrong direction. If it hadn't been for his white spats, I wouldn't have known who it was.

Sitting there, just outside the ICU of the Bedford County Memorial Hospital, I hardly felt any better. Doc had been cleaned up, of course, and was on medication to reduce the swelling in his brain, but he still hadn't come around. As for his arm, not only had it been dislocated, but it had been broken in six places. His pelvis had a hairline fracture as well. His doctor said he was lucky to be alive.

Chief Chris Ackerman of the Hernia

police department squatted at my feet, a look of intense concern spread across his uncommonly handsome face. "Miss Yoder," he said in a soothing voice, "he's going to be all right. The doctor promised."

I shook my head. "But he's an old man. How can someone have done that? *Who* could have done that?"

"We'll find out. Trust me."

"But it's just you — I mean, no offense, but we haven't gotten around to replacing Chief Hornsby-Anderson yet."

"Yes, but there's you."

"Me?"

"Miss Yoder, with all due respect to Sheriff Dewlapp's competent department and the Bedford police, who is the single best sleuth in the county?"

Despite my deep concern for Doc and the overall gravity of the situation, I felt myself blush. If Chris Ackerman had been attracted to women, and I not married to a very attractive and successful man, I would have pursued him like a hen after a junebug. Not only is he drop-dead gorgeous, but he's kind and sensitive, and he smells like Irish Spring soap.

"That would be me," I said shyly.

"What is your success rate?"

"One hundred percent?"

"That's a fact, Miss Yoder, not a question."

"You're right." I pounded a shapely fist into a shapely palm. "By jingle, you're right."

"Then what are you doing sitting here? I doubt Doc Shafor's assailant is lurking these halls — although he might be. Tell you what, I'll speak to the Bedford chief, since the hospital is his jurisdiction, and get a guard posted at the ICU door. And not to worry, I'll get hospital security to send someone up to keep watch in the meantime. As for you, your family is waiting for you in the cafeteria. So go down there, get yourself a much-needed cup of hot chocolate, and then go home and get some rest. Tomorrow morning, bright and early, you can start grilling your suspects like wienies. Isn't that how you put it?"

"Charming, is it not?"

"It is. Now go on."

I got up, fluffed my wrinkled skirt, and had just retrieved my pocketbook from a Formica end table piled high with tattered golf and fishing magazines when the thought struck me: why was Chris Ackerman trying to get rid of me so quickly? I turned to see his back disappearing down the hall.

"Yoo-hoo."

He obviously hadn't heard me.

"Yoo-hoo!"

He continued to get smaller.

"You forgot the chocolate brownies!"

Chris is twenty-three, but still has the appetite of a teenager. Even so, there isn't a spare ounce of fat on him — just deeply tanned, rippling muscle. Anyway, since he lives by himself, and receives a pitiful salary, he has never been known to turn down food. In the past, he has stated he'd walk twenty miles for one of Freni's brownies.

He appeared to fly up the hall. "Are they Freni's?"

"Indeed, they are. Except they're not here; they're back at the inn."

"Hey, that's a dirty trick."

"You haven't seen anything yet, dear. Now tell me what gives."

"Gives?"

"And don't pretend to be ignorant. I didn't fall off the cabbage truck; I have brassieres older than you, for Pete's sake. I know when I'm being had. You couldn't wait to get rid of me and go somewhere."

"Okay, okay, I'll confess. Miss Yoder —"

"Isn't it about time you called me Magdalena?"

"Yeah, but you're my mom's age. Somehow it doesn't seem right to call an older woman by her first name."

"I'll pretend I didn't hear that. Now cut to the chase."

7

Chris studied his imitation fine leather Italian shoes. "Back there in your barn — well, there was a message scrawled on the stall where Doc was attacked."

"Message? Scrawled? You don't mean in blood, do you?"

He nodded. "How'd you know?"

"Unfortunately, from years of experience. What did it say?"

"*Mind yer own beezwax.* Two of the words were misspelled."

My legs felt weak, so I groped for a chair. Like I said, I was no stranger to crime, but this was especially appalling. What on earth has happened to our educational system in this country? I learned spelling to the tune of a hickory stick, and though I'm most probably emotionally scarred for life, I'm quite capable of spelling three out of four words correctly. It's only math that still gives me trouble.

"What do you think it means, Chris?"

He shook his fine young head. "The obvious conclusion to draw would be that it has to do with the contest; Doc saw or heard something he wasn't supposed to. It could, however, be something totally unrelated. Did Doc have any enemies that you know of?"

"Of course. He was an irascible old man, sometimes downright cantankerous. He always used to say that if a man doesn't have any enemies by the time he reaches eighty, then he hasn't been living his life right. But I'm not sure how much of that was just bluster."

I yawned. "Sorry. It's been a busy day. Check-in days are always hectic, and now this." I yawned again.

"Just one more question, Magdalena. You were having dinner when Doc crawled to the door. Were all your guests with you at the time?"

"Yes, every single one."

"And Freni?"

"Don't be ridiculous. Freni feels bad when she kills flies. Besides —"

"She might have heard something that the rest of you didn't."

"Maybe, but not likely. She was in the kitchen talking to her buns. She tends to tune everything else out when she does that."

"I beg your pardon?"

"Cinnamon buns for tomorrow morning. Freni believes in talking to the dough; she tells it how much to rise, and when. It's quite a little speech she gives them."

"They must listen, because her buns are the best."

"So what happens now? What if some of my guests decide to check out on account of what happened?"

"Don't let them. Not until I've had a chance to interview them."

"How do I stop them?"

"Stall them; you're great at obfuscation, aren't you?"

"One of the best," I said modestly. "Chris, you were hoping to get to the barn before I got home, so that you could clean up Doc's blood. And erase the message, right?"

"Right."

"Thank you."

"No problem."

For a split second, I considered hugging his handsome self to my somewhat comely self, but genetics took over. We Yoders are incapable of spontaneous expressions of emotion, especially if they involve physical contact. If we must, we can schedule hugs, but they must last less than thirty seconds and be accompanied by constant backslapping. Show me a Yoder who can hug without backslapping, and I'll show you a Yoder with rigor mortis. Okay, so there may be a few exceptions.

"Well, I better get a move on down to the cafeteria before my loved ones ingest anything more than coffee. One person at death's door is quite enough for one night."

He laughed, before giving me a Presbyterian hug. I must say, it didn't feel all that bad.

My groom drove me back to the inn, and not a second too soon — my guests were in the process of mutinying. My lovely front lawn had been turned into a traffic jam of trucks and cattle carriers. Horns blared, men brawled, women brayed, but the cows, ignorant as they were of alliteration, merely lowed.

Gabe stared in disbelief. "Holy guacamole!"

There was no time to waste. I threw myself from the still-moving car, hiked my skirts to about knee level, and then leapt onto the hood of the Dorfman brothers' pickup. Their truck, by the way, was not moving, and I may have glossed over a few clumsy moves on my part, but you get the point.

Cupping my hands to my mouth, I gave the infamous "Yoder yell." The Yoder yell, for those unfamiliar with its history, is said to have originated with Eve Yoder when she gave birth to Cain Yoder, after having been banished, along with Adam Yoder, from the Garden of Eden. I'm not saying I believe that; my point is that we've long been known for our lung power.

When the mutineers and their livestock heard me, they froze. Then, one by one, they gasped as they realized where the unearthly sound was coming from. Indeed, I must have appeared as an evil apparition, perched as I was three feet off the ground. Even the cows regarded me, their eyes wide with terror.

Harmon Dorfman was the first to react. "Miss Yoder, what in tarnation are you doing atop my truck?"

Using my chin, I gestured to my feet. "No harm done, Harmon. These sensible black brogans have soles as soft as sponge cake."

"That may be, Miss Yoder, but I paid a pretty penny for her. Please get down."

"In a minute, dear."

My darling husband held out his arms, as if he intended for me to jump into them.

"Hon, you heard the man. Get down."

It was, in retrospect, a reasonable request. However, in addition to being genetically gifted in the lung department, and sadly deficient in the hug department, we Yoders sometimes carry the gene for contrariness. Tell us to go right, and we'll go left. Of course those of us with that gene have long since separated from the Amish, who adhere to a code of obedience, and most of us are no longer even Mennonite. But there are exceptions to every rule, I suppose, because I am still of the faith, even though I am every bit as obstinate as a second-generation president.

"Listen up, folks," I continued to holler, "none of you are leaving, because all of you were here when poor old Doc Shafor was assaulted."

"So were you," Candy Brown chirped.

I glared at the woman who dared jiggle her keester at the South Pole. Since it was dark, and she couldn't see my expression clearly, it didn't really count as mean-spirited.

"You're quite right, my dear. So I'll stay here as well."

"Suit yourself," Jane Pearlmutter muttered. "But you have no legal right to prevent us from leaving."

The Bible commands us not to bear false witness against our neighbors: in other words, we are not supposed to accuse them of something of which they are not guilty. Nowhere in the big ten does it say "thou shalt not lie." The way I see it, the Good Lord gives us a great deal more latitude than we are commonly taught to believe. To not take advantage of this generous state of affairs is to be downright ungrateful. Nevertheless, just to be on the safe side, I chose my words carefully.

"As I'm sure you all know by now, Doc Shafor — the man who was mugged in the barn — was one of the judges," I said. "He's a veterinarian with a great deal of experience examining udders."

"Your point, please," said Vance Brown. As a modern dairyman, the odds were that Vance had seen a lot more udders in one day than Doc had in his lifetime. After all, Doc's specialty was horses.

"What if I were to say that he confided in me that one cow in particular stood out head and shoulders above the rest?" That was a hypothetical question, and not even a lie, much less a broken commandment.

Dick Pearlmutter, who'd been standing with one foot on the running board of his truck, stepped off and approached me. "Are you saying that the competition is still a go?"

Frankly, I'd been so busy worrying about my elderly friend, that I hadn't even thought about the competition — okay, so I hadn't thought about it a *lot.* Contrary to some reports, I am only human. But during my fleeting thoughts, it had occurred to me that the best way to honor Doc, and thwart his assailant, was to continue as best as we could, as if the assault had never taken place. Of course I needed to find a judge ASAP, but even in a very small farming community like ours, that would hardly be a problem.

"Surely you jest, Mr. Pearlmutter," I said, and forced an agreeable smile.

"But isn't it too late to find a replacement judge?"

"Nonsense, dear. In Hernia, connoisseurs of bovine beauty are a dime a dozen."

Harry Harmon turned to his brother. "I still think we should head back home, before something like what happened to that old man happens to one of us."

"You won't be getting refunds — not for your rooms or your stable fees."

"Then we'll sue," Jane said.

Gertie Fuselburger shook her dyed head vigorously. "I'm afraid that would be useless, Mrs. Pearlmutter," she said. "I read

72

Miss Yoder's contract, and it's ironclad. You did read it, dear, didn't you?"

"No contract is ironclad, you old biddy. We'll hire the best lawyer on the East Coast."

I am proud to say that my husband stepped up to the plate. "Hey, watch the name-calling."

"And you don't get to speak to my wife that way," Dick said. I must say that for a former stockbroker, he looked remarkably, and worrisomely, fit. That is the problem with the trend these days of providing exercise equipment at the office. A white-collar worker is *supposed* to be a ninety-seven-pound weakling incapable of slinging a calf over his shoulder.

"Oh yeah?" the Babester said. "How about the way you've all been treating my wife? Her oldest and dearest friend is lying in the ICU, and what does she find when she finally gets back home from the hospital? Renegers, that's what."

Harry turned to his brother. "Did he just use a racial epithet?"

Sensing that bedlam was about to ensue, I flapped my arms and crowed like a rooster. That got their attention. I'm pretty good at crowing, if I do say so myself. So good in fact that a real rooster, my beloved Chanticleer II, responded in kind, even though it was still the dead of night.

Gertie Fuselburger, bless her fossilized heart, clapped her hands with glee. "Oh, Miss Yoder, everything you do is positively delightful."

"I think Miss Yoder might be crazy," Candy Brown said.

When no one, not even Gabe, jumped in to contradict her, I knew it was time to resort to drastic measures. "I'm going to up the prize money by fifty thousand dollars," I said.

Gabe tried to grab one of my slim, shapely ankles. His intention, I believe, was to pull me off the Harmons' truck, and haul me indoors before my lips could get me into any more trouble. Fortunately, having played oodles of hopscotch as a girl, I was able to elude his grasp.

"Are you sure, hon?" he whispered. "Where's this money coming from?"

"I'm sure," I hollered. "Okay, folks, how about you all turn around, unload your trailers, and go back into the inn for a good night's sleep?"

This time, not a soul objected.

8

My sleep was punctuated by nightmares. In between dreams, I must have tossed and turned like a princess on a pea, because when I finally woke up, even though I was still under the covers, my head was at the foot of the bed. Thank heavens I am not claustrophobic.

But what surprised me even more than my new location, was the fact that, sometime during the night, my dear husband had chosen to join me. This discovery made me almost as happy as the moment, under the chutzpah, when he pledged himself to me until death do us part. Or was that a chuppah? It certainly wasn't a Chanukah; that I know is the Jewish festival that generally takes place in late December.

At any rate, I should be ashamed to confess that discovering the Babester in my bed gave me an enormous amount of schadenfreude. Ida was going to be fit to be tied, and with any luck she would become tongue-tied as well. Of course this wasn't a Christian attitude to take; it was actually rather sinful of me. But I fully intended to confess this sin as soon as I'd indulged in a few minutes of this guilty pleasure. Failure to enjoy life's little blessings is also a sin, if you ask me.

Nevertheless, as a good Mennonite, I do not believe in fancy forms of sexual foreplay, seeing as how they might lead to dancing. "Brace yourself, Magdalena" is good enough for me. Still, I thought Gabe deserved a reward for ditching his ma in favor of *moi*. Although it is no one's business but my own, I will admit that during the height of my gratitude-inspired passion, I went so far as to engage in a wanton act so private I don't even think it has a name. Alas, it was far less satisfying than I had imagined.

For one thing, I didn't remember the Babester as having one foot so much hairier than the other. The hirsute tootsie also smelled a great deal worse. In all frankness, kissing his right foot was not only bad enough to dampen my ardor, but I fleetingly considered becoming a nun. Yes, I realize that would require a change of religion, but in one fell swoop, I could lose the mother-in-law and pick up some new habits.

But, like I said, it was only a fleeting thought.

"Really, dear," I said, my voice muffled by the covers, "a good depilatory and some foot powder could do wonders."

My beloved's voice was equally as distorted. Funny, but he sounded almost like a woman.

"I can't believe you said that, Mags."

Uh-oh, now I'd hurt his feelings. Gabe, as befits an only son, is a world-class pouter. He once sulked for six days straight just because I washed a cashmere sweater of his. In my defense, it was in the laundry basket along with everything else, and everything I own is either cotton or that staple of sensible women everywhere: polyester blend.

"Darling," I purred soothingly, "I still love you, no matter how much your feet stink."

Gabe even laughed like a woman. "Who knew you had a sense of humor?"

"I had it transplanted, dear. John Kerry had an extra one lying about, and generously decided to share. Of course, I had to agree to donate part of my brain to Bush when I die; they said anything was better than nothing."

The Babester found this enormously funny, and thrashed about like a trout on a stream bank. Ever the good sport, I decided to add to the jocularity by lightly pinching his hairiest toe. Boy, was I in for a surprise; my husband's toes are capable of pinching back! And hard!

Quite understandably, I screamed and threw back the covers. When I beheld who, and what, were sharing my bed, I screamed again. Then again, and even louder, just for good measure.

"Mags," my sister said, as she tried unsuccessfully to put her hand over my mouth, "calm down. It's not the end of the world."

"You've got that right. Because neither of us is budging from this one until I've given you a piece of my mind. And as for that mangy little mongrel of yours, you get that horrid little beastie out of my bed this instant!"

In 1984, when Susannah was a teenager, she won first place in Hernia's third annual Who Sighs The Loudest Contest. The sigh she emitted now put that one to shame.

"All right, but you've got to stop calling my iddle-widdle Shnookums a mongrel. It hurts his teensy-weensy feelings. I've told you a million times that he's a purebred Russian terrier."

"A Russian terrorist, maybe. Now get that rat out of my bed before I call an exterminator!"

Even Susannah got nipped when she tried to evict the two-pound canine with the one-pound sphincter. But when the task was done she crawled back under the covers and laid her head on my shoulder. I can't recall her doing that since she was three, and had just finished sobbing herself into a comatose state. That happened just after Granny Yoder told her that the Easter Bunny was a Catholic creation thought up by the pope as a plot to rot the teeth of Protestant children. Anyway, this sudden display of intimacy was a shock to my nervous system, and I almost went comatose as well.

It was a struggle to string two words together. "What gives?"

"What do you mean? Aren't I allowed to snuggle with my own sis?"

"Probably not in at least six states."

"That was actually funny, Mags. You know, marriage has really changed you. You even look different."

"How so?"

"It's hard to describe."

"Give it a shot, dear. If it's complimentary, I have all the time in the world."

"Well, you kinda have this glow about you."

"That's because I'm burning with rage. I know I'm not supposed to think like this —

that it's totally against everything I believe and hold dear — but if I ever get my hands on whoever did this to Doc, I'll — uh —"

"Rip his or her head off? Smash them with a crowbar? I hear you, sis. Doc Shafor is a dirty old man, but a sweet one. I'm mad too."

"Tell me, Susannah, how did the Amish — the ones whose children were gunned down in the schoolhouse — forgive so easily?"

"Beats me. But then again, I couldn't even handle being a Mennonite."

"Or a Presbyterian," I said. Perhaps that was unfair of me. The day she came of age, and much against our parents' wishes, Susannah ran off and married a nominal Presbyterian, one who didn't even believe in predestination. Shortly after the wedding, she officially changed her church membership, an act which really broke our parents' hearts, seeing as how our ancestors have been, at various times, either Mennonite or Amish since the 1500s. Less than three months later, she divorced Doug, and that was the end of any churchgoing for my baby sister. To call her a backslider would be unfair to millions of other nominal Christians, ones who feel guilty about their spiritual decline; Susannah didn't just backslide, she dropped like a pallet of bricks from a ten-story building.

"At least I'm not a hypocrite," Susannah said.

"Is that what you think I am? A hypocrite?"

"If the shoe fits, Mags. Or should I say the sturdy black brogan?"

"I was just being honest about my innermost feelings. I'd hardly call that hypocritical."

"Face it, sis, you and I aren't like the rest of our family. Do you think we're adopted?"

"Me, maybe. But definitely not you. I'm eleven years older than you; I remember the day you were born."

"Were you there? In the room? Did you actually see me being born?"

"Don't be silly, Susannah. Mama didn't even know she had a vagina until she was fifty-six and we made her go to the gynecologist. Before that it was just 'down below.' And since she never, ever, looked at herself, she certainly wouldn't have allowed me to. No, I was told Papa found you under a cabbage in the vegetable patch out behind the barn."

"There! You see? We *could* both be adopted."

"A sobering thought, dear," I said. "One

that might lead to a multitude of possibilities, given that we already know that Papa sowed his seed in somebody else's garden patch — if you get my drift."

"Mags, you are so old fashioned. Papa slept with Zelda Root's mother, plain and simple. He was an adulterer. It's perfectly all right to say it."

"And now I feel a migraine coming on. But I still want to know what you're doing in my bed."

"I'll tell you, but first you have to swear on a stack of Bibles that you won't breathe a word of this to a soul."

"You know I can't do that. And anyway, I should be offended; I practically raised you. If you can't trust me, then you can't trust anyone. I love you, Susannah, which means I would never betray you."

"But that's exactly it," my sister wailed. While I realize that wailing is not a common human vocalization, members of our family are peculiarly blessed in being able to do so well. And quite a blessing it is, don't you think? When we're caught in heavy traffic (admittedly quite rare in Hernia), we simply hang our heads out of our car windows and let her rip. Other cars pull over just as surely as if we were official emergency vehicles. And since half of the time we really are facing emergencies, I don't feel too guilty about taking liberties with my voice.

"I don't understand," I said calmly.

"Who do I love more than anyone else in the world?"

"Moi," I said smugly.

"Yeah, but besides you."

"Not the mantis!"

"His name is *Melvin.* And I can't believe he didn't love me back."

I didn't need a crystal ball to see where this conversation was headed. "Insect or man, he's still a murderer. He killed my minister, for crying out loud. And if it wasn't for my sturdy Christian underwear, he would have killed me too. Every day I thank God for Sears and JCPenney. If I'd been wearing something skimpy from Victoria's Secret, I'd have been splattered at the base of Stucky Ridge."

"Oh, Mags, you're always so dramatic. If you're not even going to try to keep an open mind, then I'm not going to tell you."

"There's *more?*"

She nodded.

"Okay, but if my brain falls out on account of my mind being too open, it's your fault."

"Mags, I've been having this dream. In it, Melvin contacts me and asks me to run away with him."

My teeth settled into familiar grooves as I bit my tongue. "What is your response, dear?"

"I go with him, of course. Together we crisscross America dodging the long arm of the law, just like Bonnie and Clyde. We rob banks only when we have to eat. The rest of the time we rob fabric stores. But just so you know, we never actually shoot anybody."

Needless to say, I was fit to be tied — my tongue, however, was not. "Well, I don't care who this Bonnie and Clydesdale are. What you're saying is disgusting. If Mama and Papa could hear you, they'd die all over again. From shame this time."

"It's only a dream, Magdalena. We aren't responsible for our dreams."

"Maybe. But it's become the subject of your daydreams too, hasn't it?"

"If I said yes, would you hate me?"

"Don't be ridiculous. I'll always love you. But I'd be very, very disappointed."

Susannah's response was to burrow back under the covers until not a hair on her endangered head was showing.

9

My guests pay dearly for their food, but they can't ask for a better spread. Even though Freni was worried sick about Doc, she produced a meal fit for a queen: blueberry pancakes with freshly churned butter and real maple syrup; waffles; biscuits as light as clouds; warm, fragrant banana-nut bread; bacon, ham, sausage patties *and* sausage links; fruit salad; flavored yogurts, as well as plain; oatmeal served with raisins and brown sugar; a wide variety of cold cereals; and, of course, eggs cooked to order. She also offered scrapple and headcheese, but there were no takers for those two delicacies. It has always puzzled me that some folks object to eating organ meats, but not to eating muscle tissue. They're all parts of a dead animal, for crying out loud.

At any rate, because the dear woman has a habit of talking to no one in particular, it took a while to register that Freni was addressing me, and not the bacon sizzling in her frying pan.

"Why always a contest?"

"I beg your pardon?"

"Do you not listen, Magdalena?"

"I'm trying to listen, but that bacon is mighty loud." It was only the smallest of white lies, and told only so as not to hurt her feelings.

"The English," she said, referring to anyone not Amish. "Why must everything be a contest? We have cows too, yah, but they are humble cows."

"Who produce humble pies."

"Ach, always so quick with the riddles."

"Is it my fault I'm so talented?"

Freni shook her head. Given that she has virtually no neck, her entire body moved with the effort. Had it not been for *her* sturdy Christian underwear, it might have been unseemly.

"Your mama was my best friend, Magdalena. I was there when you were born, yah? Otherwise I am not so sure you are hers."

"You were there?" This was news to me. I'd always heard it was Granny Yoder who helped bring me into the world, with the aid of canning tongs. It was either that, or the cabbage patch story.

Freni turned the color of rhubarb sauce.

86

"Okay, maybe I am not there exactly on time, but it was spring, and I am feeling the oats. To make short the story, I did not see you born."

"It was September, and you were already happily married to Mose. Your oats should have been well felt by then."

"So now the truth, yah?"

"If you don't spill it all now, I'm telling the English that your biscuits are store-bought."

"Ach! Okay, I will spill." She turned off the bacon and took a deep breath, her enormous bosom rising and falling like a small tsunami. "Yah, it is time for the truth."

"And nothing but."

"Your mama was barren, Magdalena. Just like you. And Miss Sarah, the friend you speak so much of."

"You mean the Sahara, as in desert?"

"Please, Magdalena, this is no time for the riddles."

Her words began to sink in. "No way!"

"But your papa — well, you already know about Zelda. So anyway, there was a young woman, a teenager, who came in the family way. Some say that the baby's papa was your papa, and some say it was a stranger. To make short the story —"

"So I *am* adopted?"

Freni shrugged, which is to say, her bosom bobbled even more. "I think maybe you are half adopted, because you look just like your papa."

I felt like I'd been punched in the soft hollows behind my knees. Truly, I was in danger of collapsing. And since I also felt like throwing up, I had to be careful where I landed.

"And Susannah? Is she adopted as well?"

"Maybe not so much."

"*Not so much?* What does that mean?"

"It means that by now the desert is blooming, yah?"

I staggered over to sit in a "distressed" kitchen chair — one of several for which I'd paid big bucks, following a freak tornado several years ago that demolished my heirloom kitchen chairs. The originals had been in Mama's family for two centuries — except now she wasn't my mama. Not really.

"Magdalena, are you all right?"

"No, I'm not all right! Is Susannah my sister, or is she not?"

"Yah, of course."

"Then what's this blooming desert stuff? Honestly, Freni, you speak in riddles every bit as much as I do."

Freni removed her grease- and flour-covered glasses. Believe it or not, without them she could see even less, which was no doubt her intention. That way my quivering chin and tear-filled eyes became a meaningless blur.

"Your mama and papa loved you very much. They could not have loved more the fruit of their loom."

"That would be 'loins,' dear. But please, continue."

"Every day, they thank God for you in their prayers. Then one day, when your mama thinks the change of life has come, she goes to see the doctor. He tells her she is to have a baby. At first she cannot believe it; at her age, it is not possible. But when the day comes that she must accept the truth, she becomes historical."

"You mean hysterical?"

"That is what I said. So I ask her why she cries, and she says because now she is afraid that with a new baby, she will love her little Magdalena less. She says that you" — Freni nodded in my general direction — "meant more to her than anything in the world. More than your papa. Ach, maybe even more than God."

I gasped. "She didn't!"

"Such a terrible thing to say, yah? But for her, it is the truth, because she loves you so much. Then when Susannah is born, she gets this postmodern depression that everyone is talking about. One day she confides in my ears — you must promise never to tell anyone what she confides."

"I promise!"

"*No* one. *Ever.* Not even your Gabester."

"Yes, yes, go on."

"She wishes to drown Susannah in Miller's Pond. Like a kitten, she says."

I clapped my hands to my ears in horror. "I can't believe this!"

"I could not believe either. I ask Mose to hitch the horse to the Sunday buggy so that we could take her to see the pastor of your church. At that time, it was Reverend Amstutz — a very kind man, but maybe not so good with people."

"What did he say?"

"He said it was the Devil putting such ideas in her head. He tells us to pray. So we pray — everyone in Hernia prays, I think — but the Devil does not leave your mama, and I must stay with her every second, even though by then I have my little Jonathan to care for, because she thinks always of the pond."

I was on the edge of my distressed chair. "What about Papa?"

"Ach, a good man too. But maybe not so

— Magdalena, this I do not know how to say."

"Try Dutch," I said, referring to the German dialect that is the first language of most Amish.

"No, it is not the words, but what they say."

"You mean you have something to tell me about Papa that I won't want to hear? Give me a break, Freni. Please. What did he do, go off and father six more children?"

"Ach! Look how you talk. Your papa did not think so well in this stressful time. That is why he went to Cleveland."

"Cleveland?"

"To visit his aunt."

"How long did he stay?"

"Six months."

I was eleven years old at the time, but I hadn't even the dimmest memory of my beloved papa taking a six-month sabbatical from my demon-possessed mama. I'd always believed Papa and I had enjoyed an especially close relationship, but boy, was I ever wrong. And to think I always felt closer to Papa, and, if I were to be absolutely honest, was more saddened by his death than I was Mama's.

"What happened to Mama? How did she get rid of the demon?"

91

Using her apron, Freni smeared the grease-and-flour combo around on her glasses before popping them back on. Apparently, the worst was over, and it was safe again to make eye contact with yours truly.

"I think maybe it was not a real demon. When the prayers did not work so good, Mose and I drove your mama in to Bedford to see a doctor. One for the head."

She paused to hang her own head in shame, for having resorted to psychiatry. The woman must be admired on several accounts. For one thing, her lack of neck turned head-hanging into a daunting task. I waited patiently until she continued.

"These head doctors, they are not in the Bible, are they, Magdalena?"

"Neither are dentists, but you and Mose have both been to see one."

"Toupee."

"Excuse me?"

"Like the French say, yah?"

"Ah, touché! But anyway, was the psychiatrist able to help? He must have been, because although Mama was as high-strung as a kite in a hurricane, I certainly don't remember her as being particularly possessed."

"He gave your mama some pills, and soon she is better. Not like before the post-pardon depression, but still, much better."

I waited to see if there was more, but there wasn't. "Is that all, Freni? Is there anything else you've neglected to tell me? Do I have a brother chained in the attic?"

My kinswoman turned as white as boiled rice.

"There isn't," I cried. "*Is* there?"

"Not anymore."

"What?"

For the first time in ages a smile crept across her pale, unadorned lips. "So now you feel better, yah?"

"No, not really. I can't believe I was lied to all these years. I feel betrayed. Why did they do that? My parents, I mean. And why did *you* lie to me?"

"Ach, I did not want to hurt you. You are like a daughter to me."

"But *this* hurts!" Tears were streaming down my face. If I wore mascara, like Susannah, I'd look just like a panda bear — albeit a comely one, with the figure of a brick outhouse. So says Gabe.

Freni extended her stubby arms. Her intention was to hug me. But just seeing her attempting to perform this unnatural act opened my floodgates even wider. I bawled like an eight-year-old girl who's been told that she is too old now to get

Christmas presents other than bobby socks and sturdy Christian underwear — not that I would necessarily know about such a child.

"Shush, *meine kind*," Freni said and grabbed me in a warm and somewhat redolent embrace. (Even at this hour of the morning, she smelled of green onions.) "It will be okay, yah?"

"No, it won't! How could Mama and Papa do this to me? They're dead, and now I'll never know the truth."

It's not just we Yoders who engage in backslapping hugs, but virtually all Mennonites of Amish ancestry and, of course, the Amish. It has been postulated that this ritual behavior, usually performed upon greeting and departing, has its origins in the fact that both groups are intensely food oriented, and that the back-whacking is actually a precursor to the Heimlich maneuver. To corroborate this theory, bear in mind that the first person to deviate from normal hugs was a gentleman by the name of Heimlich Yoder. Enough said.

There are limits to backslapping too, and Freni had reached hers. "So now I will tell you why your mama lied," she said.

10

BUTTER PECAN ICE CREAM RECIPE

Ingredients:
1/2 pint (250 ml) single/light cream
2 oz (50 g) brown sugar
1 tablespoon butter

1/2 pint (250 ml) heavy/double cream
1/2 teaspoon vanilla extract (or according to taste)

1/4 cup pecans (chopped)

Place the single cream, sugar, and butter into a saucepan and mix together over low heat. Stir until the mixture starts to bubble around the edges. Remove the saucepan from the heat, and allow to cool.

When the mixture is cold, transfer it to an ice cream maker and stir in the double cream and vanilla extract. Freeze according to the manufacturer's instructions, but remember to add the pecans as the ice cream starts to harden.

11

"Your mama was afraid that if you knew the truth — that you did not share the pants — then maybe you would stop loving her," Freni said.

"Share pants? Mama didn't put one foot inside a pair of trousers until Susannah was a teenager. By then, I was out of the nest. Okay, so I still lived at home then, but I'd grown my adult plumage. I could have flown, and might have too, if Mama hadn't been so clingy. I mean that figuratively, of course."

"Ach, *du lieber!* Not the trouser pants — the jeans."

"Wrong again, dear. Mama never touched a pair of Levi's."

Freni wrung her scallion-scented hands. "Not the cloth jeans; the ones inside the body. The MBNA, yah?"

Then it hit me, like a ton of Mama's eggless dumplings. (To put it kindly, Mama was culinarily challenged.) "DNA!" I screamed. "Genes!"

"Yah, that's what I said."

"Are you telling me that Mama thought that just because we didn't share the same flesh and blood, that I wouldn't love her?"

Freni nodded, no doubt speechless upon finally discovering that my stupidity knows no bounds.

"But that's so — so — well, I'm not *that* shallow."

"Yah, not so shallow. This I tell her, but with different words."

"Thank you. And Papa, what was his excuse?"

"Your papa" — she paused, and I could tell she was praying for a Christian tongue — "he made the honky-tonky with this woman and that woman, but of your mama, he was always afraid."

"She was half his size, for crying out loud."

"But she had a giant personality, yah?"

"For sure."

"You must always remember one thing, Magdalena; Mose and I do not care about this DMA. To us, you will always be a Yoder and a Hostetler. And, of course, now a Rosen too."

"I love you, Freni!" I threw my arms around the stout woman, hugging her tightly to me. Taking her by surprise as I did, her arms were pinned to her sides. It took her less than thirty seconds to cry uncle.

"Ach, let me go!"

"Not until you say 'I love you' back to me."

"You already know that I do."

"But you gotta say it."

"Enough with the games, Magdalena. The English will have a cold breakfast."

I squeezed harder. I was rather enjoying myself. It's not every day that a five-foot, ten-inch python devours a stubby Amish woman in Hernia, Pennsylvania.

"Unh."

"Say it, dear."

"Ah unh ooh."

"Close enough."

Since, in my humble opinion, nothing says loving better than a good whiff of cow manure, after releasing Freni from my death grip, I headed out to the barn. It is no ordinary barn, believe you me.

I got married the first time in that barn. I also discovered a body in that barn, pinned to an upright beam by a pitchfork. I have happier memories as well: as a girl I discovered litter after litter of adorable kittens that

99

had been birthed in its hayloft; I learned that Beverly Neuhauser didn't wear panties, Christian or otherwise; and it was impressed on me, quite literally, that Isaac Newton was quite right about gravity. The last was a happy memory because the entire week following my bungled attempt to fly (mop heads are no substitute for proper wings), I was every bit as pampered as one of Marie Antoinette's pooches.

If two cows are capable of pleasantly stimulating my olfactory senses, imagine what a small herd can do! So entranced was I by the Essence of Holstein that I plumb, and quite shamefully, had momentarily forgotten the previous night's horrible tragedy. When I saw Doc's handwriting, scrawled in blood across the broad door, I nearly fainted. Who could have done such a thing to an eighty-some-year-old man?

While I waited for the lightheadedness to pass, I closed my eyes and prayed for Doc's recovery. Had it been permissible to pray for the slow torture of his assailants, I probably would have done so. (It was my non-Mennonite blood doing the thinking, I assure you.) Then, because Chief Chris is a good man, but still relatively inexperienced, I prayed for the wisdom and strength I was going to need to find Doc's assailant and bring him, or her, to justice.

"Magdalena, are you okay?"

I jumped so high that my left foot literally came out of its brogan. Jamming it back in, I plastered a smile across my comely face.

"Mose! Where did you come from?"

Freni's dear husband is seventy-five, but is every bit as fit as a man nine tenths his age. When Papa was alive and kept an active dairy herd, Mose worked for him full time. Now he looks after my two cows and helps out with maintenance. He does not, however, keep regular hours.

"I wanted to see the English cows."

"And?"

"Never have I seen such beautiful Holsteins."

"Were you here at milking time?" Dairy dilettantes are sometimes surprised to learn that cows must be milked twice a day, every day, come rain or high fevers, and that the morning milking usually takes place at a time most folks would prefer to be snoozing. I personally don't rise at that hour, so I've hired a nearby Amish boy to do the job. And just for the record, I would sooner accuse myself of assaulting Doc than I would accuse Seth.

"Yah, because this I must see. With such machines, Magdalena, I think it is possible to get milk from a rock."

I couldn't help but smile. As much work as it was, Papa had eschewed electric milking machines for the true hands-on approach. He thought the cows responded to his warm touch by producing more milk, and with a higher butterfat content.

"So you think these cows deserve to be in this contest?"

Mose bit his lip as he appeared to think this over.

"What is it?" I demanded. "I know you and Freni aren't too keen on contests, but there's more to that here, isn't there?"

"Ach, Magdalena, I cannot tell a lie."

We'd been having this conversation in the barn, next to Doc's bloody message. I beckoned Mose into the bright, rejuvenating sunshine of a perfect April morning.

"Okay, Mose, out with it."

He glanced around, perhaps looking for the Devil. "They are all beautiful cows, yah? But except for one, I think. This one is — ach, but I must say this — ordinary?"

"Ordinary?" Mose would not knowingly bad-mouth a flea. To hear him use such harsh language about a cow shocked me to the tips of my stocking-clad toes. I reeled like a drunk woman. Had I been wearing dentures, I might well have stepped on

them. Fortunately, my real chompers are in tip-top condition, thanks to all the milk Mama made me drink as a girl.

He nodded. "It is not a bad cow; I myself have such animals. But there are many wrinkles on the bag, and it is smaller than the average."

"Show me."

Mose led me around to a pen on the north side of the barn. It was the enclosure picked by the Dorfman brothers. Although I'd seen and admired their cows the day before, armed with Mose's information, I saw them now with new eyes. One of the Holsteins was still a beauty, but indeed, the other was, well, ordinary. She certainly wasn't worth toting all the way from North Dakota.

"So now you see."

"For sure. What gives?"

"Gives?"

"What are the owners of this cow up to?"

Mose shrugged. "The ways of the English are like piddles, yah?"

"Piddles?"

"Games for the mind."

"Ah, you must mean 'riddles.' "

"Forgive me, Magdalena, but I think the correct word is 'piddles.' "

It was time to stop yanking his chain, as Susannah would say. "Did you say anything to the Dorfman brothers about their inferior entry?"

"Ach, no, it is not my business."

"Good man. Leave it to me; I'll get to the bottom of this."

"Be careful, yah?" His look of concern was heartening.

"I will, indeed."

"But this time, really careful. Not like the other times."

"Mose, just because I've been thrown down a mine shaft, left trussed in a burning house, ordered to jump out of an airplane, and even carted off to the wilds of Maryland, is not to say that I'm a careless woman. Au contraire; the very fact that I've survived these many and varied attempts on my life is proof that I am skilled at extracting myself from the very jaws of the Grim Reaper. Or would that be Reaper*ess*? Then again, if we are to eliminate sexism from language, we cannot automatically assign gender to an entity that lacks a corporal being. But if we do, is not turnabout fair play? I mean, what's good for the gander is good for the goose, and vice versa."

Mose sighed deeply, and by doing so, informed me that he, for one, had not shied away from the scrapple at breakfast. "Again with the piddles. But I was thinking, yah?"

"As we all must from time to time."

"Perhaps it is more like the wooden duck."

"In that case me thinkest thou meanest the Trojan horse."

Mose scowled. It was the first time I'd ever seen him angry, and I immediately felt guilty. Me and my big mouth. But really, when you think about it, my flapping lips have got to be inherited from whomever birthed me, and so are not really my fault. Perhaps the woman from whose loins I slithered was a carnival caller. That would certainly explain a great deal.

"Magdalena, I do not speak of horses, but the ducks that hunters set on our ponds."

"Ah, decoys!"

"Yah, the same. I think perhaps the not so good cow has been brought all this way from North Dakota so that we do not look so closely at the good cow."

This time, I chewed my cud before speaking. "Yes, but this competition is supposed to be at a high level. Surely the Dorfman twins don't think they can win with an entry that doesn't meet objective criteria."

"Is it possible they do not intend to win, only to sell the cow?"

"Ha! An interesting theory. But you would think they could find a buyer back home for the buxom bovine."

"Not for this baby," a voice behind me said.

I whirled, and found myself staring down into the flyaway eyebrows of Harmon Dorfman.

12

"Howdy-do, Miss Yoder," Harmon said, and tipped a straw hat. He grinned.

"I'll let you know when my heart stops racing."

"And you must be an aye-mish man," Harmon said and extended a beefy paw to Mose.

"Yah, I am Amish."

"We have youse in North Dakota too. Best-looking farms I ever seen. Same thing here. Tell me, how many bushels of corn do youse get to an acre?"

"Okay, it's stopped racing," I said. "Do you often sneak up on people?"

"No, ma'am. Of course, I don't get me much chance, on account of Harry and I don't get out very much."

"I thought your brother was married."

"Oh he is, but she run back to her family after two weeks. So far he ain't seen fit to go after her."

"How long has it been?"

"Five years come July."

Mose shook his head in bewilderment. Although he's had to interact with us English his entire adult life, he still finds our ways strange. Funny, but I used to exclude myself from the category English, coming as I did from a Mennonite family that descended from Amish forebears. But that was then and this is now, as my pseudo-stepdaughter, Alison, says.

Now that I was no longer of the blood, but the unwanted offspring of a carnival caller — hmm, my biological mama might not have been the caller. She could just as well have been the bearded lady, or the amazing snake woman. What's more, short of a DNA test, I had no proof who my papa was either. For all I knew, he could have been a count from Liechtenstein who'd done the extracurricular mattress mambo with a housemaid, who then handed me off to a passing carnival. Did that, perchance, make me a countess?

"Miss Yoder? Miss Yoder! Are you all right?"

"I'm fine as the bearded lady's nose hair, and you may call me Countess Yoder-Rosen of Liechtenstein."

"Ach," Mose said. The poor man was,

however, used to my flights of fancy.

"Miss Yoder, if you don't mind me saying, you're a hoot."

"Owl accept that as a compliment. Tell me, Mr. Dorfman, why have you hauled this unremarkable cow all the way from North Dakota?"

"Because Cindy Sue — that's her name — ain't unremarkable, on account of the other one, Cora Beth, is her clone."

"Excuse me?"

"Youse know what a clone is, Miss Yoder, right?"

"I read newspapers, Mr. Dorfman, as well as the Bible." A clone! Perhaps that applied to me. Okay, so scientists had yet to clone a human forty-eight years ago — at least not one that we know of — but it was possible the government had been working on it secretly. After all, if we really knew everything that the government has been up to, it would boggle our minds to the point that we'd all go insane.

And *if* I was a clone, that would go a long way to explain the feeling I've always had that somewhere there is an identical twin just waiting to be reunited with me. But even if scientists could clone the human body, what about the soul? Would the new person have one? If not, would they still be human, or just look like one? And if the soul could be cloned, and the original person was "saved," would the clone be saved as well? What if the pope was cloned, and his clone disagreed with him on theological issues? Who would be infallible?

"You sure don't look very well, Miss Yoder."

"Yah," Mose said. "Magdalena, I think maybe you should sit down."

"Sitting is for wusses. Continue, dear, with this cloning gibberish."

"It's not gibberish. You see, Harry has himself a biology degree from the University of North Dakota. When all this cloning stuff started happening, he took special notice, and studied up on it. Then one day, he and some of his buddies decided to try and clone a Holstein. The rest, as they say, is historic."

"That would be 'history,' dear."

"That's what I'm telling youse."

"Then why haven't I heard about it before now?"

" 'Cause it's top secret, on account of this time the clone — that would be Cora Beth — turned out better than the original. I mean, see for yourself."

"I see an exceptional cow and an average one. How am I supposed to tell which is which?"

"Um — well, I guess youse is gonna have to trust me on that one, Miss Yoder. But I don't got no reason to lie to you. Anyway, as soon as word of this gets out, they'll likely be a million scientists clamoring to test this baby. They'll be lots of folks wanting to buy her too. At top dollar."

"So that's why you brought her all this way? To create a media sensation at my Holstein competition?"

"With all due respect, ma'am, I didn't know it was *your* competition."

"You know what I mean, and there'll be nothing of the kind. This is an event the sole purpose of which is to select America's best dairy cow; this is not a circus. Do I make myself clear?"

"Yes, ma'am. But could I bring my own reporter?"

"No clone, no press announcement."

"But Miss Yoder —"

"Is this a legitimate question?"

But it was Mose's hand that popped up. "Yah, Magdalena, I have a question."

"Yes, Mose?"

"What does it mean, this clone?"

"It means — well, in a nutshell it means that scientists are trying to play God, and that in this case in particular, Harry and his

111

buddies were able to take a microscopic piece of so-so Cindy Sue and turn it into the breathtaking Cora Beth."

"Ach! Like at creation?"

"Pretty much."

"Get behind me, Satan," Mose said, and wisely fled the scene.

"Just so you know," I said to Harmon Dorfman, "if fire and brimstone rain down on my farm, you'll have to reimburse me."

Hernia, Pennsylvania, is a charming little town — or so I've heard — set, as it is, in a valley between two wooded mountain ridges in southern Pennsylvania. It's a nice place to live, but I wouldn't want to visit. After one has spent several hours staring at its inhabitants, there is nothing else for tourists to do. We have no movie theaters, no shopping malls, just a feed store and a dismal little grocery that sells outrageously priced products bearing expiration dates written in ancient Phoenician. The last is only a slight exaggeration.

We are a simple people, and although we tend to be conservative, we do not vote for the shedding of blood. Yes, we do have Baptists and Methodists in our midst, but for the most part they have been tempered by their proximity to folks of the Amish and

Mennonite faiths, both of which abide by pacifist principles.

Many people think that Mennonite and Amish are interchangeable terms, but they most certainly are not. The Mennonite Church began in the 1500s and was named after Menno Simons. A century later, the Amish Church, under the leadership of Jakob Ammann, broke away from the Mennonite Church, claiming it was too liberal. Both churches have undergone many changes over the centuries, but their relative differences remain.

The First Mennonite Church is the most liberal branch of the Plain People in Hernia and its environs. The most conservative is the Old Order Amish Church. Its members are the ones seen riding horses and buggies. Then there are the Black Bumper Amish, who are allowed to drive black cars just as long as the chrome is painted black. I belong to a conservative branch of the Mennonite Church, the one to which the Good Lord would belong if he were living on earth today. I drive and use electricity, but dress conservatively, like the Good Lord intended, and wear my braids neatly tucked beneath a white organza prayer cap. For the record, I do not consider myself better than anyone else in Hernia, not even the Presbyterians. I believe that in Heaven, we will all be to-gether — except for some Baptists, who will have their own neighborhood.

Oops, I may have fibbed: try as I might, I can't help feeling that I am a little bit better than Samuel Nevin Yoder, the owner of Yo-der's Corner Market. Sam is — or at least was, until certain recent disclosures — a first cousin of mine. We are the same age, which means I sat in front of him all through grammar school. Not only did Sam dip my braids in the inkwell on his desk, he often sat on my lunch bag, regularly passed gas loudly before pointing to me, and on at least three occasions clapped the chalk-filled erasers on my ears. It wasn't until high school that I learned that Sam had done all these things because of a crush on me.

As early as our sophomore year in high school, Sam proposed marriage, urging me to elope with him to South Carolina, where kinship and age were both less of an issue. I hotly refused. In the intervening decades, Sam married a Methodist woman, Dorothy, and even became a Methodist himself, but his crush on me has never waned.

One might think that his feelings for me would result in a price break at his store, but then one would be wrong. As a result, shoddy merchandise aside, I almost never shop at Yoder's Corner Market, but I do stop by regularly to get the scuttlebutt on the latest Hernia happenings. As mayor of this little burg, I see that as my duty.

The market's front door has a string of sleigh bells attached to it. "Well, well," Sam called out, in a voice so nasal one would have thought he was a native of Manhattan, "if it isn't the blushing bride."

"Good morning, Sam."

"Honestly, Magdalena, you're positively glowing. I haven't seen a face that radiant since my Dorothy was a girl."

"She had oily skin, dear — but it cleared up nicely, don't you think?"

"Everywhere but on her back. So, what can I do you out of?"

"Not my money, that's for sure. Sam, I suppose you heard about Doc."

"Agnes Mishler called last night. Around ten, I think it was. If I get my hands around the son of a —"

His last word was muffled by the gasps of several Amish women who were shopping among the stacks. Just how they knew to anticipate it is beyond me. As for *moi*, I married a man from the Fallen Apple. Enough said.

I moved closer to my cousin, but not within kissing range. "What about your customers? Anything you've heard so far this morning that might raise a red flag?"

"You know I don't gossip about my customers."

The Amish women murmured their appreciation.

"If your lips were any looser," I said, "the next time you sneezed, they'd fly right off your face."

Not only did he take that as a compliment, but he had the nerve to grin. "Well, Connie Betz said she hoped Doc had a long recovery."

"That way she can visit him in the hospital, and her husband won't be any wiser."

He looked crestfallen. "Is that so? How did *you* know they were an item?"

"They're not an item, Sam. Connie keeps pursuing Doc, but he isn't the least bit interested in her. Doc may be a Lothario, but he does set certain standards; married women is one of the places he draws the line."

"Hmm."

"Anything else?"

"Nah. You know as well as I do that Doc is everyone's favorite old geezer. Almost makes me wish I was his age."

"Trust me, dear, it isn't just Doc's age that makes him attractive to women."

116

"Ouch, that hurt."

"I'm referring to his cooking. Just because food is the way to a man's heart, doesn't mean women can't be seduced by it as well. Besides, not only can Doc cook, but he knows how to make a woman feel waited on hand and foot."

"Magdalena, are you smitten by him?"

"*What?* No! I am happily married — and glowing. You said so yourself."

Sam had the temerity to look relieved. Apparently, the Babester didn't count as competition, given that he was an outsider, and as such wasn't likely to stick around.

"Yup," he said, "you're glowing like a jack-o'-lantern with two candles inside."

"Thanks — I think. Sam, you wouldn't happen to know of anyone who'd be qualified to judge the Holstein competition on a minute's notice, would you?"

"You betcha."

"Who?"

"You're looking at his handsome mug."

"You?"

"Do you forget, oh my fair one, that I was raised on a dairy farm, just like you were? In fact, my pops was in charge of the breeding book for the tri-counties. He had me milking by the time I was four — and not with machines either. No sirree, Bob, my

117

little hands were squeezing teats before they'd even picked up a pencil."

That certainly explained a great deal; no wonder Dorothy Yoder walked around with a pained expression on her face. I shook my head vigorously to clear it of some very unpleasant images.

"But I did," Sam insisted.

"The judges don't get paid, you know."

"Magdalena, what must you think of me? I wouldn't be doing it for the money. Even a lowlife like me can want to give back to the community."

"I've never called you a lowlife!"

"Then maybe it's because you have your hair pulled back in that severe bun that I can read your mind."

"Who knew it was in large print? But seriously, Sam, who will watch the store?"

"I'll get Dorothy. She can bring chocolate-covered bonbons with her. I'll drag in the couch from the back room and set up a little color TV here by the register. She won't even notice the difference."

"I need you tomorrow morning. Can you rent a forklift truck that soon?" In the twenty years she's been married, Dorothy, bless her dear Methodist heart, has eaten her way from a size six to a special-made size sixty. Sam has had to install double doors throughout his house, but getting his wife from the house to another location always presents a challenge.

"I'll manage. If I have to, since it's downhill all the way, I'll wrap her in bubble wrap and roll her."

"Sam, that's awful — still, it did work for the Taste of Hernia Festival last summer. And if I recall correctly, it was her idea."

"Yup, the only bad part was that she had to wait two weeks before I could roll her back up. So, see you tomorrow?"

"Nine o'clock sharp. And bring your glasses."

I waited patiently for two tourist-driven cars and the Gindlespergers' buggy to pass before hoofing it over to pay my regards to young Chris.

13

The Hernia police station is directly across the street from Sam's. While standing in the doorway of the grocery, one could literally throw a stale roll and hit a police officer as he, or she, exits the building. I'm not advocating such behavior, mind you, but recalling those good times are the only decent memories I have of Melvin Stoltzfus, our erstwhile chief. Although the police station was my next order of business, the Devil had other plans for me.

Adjacent to Sam Yoder's Corner Market is Hernia's only public phone booth. For all the difference it would make, there may as well be a sign out front restricting its use to Amish only. We Mennonites have cell phones, but the Amish don't even have landlines in their houses. For so-called "matters of importance," they wait patiently in a queue for the opportunity to call other phone booths in distant Amish communities. To my knowledge, I, Magdalena Portulaca Yoder, am the only non-Amish person to have used the phone in the last ten years. But like I said, the Devil had my number now.

Of course, it wasn't all my fault; although the Amish are long-suffering, I could see that Rebecca Bumgardner had used more than her fair share of minutes, as well as goodwill. This was evident in the body language of the others waiting in line, some of whom were asleep on their feet. When I saw Rebecca hang up and dial again, that's when I listened to Lucifer. After five minutes or so, just as the loquacious Miss Bumgardner was fishing in her apron pocket for another phone number, I hit the speed dial on my cell. Since calls frequently come in to that phone, Rebecca answered as a matter of course.

"Hello?"

"Gut marriye," I said in Dutch. I spoke as low as I could.

"Yah, *gut marriye.*"

Having all but exhausted my Amish vocabulary, I switched to King James English. "Rebecca Bumgardner, dost thou not know that selfishness is a sin?"

Rebecca's first reaction was to look skyward. A solitary cloud was drifting slowly overhead. In a theology where Heaven is "up," this phenomenon added a great deal to the atmosphere.

"Who are you?" she whispered.

"I am who I am."

"Ach!" The poor child — she is only fourteen, after all — nearly dropped the receiver. "Are you *He?*"

"Do I sound like a he?"

"Not so much."

"Rats — I mean wrath. My wrath shall be visited upon teenage girls who hog the phone."

The girl was more intelligent than I'd anticipated. This time she glanced around.

"Ach, it is only you, Magdalena Yoder."

"Nonetheless, you need to relinquish the phone so others can use it."

"What does relinquish mean?"

"It means *give it up.* You've yammered on long enough, dear."

It was soon quite apparent that Rebecca was not an Amish teenager, but a teenager who happened to be Amish. "I can talk to my friends if I want to, Miss Yoder. You are not my mama."

"No, but I am the town mayor. This phone belongs to the municipality, and I am hereby ordering you to hang up immediately, or I will embarrass you in front of this group by placing you under citizen's arrest."

Okay, so maybe I was going a little bit overboard, but better safe than sorry, right? Besides, I was such a goody two-shoes growing up that a threat like that would have had me shaking in my brogans. Surely, Miss Bumgardner would crumple like a starched bonnet left out in the rain.

"Yah? Do you think I care, Magdalena Yoder? I will tell them that you pretended to be God. Ha, so there."

"But I didn't! I was only pretending to be a heavenly hostess. You drew your own conclusions."

"Then I will tell them that you hired those inalienable legals to take care of your cows."

"The *who?*"

"Mexicans," she hissed.

"But I didn't!"

"Again with the lies, Miss Yoder. My brother, Amos, had to go into Bedford this morning to deliver eggs to the IGA. I rode with him in the family buggy as far as here. When we passed your place, we saw two of these Mexicans leave your barn and head for the woods."

"What? When?"

"Just after milking time."

"And you've been blabbing on the phone ever since then?"

"It's my *rumschpringe* — if you must know." She was referring to the community-sanctioned period of rebellion every Amish young person is entitled to before baptism at age twenty, when they must choose whether to put away the world for good.

"You're *sixteen* already?"

"Ach, no. I am seventeen next week."

Although I do not watch television, I do listen to the radio upon occasion, therefore — oh, whom am I kidding? I confess! Gabriel talked me into going with him and Ida to see a theatrical production in Pittsburgh last month. *Fiddler on the Roof*. Frankly, I was pleasantly surprised by the number of traditions his people and my people have in common. In addition, some of the tunes were quite catchy.

"Sunrise," I began to sing, in my not too unpleasant voice. I began softly at first, building to a crescendo by the time I got to the word "years." One by one, the good folks in the queue awoke, and by the time I had finished this astonishingly moving ballad, I had everyone's attention — even that of three stray dogs. Sam, however, was the only one who clapped.

"Brava," he yelled from the doorway of his shop. "Brava!"

Rebecca Bumgardner, who had turned a

frightening shade of fuchsia, was definitely not amused. "I am not your little girl, Miss Yoder; you did not carry me!"

"All the same, dear, *tempus fugit.*"

Having jumped to the wrong conclusion, more than one person gasped. It goes to show you how much the outside world, with its obscene speech, has already rubbed off on these gentle people. I didst protest my innocence, and whilst doing so, Rebecca took off running. I cast my reputation asunder and took off after her, but, alas, I could not overtake the fair maiden. By the time I showed up at Chief Ackerman's office door, I was panting like a two-headed bride on her wedding night.

Chris was on the phone when I walked in, just saying good-bye. He stood and smiled.

"Not a bad parody, Miss Yoder."

"I beg your pardon?"

"Your singing. The way you hammed it up, pretending to be a female impersonator."

"I did no such thing!"

"That was supposed to be a serious rendition?"

"Yes."

"Oops. Of course I was listening with only one ear, seeing as how I was on the phone, and these windows seem to have exceptionally thick glass that distorts sound."

"Harrumph. I'll have you know that others have said — well, never you mind. And please, I've told you a million times to call me Magdalena."

"Magdalena, that was the hospital on the phone. Doc opened his eyes this morning. It was just for a second, but still, that's supposed to be an excellent sign. The nurse said that the next seventy-two hours are critical. But if Doc does wake up, there is a chance he could make a full recovery."

"Praise God and pass the mashed potatoes!"

"What was that?"

"Oh, just something Alison says when I ask her to recite grace. It was the first thing that popped into my mind."

"Yeah, well, I'm really glad about Doc too. So, have you come up with any leads so far?"

I told young Chris about the supposed clone and Rebecca's sighting of illegal aliens. He dismissed the former out of hand.

"Are there any Hispanics in Hernia? If so, no one's ever mentioned them."

"Alice Beckerman's father was born in Paraguay. But his parents were Amish emigrants from Pennsylvania. I don't think that counts. You see, Chris, folks in our community are still willing to do menial labor. When the Amish need to put up a barn, the entire community pitches in — sometimes even non-Amish get involved — and the barn is built in literally one day."

"That's incredible."

"You're darn tooting — oops, I didn't mean to swear. I sort of got carried away with pride — oops, that's an even bigger sin. Before these lips sink my shapely ship — oops! Spit it out, man — why are you asking about Hispanics?"

Young Chris smiled. "Miss Yoder, have you ever been in therapy?"

"I was shrunk once by a visiting shrink, but I'm not so sure it took. But again with the questions. You're not planning to convert to Judaism, are you? I mean, not that there's anything wrong with that — especially in your case, given that you're doomed to Hell anyway. Of course, that's not me talking, but the Bible."

"What?"

"Never mind. Get back to the Hispanics."

"It's just that several people have called in, reporting two brown-skinned men crossing their fields, or loitering about at the edge of their woods. No one has seen them close up, so they can't get any more specific than that."

Then a candle was lit in my feeble little brain. "They're Gertie Fuselburger's hired hands. She promised to look after them. Implied they weren't lacking for a place to stay. But I have a hunch they slept in my barn last night."

"And you're okay with this?"

"I most certainly am not! You can be sure Miss Fuselburger is going to pay extra for the privilege of bunking her help in the most exclusive accommodations this side of the Wyoming state line."

"Forgive me, Miss Yoder, but do you honestly consider sleeping on hay to be an exclusive experience?"

"They'll each get two burlap bags, which they can keep, and a large coffee can — the six-seater outhouse I have now is just for show. Plus, the ambiance of sleeping in a replica of an authentic Amish barn. What other inn that you know of offers such perks?"

He smiled again. "You've got me there. But I would think that allowing Miss Fuselburger's employees access to the cows all night could lead to some interesting problems."

Just because my police chief has a very attractive head does not mean it's empty. "Oh? What sort of problems?"

14

"Well, for starters, they could poison the cows."

"You mean like with jimson weed?"

"Yeah, or anything. And it doesn't even have to be lethal — heck, it doesn't even have to be anything at all. What I'm saying is that if the other contestants find out about this — about letting those men sleep in the barn near their cows — they could demand the cows all be tested. That means that the competition could be delayed."

"Over my dead body."

"Miss Yoder, please don't say that."

"Are you superstitious?"

"Is the pope German?"

"Tell me, Miss Yoder, what have you managed to learn from your guests?"

"Well, the Pearlmutters danced the bedroom bossa nova *six* times last night; both Dorfman brothers tried to show up for breakfast wearing only wife-beater T-shirts and jam-jam bottoms; Gertie Fuselburger left her chompers unattended in the downstairs powder room; and as for that dear, sweet Candy Brown, I think she's lying about being Polish. Neither she, nor her husband, had ever heard of pierogies. Now why would someone lie about being Polish, I ask you? Where there is one lie, there are sure to be many — that's what Granny Yoder always used to say, although she seemed to have no trouble *not* telling me that my birth mother was really a gypsy girl from a traveling carnival. If you ask me, withholding information is just another way of lying. But when it comes to lies, the one that really takes the cake is the whopper the Dorfman brothers think we're stupid enough to swallow. Ha, a cloned cow indeed!"

"Excuse me, Miss Yoder, do you think the Dorfmans are serious about the cloned cow story?"

"They at least *want* us to believe that Harry was able to turn a plain cow into a show-quality specimen via some secret process. What's even worse is that they're hoping to create a media sensation by announcing their hoax at my — I mean, our — Holstein competition."

"Hmm. That might not be all bad."

"Et tu, Brute?"

"You see, Miss Yoder, the kind of person who'd assault an old man like Doc is the same kind who tends to love media attention. It wouldn't surprise me if that wasn't Doc's handwriting on your barn stall, but the assailant's. At any rate, wouldn't Hernia benefit from the additional coverage? You know what they say: there is no such thing as bad press."

"I take it then that no one has ever publicly accused you of being Bigfoot and interbreeding with Melvin the Mantis?"

"I beg your pardon?"

"Never mind. Look, I have an idea that may flush this creep out into the open before tomorrow and the official start of the competition. If it works, I'm pulling the plug on the Dorfman entries."

The handsome young man leaned forward eagerly. "What's your plan?"

"What do cows say?"

"Moo?"

"Bingo."

Twenty thousand dollars is a lot of moola, even for *moi*. Well, not really. Over the years since I inherited the PennDutch Inn, I have learned to pinch a penny until it screams for mercy. But my point is that, for most folks, twenty big ones was not chump

131

change. The police station has a copy machine, paid for by yours truly, so I had no compunctions about using it to print up flyers offering a reward for any information leading to the arrest of Doc's assailant.

I had just taped a flyer to a telephone pole in the historic part of town, when the driver of a passing vehicle slammed on the brakes and jumped out. As my eyes refocused, my heart sank. One of the Dorfman brothers was striding toward me, now completely sans shirt, while his shorts hung precariously low. His hairy belly swayed from side to side with each step. I stood rooted to the sidewalk, too mortified to move. It was like watching the approach of a wooly mammoth — although of course such a creature never existed, and even if it had, it would have perished at the hands of the first Americans, who paradoxically arrived on this continent at least four thousand years before the world was even created.

"Miss Yoder, I need a word."

"Extraneously."

"Is that Aye-mish?"

"Nay, 'tis not."

"Miss Yoder, I don't speak Aye-mish. Just regular ol' English."

"Alas and alack, we lack an interpreter. But speak loudly, and then maybe I'll understand. What is it that you want, Mr. Dorfman?"

"Harry."

"Indeed, you are. And since you brought up the subject, going shirtless is just not done in Hernia. Besides, aren't you freezing to death?"

"Ma'am, it's seventy degrees. Back in North Dakota we don't get this kind of weather in April."

"Harrumph."

"Is that Aye-mish too?"

"*Nicht, nein, nyet.* Please, hairy Harry, cut to the chase. But just don't run; the sight of your unsightly abdomen swaying at high speed may cause me to poke out my mind's eye."

"Uh . . ."

"The word you wanted with me. What seems to be the problem? It isn't about that rust brown stain on the carpet, is it? Because it's ketchup, not blood. The man who died in your room was strangled to death."

"I beg your pardon?"

"Oops. I must have lapsed into Amish again. A lot of their words sound like English, but have different meanings." Okay, so that was an out-and-out fib. But the truth might have upset him so much that he'd have a heart attack.

He nodded and pulled a crumpled flyer from a pocket of his khaki shorts. "I seen this outside the feed store. Is this for real?"

"Yes."

"Hot diggity dog! I'm getting me a new water tank for my herd with this here reward money."

My heart began to pound. "You know something about Doc's assailant?"

"Yes sirree, I reckon I do. And what are the chances I'd find you just by driving around this pretty little city, looking up and down the streets like I did?"

"Spit it out, man!"

"Well, you remember dinner last night?"

"Vaguely — of course I do!" To my credit, I did not vocalize some of the epithets swirling around in my mind, only a tongue's reach away from twitching lips.

"You remember when that, uh, exotic dancer — Candy's her name — got up to use the ladies' room?"

"Just so you know, I do not suffer from dementia, Mr. Dorfman. I remember everything you're about to ask me."

"Oh, I ain't gonna ask you nothin' else. Anyway, I was thinking to myself that Candy was taking an awful long time in the powder room, even if she was doing all them things ladies sometimes do. Then I happened to glance out the window, and even though it was dark outside, on account of you have that security light, I could see her come out of the barn. She looks around, and then runs back up to the house. That's how come she was breathing so hard when she got back to the table. That weren't no asthma attack like she said."

My jaw dropped so far that I could have swallowed a sparrow, had one perchance flown into my mouth. To my recollection, Candy had not been gone that long — just long enough to do her business, wash her hands for thirty seconds using soap and hot water, and then tidy up the basin. But folks didn't tidy up after themselves anymore, did they? A lot of them didn't even bother to wash their hands — or so I've been told.

"What motive would she have? She didn't even know Doc. He's a sweet old man who wouldn't hurt a fly. His only fault is that he, uh, loves women."

"You mean he's as horny as a billy goat?"

"If one must be crude." A flock of geese walked across my grave. Maybe that was it; old Doc had made a pass at Candy, who interpreted his attention as sexual harassment. Rather than come to me with the problem, she'd taken the matter into her own hands. Perhaps she'd clobbered him with a pitchfork handle, or a piece of siding that pulled loose. Although nothing appeared to be missing, barns, like most folks' garages, tend to accumulate stuff, making it hard to account for things.

He chuckled, as if proud of himself for shocking me. Which he hadn't, of course.

"I'm ready whenever you are," he said with a leer.

"Why, I never!" Well, actually I have, but only within the confines of holy matrimony — although the first time wasn't quite so holy, given that the billy goat in question was still hitched to that harlot up in Minnesota. I'm exempting washing machines, of course, not that it's any of your business.

"Believe it or not, Miss Yoder, I am not the least bit interested in your past, no matter how checkered it might be. I just want the twenty thousand dollars you promised in this here flyer."

"I'll have you know that my past is *not* checkered. Lightly speckled, perhaps, but that's as much as I'll concede. As for the twenty big ones, first we'll have to see if your information leads to the arrest of Candy Brown for the assault on Doc Shafor."

"What's there to see? You are the power in this town, ain't you?"

"Well, I *am* mayor, and I *do* pay the chief's salary — get behind me, Satan!"

Harry glanced around nervously. "Where?"

"At the moment, he resides in you, dear. I will not be tempted to use my power — such as it is — to railroad that sweet little Polish girl, even if she dances for money."

"What sweet little Polish girl?"

"The one with all the freckles and the strawberry blond curls."

"Excuse me, Miss Yoder, but boy howdy, have you been bamboozled. That girl ain't Polish, and she don't dance at no South Pole neither. She dances in them topless bars where she wraps herself around a metal pole in all manner of suggestiveness."

I let that sink in before opening my big trap. "You mean — you don't mean *that,* do you?"

He nodded gravely. "I'm afraid I do. I don't know about youse guys, but in North Dakota, we consider that a worse sin than the real thing."

"Indeed!"

"So you'll arrest her?"

"Tempus fugit," I cried, and then, remembering the most recent reaction to this quite respectable Latin phrase, I fled like a roach when the light's been turned on. Unfortu-

nately, I was headed right into Harmon's way.

15

CHEESECAKE ICE CREAM RECIPE

Ingredients:

6 oz (150 g) cream cheese

3/4 cup granulated sugar
1/2 pint (250 ml) sour cream
1/2 pint (250 ml) double (heavy) cream

1/4 teaspoon vanilla extract
3 tablespoons fresh lemon juice

Place the cream cheese into a mixing bowl, and beat until soft and smooth. Slowly add the sugar, and then beat in the sour cream followed by the double (heavy) cream. Add the vanilla extract and lemon juice, and mix until thick and smooth. Cover and chill in the refrigerator for two to three hours. Take the chilled mixture and beat until creamy, then transfer the complete mixture into an

ice cream maker, and follow the manufacturer's instructions.

16

I'd driven straight for the inn, and knowing the shortest route, I quite reasonably expected to get there first. So you can imagine my surprise when I stepped out of my car and was greeted by Harry.

"How did you do that?" I cried.

"Gosh, Miss Yoder, you heard that inside your car? Well, it was a good one. Didn't last long, but great resonance. Heck, they earned me quite a reputation with the frat boys."

"TMI!"

"No, MIT — Mid–North Dakota Institute of Techno-biology."

"Mr. Dorfman, the sound quality of bodily functions is not much admired in Pennsylvania, and, as I told you before, neither are bare bellies."

"You never said no such thing."

"But I did. Just a few minutes ago. And pray tell, how didst thou get here so fast?

141

Thee hadst to have broken the speed limit. I know whereof I speak, having broken the speed limit myself. As a God-fearing woman, I am supposed to obey the law, but I was helping the chief solve a crime, therefore, at least in mine eyes, I had pseudo-dispensation. But verily, thou didst drive like Jehu, son of Nimshi, except thou didst not drive a chariot, and thus, perchance, drove a great deal faster."

"Huh? Was that English?"

"King James — to a degree. Now tell me, Mr. Dorfman, how did you get here so fast?"

"Well ma'am, once we caught the interstate in Grand Forks, it was pretty much smooth sailing all the way."

"No, I mean just now. Between the historic district and here."

"Uh — you must be talking about Harry, ma'am, 'cause I ain't left your place since we arrived yesterday. I'm Harmon."

"You're sure?"

"Sure as shooting."

"My apologies, then. But please, cover yourself. Global warming notwithstanding, we are a conservative community, and do not bare our vulnerable parts outside the bondage — I mean bonds — of marriage."

"That's a shame, Miss Yoder, because you have yourself a great body. Them clothes you're wearing don't hide that fact neither."

A compliment from any source, short of the Devil, is a gift to be appreciated. If only for a moment. To ignore the giver is to be arrogant, which is the third worst sin in Magdalena's lexicon of the Ten Greatest Spiritual Boo-boos, right up there under sex and dancing.

"Thanks," I said. "Just don't get any ideas, because I'm a happily married woman."

"You are? How come I ain't seen a husband?"

"Because he's staying at his own house across the road, on account of there's a maniacal mantis on the loose — oh, never mind. It's a long story."

He shook his not so handsome head, his overgrown eyebrows flowing in the breeze he generated. "And some folks think we cornhuskers is backward."

"Embrace the truth," I said and tried unsuccessfully to move around him.

"Miss Yoder, I got something you hafta see."

"Seen one, seen them all — which is not saying much, believe me."

He pulled something out of his shorts pocket. Mercifully, in doing so, he hiked them up a bit.

"See this here cigarette?"

143

"Um — yes."

"I found this in the paddock where my cows are."

"That's impossible. There's no smoking allowed on my premises, and besides, if a cow ingested a cigarette, it could get very sick. It might even prove to be fatal."

"Exactly. And that's my complaint."

"You mean you really did find it here?"

"Miss Yoder, I don't know how it plays in Pennsylvania, but folks in North Dakota don't lie."

"Not even your politicians?"

"No, ma'am."

"More's the pity." I closed my eyes for a second as the gravity of the situation sunk in. "You think it was deliberate? This cigarette, I mean."

"Had to be. It was out near the middle of the paddock, and it's fresh. Whoever it was, she wanted to stop us from competing."

"She?"

"Look closely, ma'am. There's lipstick on this end."

I whipped a tissue out of my purse, and lifted the stub from his hand. There was indeed a splotchy ring of scarlet around the filtered end. "The only woman here who wears scarlet lipstick is Gertie Fuselburger. And hers is always partly worn off — not that I've been keeping track, mind you. But if *I* was going to paint my face like Jezebel, I'd at least keep up with repairs."

"You gonna call the police, or do you want me to?"

"I will. But just so you know, in a way, I *am* the police."

He rolled his eyes like a petulant teenager. "Somehow I don't think so."

"But I am!" I wailed, and then realizing that my wailing tends to annoy people — besides being humanly impossible — I decided to set my sights on results, rather than tend my wounded pride. "I'll take care of it, I promise."

"After I found this one, I searched the paddock real well. But just because I couldn't find any more, doesn't mean that my cows didn't already eat them. No hard feelings, ma'am, if they come down sick, I'm gonna hafta sue."

"What?"

"Cindy Sue is worth about two grand, but Cora Beth, on account of her historic scientific significance, I'd say is worth upwards of fifty grand. Maybe even as much as one hundred."

"Does this cigarette contain marijuana?"

"Come again?"

"Is this coffin nail illegal in all fifty states

as a recreational substance?"

"Ma'am, anyone ever accuse you of being Looney Tunes? 'Cause this here ain't no nail; it's a cigarette."

I would have bitten off the tip of my tongue, but that thip thailed long ago. "I can see that, Mr. Dorfman. I'm asking if there's marijuana in it. Because if you've been puffing your way into this fantasy, I'm issuing a citizen's arrest."

His brows bristled. It was like watching a pair of porcupines square off.

"You take back that insinuation, or I'm suing you for slander as well."

Thank goodness for high school gym class. Although I hated it at the time — it was first period, and I had to attend all my classes with wet, stringy hair and smelling like eau de locker room — Mrs. Proschel made sure her girls were at least adequate touch-football players. (We suspected Mrs. Proschel was once an NFL linebacker, but that's another story.) At any rate, when push comes to shove, I can shove with the best of them.

First I pushed, and when Harmon was dancing about, trying to catch his balance, I shoved him to the ground. Then I made a beeline to the kitchen. I know, what I did is not Christian, and I have since confessed this most un-Mennonite of sins to the Lord. But at least I've never smoked a cigarette — well, not an entire one. And my adultery, as well as all three of my drunken episodes, was inadvertent.

I slammed the kitchen door. "I can't stand that man," I bellowed.

"Ach!" Freni pointed to the oven. "Now the cakes have fallen, yah?"

"I'll help them up as soon as I catch my breath."

"Always the jokes, Magdalena. But what will we serve the English for dessert? Pudding from a box?"

"If it was good enough for the box, it's good enough for them. Speaking of the English, where are our guests now?"

"They have all gone to inspect the show ring. Some of them are spectacle. They think we in Hernia cannot put on a real competition."

"You mean skeptical, dear."

"Yah?"

"Then they are in for a surprise. Team Magdalena has turned the high school stadium into a world-class arena. We're even selling popcorn. And Gummi Bears. You can't get any higher class than that. But by the way, not all of the English are in town;

one of the twins is standing by the driveway. If you go outside, you may wish to avert your eyes. He isn't wearing a shirt, and it's not a pretty sight."

Freni wiped her hands on her apron, and then shuffled to the nearest window, where she gingerly pulled back the curtain. Apparently, the opportunity to spy on a half-naked man was too rare of an occurrence to pass up. I could see her eyes widen behind the bottle-thick glasses.

"Ach, *du lieber!* It's Sodium and Gomorrah."

"Close enough. Now turn around and don't look back, lest you turn into a pillar of salt."

She turned reluctantly. "Why does he do that?"

"Because he thinks it's a warm day, and wants to tan. Plus he probably thinks that because we're a small town, we're all hicks. But even that's no excuse. I wouldn't go to North Dakota and take off my dress."

Freni clucked like a hen that had just laid an egg. "How you talk! Your mama would roll over in her grave."

"Ha. Right now, my mama is probably telling fortunes in a tent. Either that, or swinging from a trapeze. Either way, I don't think she'd be bothered by a reference to partial nudity. After all, I didn't say anything about removing my slip."

"It is not good to be so bitter, Magdalena. It hurts only you — and the ones you love. Your daughter needs a normal life, yah?"

Despite the fact that she was lecturing me, my heart overflowed with love for Freni. She'd called Alison my daughter! Plain and simple. The words "step" or "foster" hadn't even been mentioned.

"Freni," I cried, as I attempted to throw my arms around her, "I love you."

"Ach!"

Freni, responding to five hundred years of inbred reservation, ducked, while my arms closed around an empty prayer cap. The second I caught her, I plopped the cap back on her head.

"I'm sorry, dear. But now that I know that my birth mother wasn't a Mennonite, my body has been acting in strange ways. You don't suppose my birth mother could have been from Kazakhstan, do you?"

"More riddles. But speaking of Alison, she asks me to give you a message."

"Oh?"

"She called from school and said that Mary Ruth Westheimer has invited her to spend the weekend at her house. She said that since it is Friday, and they wear the same size clothes, could she go straight home on the bus with her friend?"

"What did you tell her?"

Mary Ruth is "Church Amish," as opposed to "House Amish." That is to say, her family is so liberal that they constantly totter on the brink of becoming Mennonites. They even allow Mary Ruth to attend public school, although her distinctive dress still sets her apart. Alison, always the champion of the underdog — that's how she sees herself — immediately took the girl under her wing, and they have become fast friends. A weekend spent with the Westheimers would benefit both girls, and absolutely no harm could come of it. Perhaps if I could steal a minute from the competition, I would drop by and snap a photo of Alison decked out in Amish clothes. The next time she tries to wear a hoochie-mama outfit to school, I could threaten to blackmail her with it.

"I said that her mama would call the school if the answer was no. Otherwise, she could let the good times roll, yah?"

"A good enough try at slang, albeit several decades behind the times. Well, dear, if you'll excuse me, I'm going to hoof it upstairs to the guestrooms to do a little legally sanctioned snooping under the guise of housekeeping."

"But all the guests are on ALPO plan; they must clean their own rooms."

"So they get a break today, and I won't charge them a penny less, if that makes them feel any better. And if the bare-bellied North Dakotan heads upstairs, whistle for me."

Then, before my wise mentor and friend could talk any sense into me, I hightailed it from the kitchen.

17

If one is to snoop into guests' drawers, 'tis wise to be schooled in the ways of the world. One is sure to find things that would make Beelzebub blush: lingerie every bit as revealing as a spider web; magazines with pictures so obscene that one must flip through them a second time in order to grasp the gravity of the situation, so that one might properly pray for the owner's redemption; and hand-held, battery-operated gizmos that make even the best washing machine, the ones with the most unbalanced load imaginable, obsolete — if you know what I mean. Such are the burdens that an amateur sleuth like me must bear. And in all humility, I bore them cheerfully.

The Dorfman brothers, it was immediately clear, had diametrically opposed tastes in magazines, and packed a paucity of underwear.

Jane and Dick Pearlmutter, despite their

highfalutin ways, bought most of their clothes from JCPenney, and the only thing one might consider contraband among their possessions was an open packet of gum. After all, I eschew gum-chewing, and prohibit my guests from bringing it on the premises, on the grounds that it makes one look like a horse, besides being impossible to remove from asphalt, let alone shag carpets.

Vance Brown, the dairyman, and his trollop of a wife (I say this with objectivity, not malice), had acquired most of their clothes from Wal-Mart, and might have passed my inspection with flying colors had I not noticed a lump in one of their pillows. Normally, this might have gone unnoticed, as I am not averse to supplying my guests with lumpy pillows. (They build character, don't you agree?) However, this particular lump extended beyond the case. Grateful yet again that I had thought to wear surgical gloves, I gingerly withdrew the suspicious item, and held it at arm's length.

What on God's green earth could even the most depraved English do with a pulley and a length of rope? Well, whatever the answer, the Browns were not going to see it again. Fueled by righteous indignation — it is an excellent source of energy, by the way

— I tugged open a stubborn window and dropped the offending article on the lawn, from which I fully intended to retrieve it later and tote it off to the burn barrel.

Then it was on to Gertie Fuselburger's room. Because she'd made such a fuss over me, I'd given her the best room — one with a marvelous view of Miller's Pond and, if one leaned out far enough, a sliver-wide glimpse of Stucky Ridge. Of course, I reminded Gertie to tie herself to a bedpost when viewing the mountain, lest the same thing happen to her that happened to that televangelist, Reverend Dilbert Gillwater.

Dear dogmatic Dilbert had riled the nation the day before by announcing that God had spoken to him personally, warning him that unless American women agreed to be subservient to their husbands, the Good Lord was going to punish them by simultaneously releasing the bubonic plague in seventeen of our country's largest cities. Then, obviously quite pleased with himself, Reverend Gillwater took a gander at Stucky Ridge without first tying himself securely to the bedpost. When he met his Maker, one of our nation's most controversial figures was wearing a pair of women's black lace panties and fishnet stockings. Only one of his crimson pumps made it all the way to the ground with him. Later the other pump caused me a tremendous amount of tsuris when it plugged up the rain gutter.

Now where was I? Oh, yes, not only did Gertie get the best room, but she got the best grade from yours truly. No trashy magazines hidden between the Hanes Her Way pairs and the polyester half slips from Sears. And certainly no cigarettes, as I'd suspected. Even the contents of her American Tourister train case — in classy avocado green — were not incriminating. The only thing in there that even approached makeup, was a small tube of lip balm. The color? Clear.

"Why, shoot a monkey," I said. Yes, it is a terrible expression, given that monkeys are primates, and we are said to be primates as well. Fortunately, those of us in the know are aware that this supposed cousinship simply isn't true.

"Are you originally from North Carolina, Miss Yoder?"

I whirled. The grand old dame herself was standing in the doorway, her thin body in silhouette.

"North Carolina? No, ma'am — actually, I can't say that for sure. For all I know I was conceived in a linen closet in Buckingham Palace and should be calling Prince

Philip 'papa.' "

Gertie smiled. It must have taken a lot of effort to lift and rearrange all those wrinkles.

"I've heard that expression back in Wilmington. But it may be something just my family said. Sometimes they could be quite colorful in their speech. If I dare say so, just like you."

I recoiled in surprise. *"Moi?"*

"A true original. Although you can be a bit verbose at times. Some might find it objectionable, but I rather enjoy it. Of course we Southerners are quite fond of words."

"That's it!" I held my right arm out, all the better to examine my wrist. "I have Southern blood running through these veins. I should have known it. I visited Charleston on vacation a few years back, and found shrimp and grits absolutely delicious."

"In that case, we are sisters under the skin. I told you we'd get along famously."

If something is going very right, you can be sure it's really going wrong. I will be the first to admit that I am a pessimist by nature. It is, after all, the wisest way to be. We pessimists have everything to gain, whereas optimists have a fifty-fifty chance of being disappointed.

"Aren't you going to at least ask what I'm doing in your room?"

"Whatever for? This is your inn, after all. I have every reason to believe that your motive for being here is legitimate."

"But suppose it isn't?"

Her laugh sounded like a can of loose coins. "Well, then I would at least find it quite interesting."

"I was looking for cigarettes." I waited for her to be shocked.

"Really? Did you find any?"

"Nary a one."

"That's because I gave up smoking the day I turned sixty. I looked in the mirror to give myself an honest appraisal, and when I saw how much damage cigarettes — and the Carolina sun — had done to my face, I threw almost an entire pack of Marlboros down the john." She cackled. "My reaction was a trifle dramatic, and not at all wise. The toilet plugged and overflowed, and I spent a good deal of my birthday mopping the floor. Since that day, ten years ago next month, I haven't had a puff."

Ten years ago? Oops. Gertie Fuselburger hadn't played with God as a child; she hadn't even played with Jesse Helms. That should show me not to judge a book by its cover. At any rate, it was time for me to skedaddle, and since graceful exits have never been my forte, I tossed a carefree laugh over my shoulder. Alas, it landed on the floor.

"Miss Yoder, are you all right?"

I managed a wan smile. "Never been better."

"I don't believe you for a second, but, for the moment, I shall settle for that. Now, besides the ban you impose on smoking, why were you rooting through our rooms looking for cigarettes?"

"Don't be silly, dear."

"Don't lie to me, please. I respect you too much for that."

"You do?"

"Of course. A single woman like you, making a thriving go of this inn with only an elderly Amish couple to help you."

"And despite a very lazy, needy sister, I might add."

"And an orphan charge."

"Well, she's not an orphan — but she may as well be, for all the attention they pay to her."

"And let's not forget a domineering mother-in-law."

"How did you know?"

"That sweet child we just mentioned filled me in a bit. I hear that she cuts your husband's food for him."

"Yes, but not his cheese."

"Understood. So, will you be truthful with me?"

"Most probably not, but we can give it a try." I sighed. "You're sure to find out anyway from Harmon Dorfman."

"That magnificent young specimen of manhood?"

"Perhaps in the eyes of a manatee. Anyway, he found a cigarette butt in his paddock this morning."

"Why, that's terrible! Any harm come to his cattle?"

"Apparently not — at least not yet."

"And you inspected the other paddocks?"

"Uh — see you later, alligator."

When I got to the barn, there was no sign of Harmon the Magnificent. But I quickly found Mose and together we searched every square inch of the barn and all of the paddocks. Thank the Good Lord there was not another butt to be found.

I was doing just that — thanking God — when the Pearlmutters' fancy-schmancy pickup pulled up the driveway. I watched, only slightly envious, as they, along with the Browns, piled out. The four of them were yakking and laughing up a storm. I have plenty of friends, but none of us can muster up that much abandonment. Fortunately for me, Gabe loves my quiet, gentle ways.

Frankly, I was also surprised to see that the two couples were getting along that well; at breakfast, Jane Pearlmutter had thrown a roll at Vance Brown when the latter had suggested that she too take up this pole dancing. Although I do not tolerate food throwing in my dining room, I was secretly pleased that plain Jane had no interest in wiggling her tuchas — as Gabe's mother refers to the human hiney. Upon further reflection, I wasn't even all that displeased to see a perfectly good clump of carbohydrates go to waste. At least not for a good cause.

I was even more surprised when, upon spotting me, the foursome bounded up like pups that had spotted a bone. Candy Brown was the first to reach me.

"Did you have a pleasant outing, dear?" I asked, ever the solicitous hostess.

"Oh, it was wonderful. We went shopping for antiques, and this one store had estate jewelry, and look what my Vance bought me." She held up a pendant that hung from her neck. "See? There's a sapphire in the center. Isn't it beautiful?"

I strained to see something blue, but to

no avail; the stone appeared inky black. Some unscrupulous sellers of cheap — often Australian — sapphires tell their customers that the darker the stone, the more valuable it is. Au contraire — to a point. The preferred color of corundum labeled as sapphire is cornflower blue. Of course, I wouldn't know any of this, were it not for the wallopalooza the Babester had set in my engagement ring. In fact, the color in my ring is so intense that strangers have often insisted that it's fake, or some other stone such as enhanced topaz.

"Isn't it something!" I declared. This is a little trick I've learned from my Southern friends, kind women all, who do not wish to be rude. A variation of this phrase can be employed when one is forced to admire a truly homely baby.

Having adequately praised Candy's newest acquisition, I scanned her lips. They were the color of the bubblegum that Alison sneaked into her room — certainly not a match for the lipstick on the cigarette butt. By that time, the others had caught up with Candy, so I turned my attention to Jane Pearlmutter.

"And how about you, dear?" I asked. "Did you have a fabulous time as well?"

"Fabulous would be stretching it, Miss

161

Yoder. But it's a charming little town, and the natives were friendly."

"*Little?* My dear, there are forty-five hundred people in Bedford."

Dick Pearlmutter laughed. It was the first time I'd seen his teeth displayed in a pleasant manner.

"You'll have to forgive my wife, Miss Yoder, but she did her residency in Manhattan. Since that time, everything seems small to her."

I continued the small talk while I surveyed his wife's lips. They were, by the way, completely unadorned.

"You're a plastic surgeon, right?"

"I am — or I was. My specialty is facial reconstruction, but I completed my residency at Manhattan General in the burn unit. I met Dick at a coffee shop down the street."

Oy vey, as Ida Rosen would say. And here I'd been judging Plain Jane harshly. I'd done nothing significant with my life, whereas the object of my distaste had been grafting skin onto poor children's faces. It just goes to show you how we truly make donkeys of ourselves when we assume.

"You are much to be admired," I said.

"I've spent my time in the trenches," she said, and then suddenly lost interest in me.

In fact, like a school of zebra fish that once occupied my now defunct aquarium, they turned in unison and started to walk away.

"Just one ding-dong minute," I hollered at their retreating backs. "Unless the bunch of you would like to spend this afternoon getting acquainted with our fabulous — and I do mean *fabulous* — jail, I suggest you turn around this very instant."

18

They turned, moving as a single entity. This time, I got straight to the point.

"Somebody tossed a cigarette butt into the Dorfman brothers' paddock. Since it wasn't them, and it wasn't me, the odds are it was one of you."

As a former stockbroker, Dick Pearlmutter was used to thinking fast on his genuine Italian leather-clad feet. "I don't know what makes me angrier, Miss Yoder, the fact that somebody has tried to compromise our livestock, or the fact that you have just accused me of this heinous act."

"I haven't accused all of you, dear: just the guilty party."

"What about Miss Fuselburger? She looks like a chain-smoker to me."

"How rude! True perhaps, but nonetheless rude. And for your information, I've already put her through the wringer. I'm satisfied that she's innocent."

Vance Brown stepped out of the pack, stroking his handsome brown beard. Although a lifelong dairyman, he had the demeanor of a trial lawyer.

"What about that Amish fellow who oversees the barn?"

"*Mose?* He doesn't smoke, and he certainly doesn't wear dark red lipstick." Oops. I'd let the cat out of the bag, and believe me it's a whole lot harder to stuff a feisty feline back into the bag — or bra, for that matter. (I once had a pussy that lived in my Maidenform.)

"Lipstick!" the ladies cried in one voice.

"Did I say that?"

"You certainly did," Vance said. "And a card laid is a card played, Miss Yoder, so please don't try to duck the question."

"But I didn't ask a question."

"Show us the cigarette butt, please."

He was so calm, so soothing, even, that I immediately extracted the tissue from my dress pocket. If pressed, however, I will admit to taking my own sweet time to unwrap the disgusting thing.

"There," I said, and literally waved the butt under their noses.

"It smells like cherries," Jane said. "As you can see, I don't even wear lipstick, and if I

165

did, you can bet it wouldn't be cherry flavored."

"My wife is allergic to cherries," Dick said. "She ate cherry cobbler in the cafeteria of her grammar school, and it put her in the hospital for two weeks."

Candy nodded vigorously. "A peanut nearly killed my friend Ophelia."

"Ophelia," I repeated, letting the word roll off my tongue. "What a beautiful name. Her parents must have been fond of Shakespeare."

"Huh?"

"As in Hamlet. Why, is there another Ophelia that I am not aware of?"

"I dunno, Miss Yoder. My friend spells her name O-H-F-E-E-L-ya."

"Why, that doesn't make a lick of sense!"

"But hey," Vance said quickly, "isn't arsenic supposed to smell like cherries?"

"Perhaps there's arsenic in that cigarette stub," Jane said. "Shouldn't you be taking it to a lab and having it analyzed, instead of harassing us?"

"Really," Dick said. "We never expected this kind of treatment from a four-star establishment."

Four stars? Where ever did he hear that nonsense? The PennDutch doesn't have *any* stars — well, except for the movie stars that

166

often stay here. Thank goodness the reviews of my little establishment were initially quite good, which eventually led to word-of-mouth business. Since then, I've had mostly bad publicity, thanks to the murders and a few bad sports who refuse to get into the spirit of ALPO. But, like they say, there's no such thing as bad publicity. The more folks grumble about my business when they get back home, the more free advertising I get. And since Freni is getting ready to retire soon, I might consider serving only bread and water for meals. . . .

"Miss Yoder!" Dick roared. "You look like you've totally zoned out."

"I was lost in thought; it was unfamiliar territory."

"That's an old one," Jane sniffed.

I treated her to a look that should have frozen Miller's Pond. Then, after carefully pocketing the cigarette butt, I hightailed my own tail across Hertzler Road, fairly flew across Gabe's front meadow — but still taking care to skirt Miller's Pond — and dashed up my true love's front steps. After all, the only other two people I knew in Hernia who smoked were my sister and my mother-in-law.

Unfortunately, I was still panting when my worst nightmare answered the front

167

door. "Oy, it's only you."

"I — I — I —"

"It's alvays about you, right?"

"Aye, aye, sir."

"So now you mock me. Vhat else is new?"

"The amount of rancor with which I do. Heretofore, the bonds of holy matrimony not yet tightened snugly into place, my tongue shied not from being glib. At times it even gyred and gimbled in the wabe. But now that I have cloven to your son — if that is indeed the past tense of cleave — I feel much more inclined to treat you as if you were flesh of my own flesh. Although surely said phrase must make even the most accommodating vegetarian feel slightly queasy."

"You're meshugah, Magdalena."

"No doubt because my birth mother was an escaped mental patient who gyred and gimbled in the hayloft with Papa. At least, that's another theory — one which I have yet to explore."

"Lies! Vhatever you are saying is lies."

"I am merely saying that Gabe loves me ten times more than he loves you."

"More lies!"

"While we're on the subject, dear, could you explain this?" I fished out the stub.

"Vhat's the meaning of this? Vhere did you

168

get my cigarette?"

"So it *is* yours?"

"You tink a person can buy this brand at Sam's? Of course it's mine; only in New York can one buy such a ting." She made it sound as special as the Hebrew National salamis she schlepped back in her suitcase each time she went home for a visit.

"Excuse me for not knowing the provenance of every brand of coffin nail on the market. Just tell me what it was doing in one of my cow stalls."

Her hands are even stubbier than Freni's, but she put them to good use by snatching the butt away from me. She held it at arm's length for a good look, which put it about a foot from her face.

"Dis isn't mine," she said at last.

"But you said it was."

"Den maybe I was wrong."

I studied her face. Gabe had her eyes, but not much else. But that was enough. Ida Rosen was lying through her dentures.

"You're lying."

"Such chutzpah I never hoid!"

"Touché. Fess up, Ma Rosen, before I call your son out to arbitrate."

"Your daughter."

"You mean my husband."

"Now you're hard of hearing as vell?"

"But you said — wait, are you talking about Alison?"

"You heff another daughter, perhaps?"

My blood began a slow simmer. "Do you have proof that Alison stole your cigarette?"

"Believe me, eef I did, I vould have come to you. Deese tings are killers. I vouldn't vant dat my shtep-granddaughter should end up like me. But dis" — a liver-colored nail traced the red edge of the filter — "dis is Kool-Aid. Cherry, I tink. *Mit* sugar. Alison likes to leek it from da package. I give her dis last night vhen she vas here."

Instantly, my blood temperature went from simmer to cold. "She was *here?* When, exactly?"

Ida shrugged. Unlike Freni, she has a neck and can do a decent job of this gesture. Her bosoms, however, seem less secured, so that any movement of the shoulders sets the volleyball-size pair on a heaving frenzy. Should one or both break loose, there's no telling what the fallout might be. I stepped back just to be on the safe side.

"I tink it vas around ten o'clock. She came to say good night to my Gabeleh. Maybe to me as vell, yah? Den my son valked her back to your place."

I growled aloud. Didn't either of the adults think to tell me about this? While it was sweet of Alison to come say her good-nights, she did so alone, with an escaped murderer gunning for our family — not to mention that brute who'd nearly killed an eighty-year-old man. Then no doubt, because she'd gotten away with it, Alison had sneaked out to the paddocks to enjoy a stolen cigarette. Someone, not just Alison, was going to pay for this oversight.

"Dun't be too hard on her, Magdalena. She is a teenager, and dis is vhat teenagers do. My Gabeleh vas no picnic lunch either, yah?"

"But she could have gotten herself killed coming over here — or worse. Melvin is a psychopath. There's no telling what he'd do."

"True. But she didn't get killed, so eet is important to keep perspective. Een Germany — but never mind."

I was stunned. I knew Ida was a Holocaust survivor, but she has never, ever talked about it. Not even to Gabriel and his sisters. To my knowledge, this is the first time she has even said the G-word since coming to Hernia, where our Amish speak a dialect of German, and which has to be a constant reminder to her of a painful past. Finally, but only after a great deal of stammering, I was able to speak.

171

"Ida, would you mind —"

"I mind."

"But —"

"Vee are done talking about me. So, you vill let me get back to my houseverk now?"

"Can't you at least tell me how Gabe misbehaved?"

"Vhat?"

"You said that he wasn't a picnic."

"Oy, the stories I could tell. Perhaps another time, yah?"

"Another time, then," I said.

Frankly, I was stunned into acquiescence by a trace of warmth in her voice. This was a side of Ida I had never seen before. Besides, she was so right: I should concentrate on being grateful that Alison was alive and well, and enjoying a sleepover with a friend. There would be plenty of time later to make heads roll. Metaphorically, of course.

19

After lunch at the inn — you can be sure the Dorfman brothers donned shirts — I drove the twelve miles in to Bedford County Memorial Hospital. Doc was still unconscious and in the ICU, but, nonetheless, it was important to me that I see him.

The hospital is famous for its good-looking interns of both genders, so my walk from the parking lot and my elevator ride up to his floor were shamefully pleasant. I might even have been joshing with a young doctor named Josh as I exited, but even if that is true, I certainly did not deserve what happened next.

First of all, how was I to know that a nurse would be walking past the doors when they opened? And, pray tell, how on earth was I to know that said nurse, whom I just happened to run into — quite literally — would be the dreadful Nurse Dudley?

"I'm so sorry," I said as I stooped to pick her up.

She turned at the sound of my voice, and then exploded like a waterlogged frankfurter. "It's you!"

I staggered backward in surprise, rebounded off the opposite wall, and then teetered back in her direction. Perhaps we might have gotten past this awkward reunion, had she not stuck a foot out to trip me, *and* had I not, whilst in the process of trying to keep my balance, reached out and grabbed one of her female appendages. Even then, all might not have been lost, had she not suffered a wardrobe malfunction of the first degree.

Nurse Dudley — or Nurse Ratched, as I am wont to call her — is one of those women whom one tends to find more frequently amongst the very devout — whose underpinnings are not only extraordinarily large, but inexplicably stiff, as if made from steel. A mighty fortress, as it were. A citadel of womanhood — although one is loathe to imagine what lies beneath these formidable structures.

At any rate, as I fell to the ground, my fingers not only got caught in the pocket of her uniform, but somehow became enmeshed in the engineering marvel that lay beneath. Without meaning to, I took with me a considerable portion of the scaffolding, as well as something that felt like a pound of raw chicken. A nanosecond later, as if part of a chain reaction, the other side of her bra collapsed, and out plopped another pound of poultry.

I staggered to my feet, all the while staring at the strange object in my hand. "You keep boneless chicken in your bra? What a clever idea."

"Those are my boobs, you idiot."

I dropped the object I was holding. It landed next to its twin, where they both quivered on the linoleum like bowls of upended gelatin. "Uh — sorry about that."

Nurse Dudley snatched her feminine wiles off the floor. "I'm going to sue you, Magdalena! I'm going to bleed you dry."

"It was an accident. You scared me, and I tripped."

"Security! Someone call security *and* the police."

"No, please don't. I'm here to see Doc Shafor."

"That's what you think; you're headed straight for jail."

"But I didn't know you wore a prosthetic bra."

"I don't, you moron. Not all of us are as

175

blessed in that department as you."

"True, although I only just recently realized the extent of my bountiful goodness, having heretofore suffered from body dysmorphic syndrome. So you see, there was no ill intent on my part, whereas you, with your booming voice, practically gave me a heart attack. Indeed, methinks that it is I who should be suing you — or, at the very least, launching a countersuit. After all, as a wealthy woman, I am sure to win. Security!"

Nurse Dudley's glares have been known to start fires if appropriate kindling material is available. She fixed those smoldering eyes on me, but the rest of her body language spelled defeat.

"Okay, I'll let you see Mr. Shafor, but only for a minute. And you have to pay for a new uniform."

"No problemo."

"And for a Bosom Buddies bra."

"Certainly."

"This particular model, Titan Twins number two, cost me ninety-eight dollars on eBay."

"That's just ridiculous." Fortunately I noticed that her sagging shoulders, which were undoubtedly powered by steam, had begun to rise. "But worth every penny," I added wisely.

"Just so you know," she hissed, "I'm going to get you someday, Yoder. Sometime when you least expect it."

"I'm quaking in my brogans, dear."

She appeared to take me seriously. "Good. That's the way it should be. By the way, that old goat is awake now."

"What old goat?"

"The one who made a pass at me within minutes of coming out of a coma."

I didn't waste a second getting to the old codger's room.

"Hey, gorgeous," he said as I entered the room.

I turned to look behind me.

"I mean you, silly. Magdalena, when are you going to get it into your pumpkin head that you're one fine-looking woman?"

"The same day you get it into your broken head that I'm unavailable — oops. I shouldn't have used the B-word. Sorry about that."

"But it is broken. I feel like — uh — uh —"

"Shiitake mushrooms?"

He laughed. "You might say that."

"I've been there, and it's most unpleasant. What does your doctor say?"

"Prognosis good. Another day hooked up

to machines, and then I get moved to a regular room. Then, with any luck, after a couple days, I'll get to go home."

"How long have you been awake?"

He looked at the bedside clock before shrugging. "I'm not certain. But I was just getting ready to call you. Honest, I was."

"It doesn't matter."

"Yes, it does. You look uh — uh —"

"Pistachio ice cream?"

"Bingo."

"Doc, what I'm feeling is unimportant. I want to know the identity of your assailant."

"My *what?*"

"The person who attacked you."

"So *that's* what happened! The real doc wouldn't tell me. Just kept shining a light in my eyes, and asking me to count his fingers."

"You mean you don't remember the attack?"

"Not one uh — uh —"

"Damp detail?"

"Yeah. Where did it happen?"

"In my barn. You even scrawled a message in your own blood."

"No kidding? Magdalena, I don't even remember driving out to your place. The last thing I remember was feeding Old Blue her supper — Old Blue! Who's been taking care of her?"

I swallowed hard. The ancient bloodhound is the other pea in Doc's pod. Not only are the two inseparable, but they help prove that adage about dog owners looking like their pets — although I say that with apologies to Old Blue. Alas, I hadn't given a thought to the wrinkled old bitch.

For Doc, who'd spent a lifetime reading horse faces, decoding my frozen mug was a piece of German chocolate cake. "Get your asteroid over there, Magdalena, and feed my best gal. But let her out first. How would you like to hold it in that long?"

"Not much, so will do. But if you remember anything — *anything* — give me a call on my cell. If you hold anything back, I'm going to tell Nurse Ratched out there that you've been harboring a crush on her for years."

Doc licked his lips. "Promise?"

"You dirty old man! Just for that, I'm changing it to Ida."

"Your mother-in-law?"

There was a time when Doc and my nemesis couldn't keep their arthritic hands off each other. Then I sent them on an all-expenses-paid trip to Tahiti. (It wasn't a sin to do so, because they were bent on doing the tatami tarantella anyway.) As it turned out, giving them unimpeded access to each other, along with my tacit blessing, was like throwing a bucket of glacial-melt water in their faces. They returned on separate flights, hating each other.

"You wouldn't!"

"Oh, Doc, what strong arms you have. Ida, allow me to pluck that chin hair; I find it a bit distracting."

"You were listening?"

"Just that once," I wailed. "I couldn't help it that I was cleaning your closet when you returned from dinner that day. And way early, I might add."

Doc smiled. "Get a move on, Magdalena, before I hop out of bed and throw these strong arms around *you* — married, or not. And just so you know, I don't mind your chin hairs one bit."

I was out of there so fast that I left my shadow behind.

Doc lives on the south side of Hernia, in the shadow of Stucky Ridge. In the summertime, if you stand on his back deck and lean way to the left, so that you can peer around the sycamore, it is possible to spot a molecule or two of Lover's Leap. Local lore has it that an Indian princess and her white settler boyfriend leapt to their deaths one foggy morning. Unfortunately for them, they didn't intend to commit suicide; they were merely horsing around, as lovers sometimes do, and thought they were leaping into a pile of leaves. Okay, I admit that is only one of many versions of this tale, but it is the one which I much prefer.

Usually when I visit Doc, he and Old Blue meet me out by the mailbox, on account of Old Blue has smelled me coming a mile away. This is not because I stink, mind you —Yoder with the Odor is a thing of the past — but because the dog is descended from a long line of champion bloodhounds. At any rate, it felt strange not having either of my elderly pals greet me, and I began to have morbid thoughts about what I might find inside.

I needn't have worried. The second I pushed the door open, Old Blue barreled past me and, as soon as she hit grass, attended to her needs. Upon finishing, however, not only did she greet me, but she was on me like germs on a day-care door.

Dogs are notoriously bad huggers, but the old gal tried her best, thoroughly raking me with her claws in the process. After she tired of me pushing her away, she attempted to bathe me with her foot-long tongue. And speaking of germs, there are those who claim that we humans carry more germs in our mouths than dogs, but Doc, a veterinarian of some renown, says that this is simply not so. "Consider what you do with your tongue," he said. "Then observe what she does with hers."

It was while trying to escape Old Blue's effusive gratitude that I shut myself up in the downstairs powder room. While the dear beast whimpered outside the door, I sat on the closed lid of the john to collect my thoughts. It can take a while to gather such scattered things, but about midway through, I became gradually aware of the draft against the back of my neck. Slowly, I turned.

20

CHOCOLATE ICE CREAM RECIPE
CUSTARD BASE RECIPE:

Ingredients:

5 egg yolks
1 pint (500 ml) milk
1/2 pint (250 ml) double/heavy cream
2 oz (50 g) sugar
3 tablespoons cocoa powder

The custard base is the essential part of what makes ice cream really creamy and luxurious. The basic principle for making a custard base is to use cream and/or milk, egg yolks, and sugar. Some people create a mix from these ingredients without heating, in which case it's generally referred to as a cream base. Others, myself included, prefer to use heat in the process and create what's known as a custard base.

This is a typical custard base method, which involves heating:

First of all, beat and mix together the egg yolks and sugar until thick. Separately, pour the milk into a saucepan and scald it (bring slowly up to boiling point). Pour the hot milk into the egg-yolk-and-sugar mix whilst continuously stirring. Then pour the mixture back into the pan and heat gently, stirring until the custard thickens — *do not bring to the boil, or it will probably curdle.* When you can see a film form over the back of your spoon, it's time to remove the saucepan from the heat. Leave to cool.

Then you can do one of three things:

A. Pour the cooled custard into a bowl, and add your chosen flavoring, then transfer mixture to an ice cream maker.

B. Pour the cooled custard into a bowl, and add cream plus your chosen flavoring, then transfer mixture to an ice cream maker.

C. Chill the cooled custard thoroughly in the refrigerator. Whip some double cream, and fold it into the chilled custard, then add your chosen flavoring, and transfer mixture to an ice cream maker.

For this recipe, we suggest option C. First,

create a custard base. At the point when you remove the saucepan from the heat to allow the mixture to cool, add the cocoa. Then chill the custard until it's really cold. Once chilled, mix until slushy. Add the cream (whipped), and make sure it mixes in well. Transfer the mixture to an ice cream maker, and freeze according to the manufacturer's instructions.

Quick Chocolate Ice Cream Recipe

This is ideal for the kids or anyone wanting something quick and delicious!

Ingredients:
1 can (large) sweetened condensed milk
1/2 pint (250 ml) milk
5 tablespoons cocoa

Mix together the milk and condensed milk. Dissolve the cocoa in a little hot water. When fully dissolved, stir it into the milk/condensed milk mixture. Transfer the whole mixture into an ice cream maker, and freeze according to the manufacturer's instructions.

21

The window was halfway open. Something was terribly wrong. Doc may be a veterinarian, and thus a man of science, but he also belongs to a generation of draft-dodgers. By that, I don't mean that he evaded military conscription; au contraire, although of Mennonite background, Doc volunteered for active service the day Pearl Harbor was bombed. What I mean is that Doc, who is not averse to spending time outside, is convinced that outside air flowing into a house or an automobile is somehow dangerous.

He is, of course, not alone on this score. For hundreds of years people in Europe sealed their homes in winter — sometimes year-round — to ward off the dangerous night vapors. As a result, houses became stuffy, almost tomblike. This approach to ventilation persisted through Victorian times, and lingers still in the groundless belief that exposure to cold air will result in one catching the common cold. As for Doc, he would no sooner crack a window — even on a cold night — than he would lie down across the fast lane of the Pennsylvania Turnpike.

"Heavens to Betsy!" I exclaimed, when the gravity of the situation had sunk in thoroughly. I quickly opened the bathroom door, whereupon Old Blue merely whimpered a final time, as she gazed at me with eyes that seemed to say, "See, I told you so."

"Is the intruder still here?" I whispered into one of her drooping ears.

She closed her eyes, then immediately opened them.

"Good doggy," I cooed. "Let's do that again; blink once for yes and two for no."

Again, she blinked once.

To be sure, I prayed for inner strength and wisdom. But even though my faith eschews violence, even armed resistance, I could not (at least at that moment) recall a single sermon or Sunday school lesson that stated, unequivocally, that the *appearance* of power was a sin. Perhaps my very inability to recall such a teaching was itself an answer to my prayer. Satisfied that this was so, I snatched a much-used plunger from the corner of the tiny room.

"I'm coming out!" I hollered. "This dog may be a wimp, but I'm full of urine and vinegar." This declaration of boldness was a paraphrase of something I'd heard Doc say.

Silence reigned.

"Be forewarned, I'm heavily armed — not to mention mentally unstable. There are those who think I belong in a padded cell." Alas, there really are folks who share this sentiment, and not just the residents of Hernia.

More silence.

I peeked out just far enough so that I could see the main rooms. I did this by slow degrees. In the meantime, Old Blue wedged herself between my legs and the toilet, her head sensibly tucked under my skirt. I mean, what better way to deal with terror than to prevent oneself from seeing it? Perhaps I should have taken a cue from her.

"Look, whoever you are, the police are on their way. The sheriff as well. But if you skedaddle now, you stand a chance of getting away, especially if you hightail it out the back and head for Stucky Ridge. There's a cave along the base of Lover's Leap that is rumored to be quite comfy. Just don't believe the graffiti on the walls — unless it's about Wanda Hemphopple. I may even have understated that."

The back door slammed. Hard. There was no mistaking that.

I did indeed call the sheriff — I've gotten to know him quite well over the years, and consider him a personal friend — and together we combed every inch of Doc's small house for clues that might point to an intruder. Unfortunately, ever since Belinda died, which was more than twenty years ago, Doc's standards of housekeeping have slipped steadily. For instance, he no longer changes out the box of baking soda in his fridge on a regular basis. One box — which I initialed with a ballpoint — was in there for three months before getting the old heave-ho. On another occasion, I watched him place a dirty skillet in the kitchen sink and not wash it for another four hours. My point is that the good sheriff and I found nothing amiss except a small fragment of a dried leaf stuck to the living room carpet, and as tempting as it was to assign criminal provenance to this, it might just as well have been due to Doc's well-documented sloven-liness.

While waiting for the sheriff to arrive, I took Old Blue outside where she was fed, watered, and walked again. Then, just before the sheriff left, seeing as how I have great fondness for all things old, I loaded the big galoot into the back seat of my car and drove all the way up to the Sausage Barn just outside Bedford. The reason for picking this destination was threefold: Wanda loves dogs, Wanda loves to gossip, and Wanda serves remarkably edible food.

The one thing that can't be said for Wanda is that she has a soft spot in her heart for yours truly. It may even be said that she harbors an intense dislike for my internal organs. As a sincere Christian, I try not to hate anyone — but if I ever did, Wanda would be at the top of my list. At any rate, when I pranced into the Sausage Barn leading a rather large dog, Wanda's face turned the color of raw liver, and she began to shake violently.

"How dare you, Magdalena!" she said. Her teeth were actually chattering from all the motion.

"It's actually easier than I thought. One need only keep in mind this face; the sagging skin, the drooping jowls, the comical ears. The dog looks pretty mournful too, doesn't she?"

"Ha, ha, very funny. Now get that beast — wait just one sausage-sizzling minute! Is that Old Blue?"

"One and the same. I'm hoping you'll agree to watch her until Doc gets back on his feet."

Wanda is happily married — well, arguably so — but I saw the anguished look of a lovelorn schoolgirl flitter across her birdlike face. When she was sixteen, her cat, Jeckle, was hit by a car. Doc was able to restore the animal to an approximation of its scrappy self, and won his owner's unflagging devotion. That was forty-two years ago, when Doc was still in his forties and still sported a real stud's physique, but it was clear that Wanda had still not gotten over her crush.

"Are you toying with me, Magdalena?"

"Is the PennDutch Inn the best full-board inn east of the Mississippi?"

"Then you *are* toying with me."

"E pluribus unum."

"I was right; you only speak Pennsylvania Dutch when you're cornered."

Shame on Wanda for not being able to recognize the sound of Dutch after having spent her entire life in Amish country, let alone being unfamiliar with a simple Latin phrase that every American worth their stars and stripes should be able to rattle off. But who am I to judge? For years I thought hip-hop was merely the way bunnies moved and that thong underwear referred to a split-toe sock meant to be worn with flip-flops.

"Wanda, will you take her in or not?"

"Of course, you idiot." She grabbed Old Blue's leash and disappeared in the kitchen with her.

While I waited for her imminent return, I seated myself at my favorite table and scanned a grease-coated menu. Not a thing on it had changed in the last twenty years — except for the prices. One day, perhaps very soon, trans fats would be banned in Bedford County. When that time came, old-timers in the business, like Wanda and me, were going to have a very hard time adjusting. Oh, my goodness! That was the one thing that she and I had in common.

"Are you going to order, Magdalena, or just drool on my menu?"

I snapped back to the present. "You're here."

"What an odd thing to say." Wanda, who serves as both hostess and waitress, tapped her order pad with a stubby pencil. "So, what will it be?"

"The usual."

She nodded. "A small glass of freshly squeezed orange juice; two eggs over medium; four strips of bacon, not too crisp; two slices of lightly toasted whole wheat bread; real butter; grape jelly; and coffee with lots of half and half. Anything else?"

"Gossip."

She slid into the booth and sat across from me. "Well, did you hear about the sixteen-pound tumor they removed from Daniel Berkley's cheek over in Somerset? Turns out it wasn't a tumor at all, but a perfectly formed second head. Of course it was hidden under a layer of skin, so you really can't blame the doctors. They say that when the skin was removed and the face revealed, that head began to talk. Marla Kuhnberger says you can't read about it in the papers because the government wants to keep it top secret. They've already whisked it off to Washington in a Black Hawk helicopter. What do you suppose will happen to it there?"

"Beats me — although I imagine it could have a fine career as a political pundit. Talking heads are in great demand. And they wouldn't have to pay it very much, would they? I mean, it could live in a very small apartment — maybe a renovated birdhouse. It certainly wouldn't need a clothing allowance. Well, except maybe for hats."

"Are you mocking me?"

"Nay, just having a bit of fun. After all, Wanda, you are known for being a good sport."

"I am?"

"Don't you think so?"

"Come to think of it, I am."

"There you go, then." I smiled pleasantly, despite the effort. "Wanda, dear, have you heard any gossip about Doc?"

"Are you kidding? Geraldine Yutzy thinks that Doc's attacker is none other than the Antichrist. She's planning to move her brood back to Lancaster, where she thinks there are fewer heathens. Meanwhile, Erma Dietweiler is convinced that it's Bigfoot."

"Oh, not again," I wailed. You'd wail too if the *National Exposer* had printed a special issue on you, naming you as Bigfoot only because your feet were — well, rather big.

"Yes, but that's not all: Jonathan Lehman is convinced that Doc's possessed by an evil spirit and beat his own self up. He's trying to convince a Reverend Haggleworth to come up here from Cumberland, Maryland, to exercise Doc. Apparently this guy not only does exercisms, but he's able to catch the demon as it exits the body and seals it inside a specially lined glass bottle suitable to place on your mantel."

"Trust me. Doc's not up to exercise just yet. Exorcism either. Anything that might be credible?"

Wanda scowled. "Honestly, Magdalena,

you have no imagination. Think of the money that we could make, if we did the exorcism ourselves — well, you at any rate. I mean, you're pretty scary, right? And I could sell the bottles right here in my gift corner. Heck, we could even advertise our product in *TV Guide.* You know, five easy payments of $19.95. Or maybe an infomercial would be the way to go: 'Act now, and you get your choice of designer bottles in the color of your choosing, *plus* a two-ounce container of Holy Talcum Powder that's guaranteed to keep demons away from you and your loved ones if used on a daily basis.' For refills, of course, we'd charge a mint."

Who knew that Wanda and I had so much in common? Under different circumstances, and if we were different people, we might have been able to be business partners — although scamming the public with a devilish scheme like that would be like playing with fire. Much better to charge them an arm and a leg for something real, no matter how paltry it might be — like little bags of barn hay tied up with fancy ribbons and labeled with cute sayings like "Hay there, miss you" or "I took a straw poll and —"

"Magdalena, have you fallen asleep? Don't tell me you're drunk again."

I shook my way out of a lucrative daydream. "Rumors of my drinking have been highly exaggerated. Anyhow, the gossip you've related so far, as stimulating as it is, will not help me find Doc's assailant. Don't you have anything else?"

Wanda sighed. "Well, there was something that Mary Anne Gingerich said — something about Doc. But I'd hardly call it newsworthy."

"Gossip never is. Now spit it out, dear."

22

"You're so pushy, Magdalena, you know that? Anyway, when Mary Anne got up in the middle of the night to go to the bathroom, she noticed a light on in Doc's house. But then it was off by the time she went back to bed."

The Gingeriches are Doc's nearest neighbors. Doc has often complained about how nosy Mary Anne is. Once he caught her going through his garbage.

"The light was probably on a timer," I said.

"That's what Mary Anne thought too, but an hour later when she had to go again, it was back on."

"That explains it!"

"Explains what? That Doc had a woman staying over? Magdalena, I hate to have to be the one to break it to you, but that ship has long sailed."

I feigned shock by clapping my cheeks

with my hands. "It *has?*"

"Honestly, you'd think an experienced adulteress like you would be a bit savvier about the ways of the world."

"I was an inadvertent adulteress — unlike some people in this room."

Wanda leapt to her feet, nearly taking the booth with her. "How dare you heap accusations at my feet? I only cheated on him once, I'll have you know — twice, if you count that time when we were separated. That hardly makes me a real adulteress."

"Hmm. That all depends; have you applied for your AARP card?"

"I'm not that old, you doofus."

"The Adulterers' Association of Rural Pennsylvania has no age restrictions, dear. Although the dues are said to be quite steep."

"Are you making fun of me again?"

"Absolutely." I stood as well.

"If you leave now, you'll still have to pay for your food."

"You haven't even taken my order back to the kitchen."

"Get out of my restaurant!"

"Certainly, dear."

I was still hungry, of course, but I knew that Freni had already served my guests lunch.

While technically it is my kitchen, in reality it is the sovereign domain of a stout, stubborn Amish woman in her mid-seventies. I would rather scavenge for bones in a lion's den than raid my own refrigerator for leftovers after my cook has "put the kitchen up." Fortunately, not only did Hernia's fifth greatest cook (I sell the complete list for two dollars) live only a stone's throw from the Sausage Barn, he was always eager for visitors.

Reverend Richard Nixon is pastor of the First and Only True Church of the One and Only Living God of the Tabernacle of Supreme Holiness and Healing and Keeper of the Consecrated Righteousness of the Eternal Flame of Jehovah. He was also one of my judges for the Holstein competition the next day. By dropping in on him, I could kill two birds with one stone.

The parsonage of this miniscule congregation is a single-wide trailer that sits adjacent to the windowless concrete block building that serves as a sanctuary. Originally, a set of wooden steps allowed one easy access to the trailer door, but they've rotted over the years, and have yet to be replaced. My guess is that the church with thirty-two words in its name is too poor to maintain its property. Whatever the reason, the lack of steps doesn't negatively impact Reverend Nixon, because he has the longest legs I've ever seen outside of a zoo.

Usually the reverend is quick to pop out of his cramped quarters, whereupon he greets his visitors with a warm smile. However, since I'd eschewed the gravel parking lot in favor of a grass sward, it is possible my approach had gone unnoticed.

"Yoo-hoo," I hollered through cupped hands.

Still receiving no response, I strode to the door, and rapped on it with knuckles that are the envy of woodpeckers. Finally, after damage was beginning to show (on the metal door, not my hands), the good reverend appeared.

"Magdalena, what a pleasant surprise."

"No offense," I said sweetly, "but are you losing your hearing?"

"Not at all. I have the TV on."

"In the daytime?"

"I'm also eating lunch. Would you care to join me?"

"What are you having?"

"Stew. And then deep-dish apple pie for dessert."

"Well . . ." I hung my head coyly.

"Home-churned ice cream comes with the pie."

"All right, if you insist. But you'll have to help me up. I'm five feet ten, but I'm no giantess — oops, sorry about that."

"No offense taken. I rather like being this tall; I can sit anywhere I want in a movie theater, and no one is in my way. The only drawback is that I can't stand in this trailer. I thought of tearing off the roof and building a sort of skylight down the middle — I'd do it myself, of course — but skylights are notorious for leaking, and then in the summer I'd have to worry about overheating this place. So instead, I'm looking into the feasibility of dropping the floor about a foot. Maybe even adding a basement."

My mouth fell open. Fortunately, it was still too early for flies.

"*You* watch movies? Isn't that a sin?"

He offered me his hand, which was slightly larger than the state of Rhode Island. "We'll talk about it at lunch. In the meantime, here, let me help you up."

I graciously accepted, and soon was seated across from him in a galley that was far smaller than the state of Rhode Island. But since he'd turned off the Devil's Chatterbox and had set a steaming bowl of delicious stew in front of me, it didn't seem right for me to complain that my own knees were practically on either side of my face, a position I hadn't assumed since . . .

"— of course, that's it in a nutshell. Feel free to ask questions, if you have any."

"Huh? What did you say?"

"How charming, Magdalena," he said, entirely without sarcasm. "How utterly like you: always off in your own little world. At any rate, I said something about it boiling down to moral selectivity."

"You're darn tootin'." I swallowed my pride along with a spoonful of delicious stew gravy. "By the way, what does that mean?"

"It means that I, along with everyone else in this world — with possibly a few *un*notable exceptions — pick and choose our moral laundry list."

"Yes, of course, but can you give me an example?"

"Take divorce, for instance. It used to be the big no-no. But when the so-called Moral Majority lined up to vote a divorced man into office — that would be Ronald Reagan — they had to pick a new cause. Enter abortion as the cause du jour. That took them through the eighties and half the nineties. However, nothing has got them so worked up and spewing hate in the name of God as homosexuality. The ironic thing is that Jesus came down hard on divorce, but he had nothing at all to say about abortion or gay rights."

"To be fair, there are a lot of other sins Jesus didn't mention by name."

"Do you think loving someone is a sin?"

"This isn't about me!"

"Yes, it is. It's all about all of us. Tell me, Magdalena, which sin do you choose to ignore? Perhaps even to justify?"

"*Moi?* Uh — nothing comes to mind."

"Be honest."

"Okay, I give up. Pull out the bamboo slivers. Lighten up on the thumbscrews. I suppose that it is possible that at times I am creative with the truth."

"You're a liar. Come on, say it."

"I most certainly will not!"

He fixed his doleful brown eyes on me, no doubt trying to guilt me into a full-blown confession. I, however, stood my ground. And it wasn't even that hard. All I had to do was pretend that he was Mama, and that she had just whipped me for stealing the last piece of her rhubarb pie. I hadn't stolen it, of course, because I hated her rhubarb pie. It was so bitter, it literally killed half your taste buds before you could gag it down. Since both Papa and Susannah vehemently denied eating the vile stuff, I could only conclude that the missing piece had managed to make its way over to the sink, where it voluntarily committed suicide by jumping into the garbage disposal.

"Wow," the reverend finally said, "you're a tough nut to crack."

"Indisputably so. Now tell me about your movie addiction."

"It's not an addiction; it's merely a sinful pleasure. I go every Saturday if I'm free. I call it my little excursion into Sodom and Gomorrah."

I gasped. "You go all the way to Maryland?"

"Don't worry, I take provisions. But I don't want to be a stumbling block to my congregation, so I have to go someplace they aren't likely to see me."

My head reeled. "Let me get this straight. You choose your big sin, and then, as they say in this day and age, you 'own' it?"

"Exactly. Imagine what a nicer world it would be if all the closeted homosexuals in this country stopped persecuting other gays from their pulpits or pews, and owned up to who they are."

"Hmm."

He fixed his doleful gaze on me again.

"Stop it — dear! I'm not a liar, merely an embroiderer of the truth. Rather skillful embroidering, if I do say so myself." I stood and stretched, and in the process whacked my hands against the metal ceiling.

"Huafa mischt."

"Excuse me?"

"You heard me. My mother was Amish, as you may recall. I know the socially acceptable way to say horse manure in this community. If you can't just flat-out admit that you're a world-class liar — well then, Magdalena, I've lost all respect for you."

I thought carefully before responding. I even cast a prayer heavenward. That it bounced off the metal roof of the reverend's tiny trailer wasn't my fault.

"If I refuse, will you still be a judge tomorrow?"

"Of course. I'm not being punitive; I just want you to stop kidding yourself."

Knowing that my prayers for a charitable tongue would be futile, I skipped them and dove right in. "Why, Reverend Nixon, you're a first-class hypocrite, despite all this liberal posturing about self-knowledge. Your congregation is the most conservative in the county, Amish or otherwise. I've heard that you thump your Bibles so hard you wear them out on an annual basis, and, according to the hospital statistics, at least once a month someone in your church is hurt by all the jumping up and down in the pews you folks engage in. If they knew you were sneaking off into Maryland to watch movies, they'd toss you out like last year's devotional guide."

The good reverend is one of those men whose virility is immediately made apparent by an enormous, angular Adam's apple. When he swallows, or becomes agitated, it bobs up and down like a fishing cork on Miller's Pond. At the moment, judging by the vigorous activity taking place in his throat, one might guess Richard Nixon had caught a large-mouth bass.

"Please leave now," he said in a tone as flat as central Kansas. Perhaps I'd gone too far.

"Certainly, but you'll still judge, right?"

"Actually, I've just changed my mind; I will not be judging. In fact, I'm not even coming. Far be it for me to sully this august event with my wicked, hypocritical ways. Besides, I have yet to wear out last year's Bible, let alone get started on this year's, so I've got a lot of thumping to do."

"But who will I get to take your place on such short notice?"

"Frankly, Magdalena, I don't give a —"

If Reverend Nixon finished his sentence with a swear word, I didn't hear it. I was too busy fainting. Fortunately for me, the pastor of the church with thirty-two words in its name made good use of those long arms and caught me before my head hit the floor.

23

Imagine my surprise when I woke to discover that I was in Hell, and I mean that literally. After all, I'd given my life over to the Lord, and was a *true* believer, and, although it's faith that's important, not good works, I'd even acted charitably at times. If anyone deserved to go to Heaven, it was me — not that any of us are truly deserving of such a wonderful place, but you know what I mean. I certainly didn't think I was bound for Hell, just because I stretched the truth on the odd occasion.

For some reason, I was lying on my back. Leering down at me was the Devil who, although *not* wearing Prada, was unmistakably female. Her voice soon confirmed that.

"Do you know who I am, Magdalena?"

"Beelzebub. Or would you prefer Your Devilship? But Sataness is just too sibilant, if you ask me. Look, a terrible mistake has been made: I've been sent to the wrong place."

"Oh?"

"No doubt about it. I should be up there" — I pointed to the ceiling — "choosing my mansion. How many styles do we get to pick from? Oops, I guess you wouldn't know."

"It's me, Nurse Dudley."

"What?"

"Focus, Magdalena. How many fingers do you see?"

"Hey, that's not nice! Just because I'm a simple Mennonite woman, you don't think I know what that means. But you're right, you do sort of look like Nurse Ratched, although frankly — and I mean this as a compliment, you're somewhat prettier."

"Shut up, you idiot! I really am Nurse Ratched — Darn, you see what you made me do? Well, I told you I was going to get you, Magdalena; I just didn't expect the moment to come so quick. But now that you're lying in a hospital bed, and I'm the nurse on duty . . ." She rubbed her hands together and cackled.

It was then that I realized Hell was merely a room at Bedford County Memorial Hospital. The real Devil, however, could not have been any scarier than Nurse Ratched. I tried to sit up, but was pushed back down by her almost supernatural strength.

"Help," I shouted. "Help!"

She clamped her other hand over my mouth. Her deadly digits were icy cold, and smelled of rubbing alcohol.

"I was only kidding, ha-ha. Or was I? I'm going to let you go now, Magdalena. But bear in mind that it will be your word against mine. And since you just came out of a near coma, and I am a respected professional, who will they believe? The woman who exaggerates everything when she's not out-and-out lying, or the kind, compassionate caregiver?"

"Why you evil, evil —"

The door opened and in strode my dearly beloved and, hard on his heels, the breathtakingly beautiful Faya Rashid. The latter is a doctor, and a friend of mine. Originally from Lebanon — as in the Middle East, not Pennsylvania — Faya has been busy turning herself into a proper American. Although she will always have an accent, and her grammar is not quite perfect, she knows more about American history and government than any six high school students combined. In fact, in less than a month, she planned to take the citizenship test.

"Babe!" Gabe ran over to the bed and practically threw himself on top of me.

Dr. Rashid peered around my husband's thick mop of still-black hair and smiled. "You are awake now, Miss Yoder. Congratulations."

"Congratulate me on being alive; this woman tried to kill me."

Nurse Dudley somehow assumed the innocent pose of an elementary school girl. "The patient is exhibiting signs of extreme agitation. Would you like me to prepare a sedative?"

"She would *not*," the Babester said.

My tormentor's innocent façade began to crack. "Are you a doctor?"

"Yes, as a matter of fact, I am."

Dr. Rashid's last hurdle in her quest to become an American is to master the tricky art of assertiveness — especially when dealing with men. Alas, I am not the one to teach her this skill, seeing as how I am a mite overqualified.

Instead of shooing my sweet baboo from my bed, she laid a cool hand gently on my arm, and looked at me when she spoke. "Dr. Rosen is a world-famous heart surgeon, but I am afraid he is not Miss Yoder's attending physician."

"I get the hint," Gabe said, and retreated to the foot of my bed.

Dr. Rashid's dark eyes shone with relief.

"Miss Yoder, is this the first time you are fainting like this?"

"To my knowledge, yes. Although I suppose it is possible I've fainted before, and then regained consciousness immediately and not realized that it happened. I mean, theoretically, just about anything is possible — well, pigs will never be able to fly, of course, unless some wicked scientist manages to splice pig genes into a bird egg and comes up with something like a peagle, which would be a sin, and maybe something Congress —"

"Hon, would you please just answer her questions? And for the record, we use pig valves in human heart patients all the time. I'd hardly call that wicked."

"Ha!" Nurse Dudley was obviously quite pleased with my reprimand.

"Nurse!" Dr. Rashid spoke with shocking, but delightful sharpness. "Please do leave the room."

"But I was —"

"Please, no buts. Yes?" She waited while my erstwhile nemesis stomped from the room like a spoiled child. "Miss Yoder," she continued, as if nothing untoward had happened, "we checked your most vital signs, and I drew some blood while you were passed out. There is much backup in the laboratory, but your most vital signs, they are very good. You have a strong heart, Miss Yoder."

"Good things come in small packages."

A look of confusion flickered across her face. "Nevertheless, we are keeping you here for twenty-four hours for to observe."

"But you can't! I have a competition to preside over."

"This competition must wait."

"It can't wait. Everyone already is here with their cows. Folks have come from as far away as Timbuktu."

"From Africa? As far as that?"

"Oh, is *that* where Timbuktu is? Never mind, that's just an expression. My point is that this date is chiseled in stone, and so is my being there."

Poor Dr. Rashid turned to Gabe. That a Lebanese immigrant has to ask a Jewish man from New York to translate for a regular American like yours truly — well, as my mother-in-law would say, that's a *shande.*

"What she means," Gabe said without any prodding, "is that a lot of people are counting on this cow competition. But don't worry, Dr. Rashid, I'll see that she stays right here."

"In a flying pig's eye," I sputtered.

214

The love of my life planted a kiss on me of such high quality that it bought him some explaining time. "Don't worry, hon, I have this covered; I'll take over all your duties."

"But what do you know about cows?"

"You'll teach me. I'm not leaving your bedside until I know exactly what to do."

"Well, the first thing is to find a judge to replace Reverend Richard Nixon."

"Why? What happened? Is he unwell?"

"Uh — no."

"You ticked him off, didn't you?"

"Remember that I'm in a hospital bed. You can't be mad at a dying woman."

"No!" Dr. Rashid gripped my shoulder. "You are not dying, Miss Yoder."

"That was for dramatic effect, dear. Gabriel, darling, if you can find a suitable replacement for the reverend, and pull off the job of emcee — well, I'll be eternally grateful. I might even do this." I pulled him close and whispered in his ear.

"No way, babe, only my ma does that."

"Cut his meat," I said to Dr. Rashid, to stop her from looking so horrified. Sadly, it was the truth.

Dr. Rashid pretended it made sense. "So, we are all squares then, yes?"

"Squares, indeed," I said in much too loud a voice. "But please, dear, do me a favor.

215

Tell the dietician that chocolate pudding is necessary for my health, and please tell someone — anyone other than Nurse Dudley — that I have yet to have lunch."

Gabe squeezed my hand. "Mags, hon, it's three in the afternoon. No hospital serves lunch this late."

"Then tell the concerned party that I'll have two suppers — one now, and the other at the appointed time. If they object, Bedford Memorial Hospital can kiss their Magdalena Yoder wing good-bye."

His and her gasps sounded almost like my old furnace starting up. "Darling, are you serious? Are you donating a new wing to the hospital?"

"Absolutely not, dear. At least I have no plans to at the moment. But should I not get my lunch, I will definitely *not* be funding a new wing."

Gabe smiled wanly at my gorgeous physician. "Gotta love my Magdalena, right?"

If I was supposed to be getting any rest the remainder of the afternoon, it was definitely a lost cause. Everyone and their uncle either called or dropped by. One of the uncles, I think, called several times. As a result, my lunch — which arrived in twenty minutes — was cold before I could finish it. In the meantime I tried to school Gabe in the fine art of holding a Holstein competition. Honestly, how is one to hold court, lecture a city-slicker husband on animal husbandry, and eat chocolate pudding at the same time?

Shortly after five, Gabe said good-bye. For the next hour or so, I read a health magazine, and bravely resisted the temptation to turn on the TV. (I haven't watched that spewer of evil since *Green Acres* went off the air.) Just as I was about to raise a fuss concerning the whereabouts of my supper — I'd heard the meal cart out in the hallway an hour earlier, but no one came to my room — the door was flung open, and the room filled with the wonderful aroma of real food.

I saw the cart first. Then, just barely sticking above the covered dishes, the hoary head of my mother-in-law came into view. Lacking someone else to pinch, I pinched myself to see if I was dreaming. Apparently, I wasn't.

"Magdalena, must you alvays scream?"

"Ida, what are you doing here?"

"I came to feed you. Vhat else?"

"Where did you get that cart?"

"Vhy the twenty questions?"

"Because you don't like me, that's why. Who put you up to this? Who brought you

217

here? My dear, sweet baboo?"

She shook her head as she rolled her eyes. "Baboon? Oy, dis voman is even more meshugah den I tink before."

"Okay, so I'm nuts! Now tell me how you got here."

24

"I drive myself," my mother-in-law said, as if it were an everyday occurrence.

"But you're not supposed to drive anymore; you lost your license. The judge said you are a menace to yourself and to everyone around you. If they catch you driving again, they could throw you in jail."

"Do they have TV in this jail? I must watch my *Yeopardy*."

"Your *what?*"

"De game show. *Mit* Alex Trebek, yah?"

I'd actually heard a lot of good things about this show. Someday — if I ever jump off the fence — I might give this program a try. But what Ida was able to watch in the hoosegow wasn't the point I was trying to make.

"You could hurt someone, Ida. Even kill someone. And even if you got lucky for the rest of your life, what kind of example would that be setting for Alison?"

"Vill you vake me vhen dis lecture is over?"

"Sorry, dear. I know you meant well. So, what did you bring?"

Ida's eyes lit up like a jar full of fireflies, and she actually smiled. "All your favorite tings, yah?"

Still beaming, she uncovered a platter of brisket, a boiled chicken, a small tureen of chicken soup *mit* matzo balls, a serving bowl of roast potatoes, a pan of noodle kugel, candied carrots, a mixed green salad, and, for dessert, a jelly roll. Oh, and a loaf of her homemade braided egg bread. Challah nagila I think it's called.

"Ida, this is fabulous. Thank you."

In the blink of an eye, she somehow hopped up on the bed and settled in next to me. Perhaps she had springs in her shoes. However she got there, I was actually stunned speechless for a minute.

"You vant dat I should cut your meat?" she asked.

"Uh — uh —"

"Is not a difficult question, Magdalena."

"Okay, I'm game. Saw away."

No doubt I would embarrass myself if I admitted that Ida not only cut the brisket for me, she literally fed me as well. When I was full to bursting, she took the cloth napkin from my lap, spit on a corner, then dabbed at my face.

"Yuck! What are you doing?"

"You have *shmutz* on your chin. You vant it should stay dirty?"

"No. I want to know why you are being so nice to me."

"Because you are family, dat's vhy."

"That's *huafa mischt.* I'm not stupid, dear; I only look that way."

"Yah. So I tell you, den: I vant to move back to New York."

My healthy heart skipped with joy. "I think that's a great idea!"

"Vill you help me convince my Gabeleh dat you tink so?"

"Absolutely."

She reached up and kissed my cheek. Then she grabbed my head, turned it, and kissed the other cheek.

"You're a mensch, Magdalena. I don't care vhat da others tink."

Jesus instructed us to turn the other cheek should someone slap us. He said nothing, however, concerning what to do about random acts of osculation.

"Vhat — I mean, what — *do* they think?"

"Dis one is so arrogant, dat one says. Tinks she is the center of the voild, another says. Oy, such chutzpah we've never seen.

Of course I shtick up for you."

"Who are these people? Names. I want names."

"Too many for to name, yah? But, like I said, I tell them where they should get off at."

"Hopefully the first station."

"Vhat?"

"Never mind. All's well that ends well." Despite the reminder that I had my share of detractors, my heart was filled with latent joy. Who could have guessed that my biggest (although certainly not in size) critic would someday be a staunch supporter? Throw in the news that Ida Rosen was headed back to Brooklyn, and I was positively giddy.

"And now vee plan, yah?"

"Plan away!"

"I vas tinking dat foist vee should move back to da city, before selling da farm. You vouldn't mind selling it for us, if vee give you commission, yah?"

Mine was the gasp heard 'round the world. "Hold your horses! What is this 'we' you keep mentioning? Does that include my husband, or is it the royal 'we'? No scatological reference intended."

"Vhat? So now you speak da Amish."

"Just tell me," I said through gritted teeth,

"are you planning to take Gabe with you?"

"Of course. I tell you dis, and you say fine."

"I meant that it is fine for *you* to go back, but not for my husband."

"He is my son!" Who knew such a thunderous sound could come from one so tiny. "He is the fruit of my looms."

"Yet far too big to be a jockey."

"Do you mock?"

"Quite often — or so I'm told. Although I'm trying to be better, I really am. Now, you listen to me, Ida Rosen. My husband isn't going anywhere with you. Not to stay. And if you don't get your fanny off my bed right now, and make yourself as scarce as a shadow on a rainy day, I'm calling security. *Comprende?*"

"Oy, the Amish again." But she did remove her buttocks as directed, and I saw no more of her that evening.

Only the dead can sleep in a hospital, and I've no doubt that even some of them can't get a full night's rest. Nurses are forever coming in and shining lights in your face, taking your temperature, and writing full-length novels on your chart. When they tire of that, they take delight in coughing into the loudspeaker system, or dropping barbells in the hallway.

Yet somehow, I managed to sleep through breakfast, and thus, as one can well imagine, was not in the cheeriest of moods when my bedside phone rang. As usual, I prayed for a patient tongue, and, as usual, that prayer went unanswered. The phone, however, was answered.

"Just for that, you're not getting the million bucks I promised you!"

"Who is this?"

"You tell me, you're the one who called."

"Hon, it's me, Gabe. You don't sound so good."

"Your mother paid me a visit last night."

"Uh-oh. What happened?"

"She brought me supper. Then, like Judas, she kissed me on the cheek, before telling me she plans to take you back to New York with her. *Permanently.*"

"You're kidding."

"Do I ever kid about your mother?"

"Huafa mischt," my husband said, although in English. "I can't believe she'd do that — actually, I *can* believe it, and it really ticks me off. I can't tell you how sorry I am." He paused wisely for several seconds. "What did you say to her in response?"

"I threatened to call security. Darling, tell me honestly, you didn't know about this in advance, did you?"

"You better be kidding now, because if not, I'm going to be angry."

"Shall I tell the truth and face the consequences?"

I could hear him counting softly to ten before speaking into the receiver. "Hon, it hurts me that you'd think, even for a second, that I would put Ma before you."

"I'm sorry you're hurting." I glanced at the bedside clock. "Say, aren't you supposed to be presiding right now? It's almost time to tally the results of round one."

He sighed. "Look, I don't want to fight. And yeah, that's why I'm calling. I did call first thing this morning, by the way, and you didn't answer. Anyway, there's something fishy going on."

"Fishy? Like what?"

"Holy guacamole! Hon, look — I'll have to call you back."

"Oh, no you don't! Don't leave me hanging like this."

There followed a lot of static, and only a smattering of words. The only two words that were said without a break were "lateral incision." Shortly after he said those, the line went dead.

Gabe had been calling on his cell phone,

which explained everything. Because Hernia is situated between two mountain ridges, aerial reception of any kind is, at best, intermittent. Sacrilegious wags have been known to say that on Judgment Day, only half of Hernia's dead will rise, the other half having not gotten the signal.

Late morning, as my stomach was beginning to rumble like an active volcano, Nurse Ratched stopped by. She looked like a small child who'd just been told that Santa Claus was a myth, one perpetuated by secular parents who believe the true Christmas story sounds just too fantastical to pass on to their children.

"Dr. Rashid says you can go. Apparently everything checks out okay — you're still alive, gosh darn it. I'm to process you. But don't think you've truly escaped my clutches, Miss Yoder. Someday, when you least expect, you'll pay for what you did yesterday."

"It was a bra, for heaven's sake. Let me pay for it now."

"Oh, I don't want your money — although you do have too much of it for your own good. I want revenge, and that is a dish best served up cold."

"Cold dishes are way overrated. Have you ever tried eating fried liver and onions cold?

Or boiled turnips?"

"You can't dissuade me."

I pushed my call button. I pushed it hard and repeatedly.

"What are you doing?" she demanded. "I'm the nurse assigned to you, and I'm right here."

"So you are. Silly me." As she watched, scowling, I rummaged through my purse until I found my cell phone. The number I wanted was prerecorded on my speed dial. "Hello, Ed?"

"Magdalena! I heard you were staying with us. How are we treating you?"

"I've been treated very well, Ed, thank you. Say, do you mind dropping by for a moment?" Out of the corner of my eye I saw Nurse Dudley turn to stone — petrified stone.

"As it so happens, I'm on your floor. I'll be there in a second."

25

FRESH COFFEE ICE CREAM RECIPE

Ingredients:

6 egg yolks

4 tablespoons fresh coffee beans, finely ground

8 oz (200 g) light brown sugar

1 pint (500 ml) milk

6 oz (approx. 185 ml) very hot water

Take the finely ground coffee, and pour the water onto it, then let it stand for about ten minutes. Strain the mixture. In a heatproof bowl, mix together the sugar and egg yolks, then whisk until thick and pale. Whisk in the milk and the coffee, then put the bowl over a saucepan of simmering (though not boiling) water. Cook until the mixture is thick (i.e., until it forms a layer on the back of a wooden spoon), being sure to stir it all the time. Take the saucepan off the heat and place the bowl to one side to cool. (If you want to prevent a skin from forming on the mixture, you can try covering the surface with a piece of damp, greaseproof paper.)

When cool, transfer the mixture into an ice cream maker, and follow the manufacturer's instructions.

26

Ed actually took several minutes to arrive, and by then I had the check written and recorded. We greeted each other warmly (we've served on many boards together), and he nodded at Nurse Dudley. Personally, I think he tried too hard to appear as if he *wasn't* trying to read her name badge. Oh well, no one is perfect.

When the pleasantries were done, and he'd turned his attention back to me, I handed him the check. "Here is a small gift to the hospital; a token of my thanks for the excellent care I've received."

The hospital administrator glanced at the check. Then he looked at the check. Next he stared at the check, his eyes bulging.

"A — a — *million* dollars? There must be a mistake."

"Oh, no mistake, dear. But strings, yes."

"Wonderful. Strings are just great."

The petrified woman to my right returned

to life enough to blanch, thereby turning herself into a white statue. Perhaps she was a pillar of salt.

"Ed, I was thinking — always a dangerous activity for me — that some of the hardest-working and least-appreciated professionals are nurses. Where would patients be without them? Or doctors, for that matter? So I would like this money to do something that makes life easier and more rewarding for nurses. I was thinking it might be a down payment on establishing a day care center — or a really special nurses' lounge. At any rate, that is really up to you and the board."

"Those are fantastic ideas, Magdalena. The day care center especially. Would you mind if it was available to all hospital employees?"

"That would be zippers with me, but there is a condition."

"Zippers?"

"You know — like *cool.* You unzip anything, you're bound to get a cool breeze." I've been trying for decades to get one of my clever expressions accepted into the lexicon of American lingo, but so far there hasn't been even one taker.

Ed smiled indulgently. "Ah, zippers. I'll have to remember that. So, what's the condition?"

"I want the facility to be named after Nurse Dudley."

There were two audible gasps, followed by two soprano voices speaking in unison. "You *do?*"

"Indeed, I doodest. The Nurse Dudley Day Care Center — has a nice sound to it, doesn't it?"

Ed managed to pull his voice down an octave. "But Nurse Dudley — and I mean no disrespect — is our least-liked staff member. Not just in the nursing department, but in the hospital in general. As a matter of fact, she's pretty much hated by —"

"Now, now, Edwin, we mustn't be so judgmental." I turned to the object of Ed's scorn. "Were the window open, Nurse Dudley, a sparrow could fly down your throat. Trust me, all those feathers in your tummy can be a mite tickly."

"But — but — Miss Yoder, I've been so bad to you over the years. I don't know how you can forgive me, much less do something so awesome in my honor. Sure, you've been even worse to me —"

"Stop while you're ahead, dear. And for the record, I'm not naming the center in your honor — although you may choose to believe so. I'm merely naming it that because it will need a name, and you're standing right here."

The tears coursing down her face were following the topography, as laid down by a lifetime of sun exposure and years of heavy smoking. "That's a lie, Miss Yoder, and you know it. But I'll take what I can get."

"You're right, that was a big fat lie. I'm spending a million dollars just to get back at you. Having your name on the center will be a daily reminder of how I countered with kindness the hot coals you've heaped on my head over the years."

Now the tears ran so freely that they overflowed the smokers' lines. "Thank you, thank you, thank you! Commemorating my meanness is the nicest thing anyone has ever done for me. How can I ever pay you back for this wonderful gift?"

"Bring me lunch, for starters — with an extra dessert. I'm so famished, I could eat even my own cooking. And then be a dear, and give me a ride into Hernia. Ed, you won't mind if she takes the afternoon off?" It was neither a question, nor a command; it was a statement that left little doubt in his mind that cooperation was expected.

"Anything you'd like, Magdalena," Ed said, as tears flowed down his face as well.

■ ■ ■ ■

I would have left the hospital much sooner, but, as I was reaching for my glasses — in order to read the ingredient list on my juice box — my hand accidentally alighted on something called a remote control. It is used to turn modern televisions on and off, and also, if one is skilled in these matters, to select various stations.

Needless to say, I'd never felt one before. It was long, hard, and disturbingly exciting. As strange as it might sound, I found that I was incapable of letting go. Then, just as surely as if Satan himself had pushed my finger, I pressed the ON button. A minute later, with Beelzebub at my side, I began to watch my first feature-length motion picture. In all sincerity, I must let it be known that I was powerless to stop.

The movie, if you must know, was *Imitation of Life,* with Lana Turner. I'd once heard my sister, Susannah, refer to this movie as a tearjerker. Boy, was she ever right. By the end of the show, I'd jerked my way through an entire box of facial tissue, and had just rung for a second box. To be absolutely honest, I never even cried that much when my parents died.

Of course, after that I had to wait for the puffiness below my eyes to subside, which took another hour, and then I had to check on Doc. He was sleeping as peacefully as a baby, although judging by the configuration of his sheet, he wasn't dreaming of mobiles and pacifiers.

At any rate, Nurse Dudley was an excellent driver, despite being such a poor winner. We hadn't so much as exited the hospital parking lot when she began in on her list of demands: the letters of her name had to be at least four feet high and chiseled into Indiana limestone — certainly *not* attached letters, ones that could be torn down at the whim of another CEO. In addition, there was to be a tastefully sized bronze bust of her just inside the main doors. And oh, if a new sidewalk was part of the package, there was to be a star embedded in it, as well as her handprints.

I told her to go on a solo picnic lunch in the Allegheny National Forest, after first smashing any compasses she might own. She then told me to take a running leap from Bedford's tallest building, which is a silly thing to say, given that I'd land on either concrete or asphalt and hurt the dickens out of myself. At any rate, after that, we got along famously, and by the time she dropped me off at Hernia High stadium (where the competition was held), we were no longer the worst of friends.

My best friend, incidentally, was one of the few people left at the stadium. She appeared to be directing several young Amish men, telling them how they should go about scooping up cow dung.

"Agnes!" I cried in bewilderment. "Where *is* everybody?"

"They're gone, Magdalena. How are you doing? *What* are you doing here? Gabriel said you were in the hospital."

"I was. But I'm good as new now."

Agnes is a short, round woman with a round face framed by round glasses. Despite the fact that she is grossly overweight, she positively brims with energy. In fact, she bounces when she walks. When she gestured me away from the Amish men, I found it hard to keep up with her.

But when we were well out of earshot, she bounced in place until I caught up. "What was your diagnosis?"

"Diagnosis? Agnes, dear, you of all people should know that, despite advancements in modern diagnostic machines, doctors are reluctant to give diagnoses. They'd rather have their egos excised."

"Why, Magdalena, what a judgmental

thing for you to say. So you *are* all better!"

"I'm fine as frog's hair, dear. Now tell me where everyone is."

"They've gone home — I guess. The first annual Hernia Holstein Competition is officially over."

"Agnes, I'm not in the mood for jokes. Besides, you've never had a sense of humor — and I mean that kindly — so why start now?"

"It's not a joke. Your handsome husband rushed things so much, he was able to cram two days of judging into one. As for the festivities, well — you can see for yourself. Three Amish men on poop-scooping detail, and they're not even cute. Whoopee." She twirled her index finger in the air.

"But what about the hot dog vendor and the cotton candy machine? And the three-legged stilt walker? Where are they?"

"The stilt walker called in last night to say he'd broken one of his legs. The vendors stayed only until the winner was announced, because that's when the crowd, such as it was, left. Everyone is angry, Magdalena. They say that they were ripped off by the high ticket prices for a show that didn't deliver. As for the contestants and their cows — they actually came to fisticuffs. I mean the contestants did. For the most part, the cows were well-behaved."

I moaned, my new alternative to wailing. "Whose cow won? Was it a local farmer?"

Agnes, like Freni, lacks a neck. Shaking her head must create a good deal of friction, but she bravely did so anyway. That's how strong her emotions were.

"A local win, suspect as it might be, would be great for the economy. I'm afraid it was one of your people."

"*My* people? I only have Mose and the Amish lad who milks for me. I don't recall either of them entering a cow."

"No, one of your guests."

I had to swallow hard to keep my heart in my chest. "Who? What were their names?"

"Hmm. Pearlman, I think."

"You mean Pearlmutter? Was she uncommonly plain, to use an oxymoron, and was he to-die-for gorgeous?"

"Yes, one might describe them like that."

"Rats. I was really hoping that, if it couldn't be one of our homegrown farmers, the delightful Gertie Fuselburger would win."

"Now *you're* joking — right?"

"Nay, I joketh noteth. I think she's a hoot."

"Wrong. You should have witnessed the hissy fit she threw when she was eliminated after the first round. I was seriously worried that she would have a stroke. How old is she anyway? A hundred?"

"Knock off a third of a century and you'll be closer. But don't stop there. Tell me what her hissy fit was like. And it's not that I just want to gossip either — a good grasp of human nature is helpful to me as an innkeeper."

Agnes chortled. "A good grasp? Magdalena, if human nature had an esophagus, you'd have long since asphyxiated it. Anyway, she cussed a blue streak — even threatened to call the cops."

"The police? What for?"

27

"Something about the contest being rigged. At the very least, she said, she'd be calling the BMC. Magdalena, what on earth is that?"

"Bovine Mediating Council. It's a little-known organization that settles cow disputes. But never mind that, could you please give me a ride home? I was planning to ride with Gabe. Speaking of whom, how did he do? More importantly, how did he manage to run through two days' events in less than one?"

"He spoke like an auctioneer, that's how."

"Well, he is a New Yorker; they all talk fast."

"No, I mean he really spoke like an auctioneer. He rattled off a million words a minute. It seemed like he didn't even stop to breathe. Everyone was complaining, Magdalena, but your husband essentially told them all to shut up. He said that you gave him the absolute authority to do things however he pleased. You should have seen the faces of the judges. That's how the Roman senate must have looked when Julius Caesar took over as lifetime dictator. Although I've seen statues of Caesar, and your Gabriel is much better looking."

I nodded. "And if there's a dish named after my sweetie, it better be more than just a salad."

We chatted amiably on the way home, as best friends are wont to do. But when we got to the juncture of Main Street and Hertzler Road, Agnes pulled over onto the shoulder, which is also the west bank of Slave Creek. Legend has it that escaped slaves followed this stream north from Maryland and to freedom. I am all for believing in legends — just as long as they don't contradict my faith — but the truth is that not only does Slave Creek begin in Pennsylvania, it ends here as well, having emptied its meager flow into the mighty Allegheny. Still, it is a nice legend, and the only other person aware of this fallacy is Doc, and neither of us intends to breathe a discrediting word.

"Agnes," I said with as much pleasantness as I could muster, "why on earth are we stopping? I need to get home pronto. ASAP.

Be a dear and press the pedal to the metal."

"Magdalena, I need to ask you something first."

"The answer is no. I will not run away with you to homestead in the wilds of Alaska. I hear that in the summer the mosquitoes are as big as starlings, and that —"

"Please don't wisecrack."

I sighed. "Okay, I'll try not to, difficult as it may be. Now, what is it?"

"I think I'm in love."

"That's exactly what I was trying to get across. I love you too, Agnes, but only as a friend."

"What? I'm not in love with *you!* Honestly, Magdalena, when are you going to learn that the world does not revolve around you?"

That stung. Yes, I am guilty of thinking that I am the center of the universe — but only *my* universe. It's called having an ego, and it's not necessarily a bad thing. As tempted as I was to retort with the argument that we all think that way, I took the high road and merely pantomimed locking my mouth with a key and tossing it out the window.

Agnes gave me a challenging look until she was quite satisfied I'd been properly put in my place. "I'm in love with Harmon Dorfman. He's in love with me too, I just know it. It was love at first sight. He wants me to move to North Dakota and marry him there. When I told him I have the uncles to care for, he volunteered to move down here."

I sat bolt upright, my eyes bulging from the pressure of unreleased words.

"Don't be such a pain, Magdalena. Unlock your mouth and tell me what you think. Tell me what you *really* think; don't hold back a thing."

I didn't even bother to look for the invisible key. "I think that you must be nuts. Not only are you off your rocker, but you must have fallen off and hit your head. Agnes, Harmon Dorfman is one of the most irritating men I've ever met, and I say that with Christian charity."

"Magdalena, I've always been glad that you're not a pagan. So Harmon isn't your cup of tea — that doesn't mean he's not right for me. I'm forty-six years old, Magdalena, and not pretty like you. The last date I had was in college, and he was a blind date. I mean that literally."

"But Harmon Dorfman walks around without a shirt."

"So what? Have you forgotten that the

243

uncles don't wear pants?"

"*And* he claims to have cloned a cow."

"His brother claims that, not him. Besides, Harry withdrew the claim this morning when the crowd booed his announcement."

"Gabe let him announce it?"

"Yes, and forgive me, Magdalena, but it was mean of your husband to allow him to hang himself like that. Gabe is a doctor; he knew Harmon was faking it."

"Faking or trying to pull the wool over our unsophisticated eyes? I think most folks would call that attempted thievery."

Agnes extended her jaw in defiance, which set her chins to wobbling. When she gets into this frame of mind, there is no dissuading her.

"When are you leaving for North Dakota?"

"Oh, Magdalena, do you really mean it? Are you really going to support me in this?"

My sigh ruffled the surface of Slave Creek. "Yes, silly, but I'm not going to stop by to check on the uncles without you there. When you've seen one, you've seen one too many, if you ask me. I still can't look at a turkey neck without blushing."

She giggled. "I couldn't ask for a better friend. And the answer is Thursday. By this time next week, I plan to be Mrs. Harmon

Dorfman."

I shuddered.

Freni must have heard the car pull up my gravel driveway, but she waited until Agnes was back on the road again before making her move. Then she burst through the back door and practically threw herself down the steps, flapping her stubby arms vigorously like a plump hen that can't quite achieve liftoff.

"Ach, where have you been?"

"In the hospital. And how are you, dear?"

"Yah, I know about the hospital. But I called them, and they said that you checked out an hour ago. Where have you been since then?"

"Agnes plans to marry Harmon Dorfman."

"Ach," Freni squawked, and flapped her arms one last time. "That one is not right in the head."

"Harmon or Agnes?"

Her eyes glinted behind the thick lenses, which meant she was trying hard not to smile. "Two pecans on the same branch, yah?"

"Yes, but at least Agnes is sincere. I'm afraid she's going to be hurt."

"She is a smart woman, Magdalena.

Perhaps she can take care of herself. But your husband — well, what does he know of life outside his Big Banana?"

"*Excuse* me?"

"It means New York." She wiped lard and flower from her glasses with a black sleeve. "How is it that I know this name, and you do not?"

A ray of light shone into my primordial brain. "Ah! You're referring to the Big Apple!"

"They are both fruit, yah?"

Sometimes I can't help myself. "A pea and a head of cabbage are both vegetables, both green, and both round, yet they're hardly the same thing."

When Freni loses an argument, she first wipes her hands carefully on her starched white apron. Then she heads to the large ceramic pot that is kept on a bench beside the stove, and withdraws from it a lump of rising dough. She proceeds to punch every last microscopic air pocket from the dough, before placing it in a new location so that it can rise again. The result is a never-ending supply of the best bread, buns, and cinnamon rolls this tongue has ever tasted. Please believe me, it is seldom my intention to goad my sweet, elderly cousin, but if we didn't disagree from time to time, I would have to buy commercial bread. Then we'd both lose.

Today, however, Freni didn't budge. "Maybe you need to sit now, yah?"

"What ever for? I've been lying in bed all day. It's about time my feet got some blood."

She sighed heavily, sending airborne those particles of flour that had not been captured by the grease. "Okay, but this is not such good news."

"Freni, in the last six years, you have quit exactly one hundred and eighteen times. Given that you'll be back here tomorrow morning, at the latest, quitting your job is hardly earth-shattering news."

"Ach, this is no time for the lecture. Your Gabe is in trouble."

"What?"

"He calls me this afternoon while I am making the shoofly pie. I am just pouring the liquid onto the crumbs, so I cannot stop, yah? So then he calls again in five minutes. Maybe less. He says that he tries to call you at the hospital, but can get no signal. He says to warn you that the contest is not going so well."

"Don't stop!"

"But that is where he stops."

"Where is he now? Have you heard from

him since then?"

Freni shrugged and shook her head at the same time, which, given her physiognomy, was an economy of motion. But not to worry; surely my Bubeleh was across the road being comforted by the stubby arms of you-know-who.

I dialed his number. His cell rang five times, and then switched me over to voice mail. If I had one of those dingleberry things, or whatever they are, I would have tried to send him a text message. But I didn't. Instead, I did what every red-blooded, able-bodied, American woman would do: I prayed for wisdom. After sending up my smoke signal to the Almighty, I hiked up my skirts, retied my sensible black brogans, and ran the quarter of a mile to the farmhouse that my beloved still, if inexplicably, owns. Fit as I am — from repeatedly jumping to conclusions — I wasn't the least bit winded upon my arrival.

Gabe's car was in the long gravel driveway, parked next to the house, but that didn't mean much. The one thing Hernia High School has a dearth of — besides students — is parking places. The Babester had already told me he planned to hitch a ride into town with one of the judges, so as to leave a space free for one of our many expected visitors. If pressed, however, my husband would undoubtedly admit that, as a New Yorker, he isn't used to driving. I've seen him freeze up when he gets behind an Amish buggy, as if he doesn't know whether to honk impatiently, or get out and snap pictures.

At any rate, I checked the barn first, where he has his writing studio, before making a beeline for the house. Of course, I didn't knock or ring the bell. Why should I? Not only is my beloved mine, so is his property. The Babester and I commingled our belongings before commingling ourselves, on the grounds that anything less was a vote of no confidence. Anyway, neither my spouse nor his meddling ma were on the ground floor, so I sprinted up the stairs to the bedroom that my Sweet Cakes used to occupy before our blissful nuptials. I screeched to a stop just inside the door.

What I saw turned my stomach.

28

Ida Rosen, clad only in her flimsy Jewish underwear, is not a pretty sight. Perhaps no mother-in-law would be. Ida apparently felt the same way, because she shrieked and fell into an open suitcase on the floor.

Let those who think I am mean-spirited pay special attention to the following: I did *not* close the suitcase, shutting her inside, and ship her off to a made-up address in Outer Mongolia. Instead, I helped her out, averting my eyes the entire time, even when she said, "Oy, the second shtrap just broke. So now vhat am I going to do?"

"Please just get dressed," I said. "Shtrap or no shtrap. I'll wait outside until you're done."

I could have single-handedly dressed an octopus with rigor mortis in the time it took the tiny woman from Brooklyn to slip a muumuu over her head. Then again, I shouldn't have been surprised by her lengthy delay. By the time she told me I could peek, the suitcase was no longer in sight.

"Where did it go?"

"Vhat?"

"The suitcase, of course."

"Dere is no suitcase."

"Ida, I haven't got time for games, and neither do you. I've come to look for my husband."

"My son?"

"Something is wrong. I can feel it. If you don't tell me where he is this minute, I'm going to make every ancestor of mine for the past five hundred years spin in his or her grave, by doing something violent to your person. After that, I'll have to become a Southern Baptist, or maybe a Presbyterian — but trust me, it will be so worth it."

I doubt if she understood my words, but something must have gotten through. "*Nu?* Are vee just going to stand here, or are vee going to look for my Gabeleh?"

"We'll look. But if he isn't here, and he isn't at my — I mean, *our* — house, then where could he be?"

"*Mit* his girlfriend, perhaps?"

Just hearing the words was a stab to my heart. "*What* girlfriend?"

"How should I know? A son doesn't tell

his mother deese tings."

"But are you saying that he has one?"

She clucked, sounding for all the world like my favorite hen, Pertelote. "Magdalena, look at you; you're as tin as a slice of lox, yah? And your hair — oy."

"What's wrong with my hair?"

"Da braids and da bun, you look like a *bubbee* already."

No doubt steam rose from my bun. It certainly spilled out of my nostrils. I pawed the floor with a size eleven, and waggled a finger at the woman who had become the bane of my existence.

"A *bubbee,* you say? I most certainly do not look like a grandmother. There are times when I may look like a mare that's been ridden hard and put away wet, and I know for a fact that there are grandmothers younger than I am, but I do not look like a stereotypical grandmother: I don't have many wrinkles, my hair is still its natural shade of mousy brown, and only a few of them are to be found on my chin. And as for having a figure like a slice of smoked salmon, I'll have you know that your son refers to my bosoms as bodacious, and claims to be quite happy with the junk in my trunk — to borrow a term from the vernacular."

"And crazy too."

"Your son," I cried. "Shouldn't we be concentrating on him? For all we know he could be lying in a ditch somewhere."

"Yah?"

"Double yah. Vultures could be circling overhead. The Grim Reaper could be sharpening his scythe. And meanwhile, your only son, the fruit of your Looney Tunes, is murmuring, 'Ma? Where are you, Ma?' "

Ida galvanized before my eyes. The transformation was amazing. One minute she was a meddling mother-in-law in a muumuu, the next she became the quintessential Warrior Mother, a lioness who would fight to the death for her cub.

"*Nu?* Vhy are vee standing here? Let's get a move on, already."

I was in need of some real moral support, so I called my normally levelheaded friend Agnes and asked her to come along. Pal that she was, I didn't need to twist her arm more than once.

And so we did.

We began by phoning all the judges, organizers, and sponsors of what was supposed to have been the shining star in Hernia's crown. Not only had my husband not hitched a ride with any of them, but no one had seen him since the closing ceremony.

253

However, plenty of people — okay, virtually everyone — were as mad as hornets. You'd have thought I'd knocked down their nests and stomped on them, perhaps even spraying them first with DDT.

Lyudmila Prendergast, who'd donated twelve dollars towards our expenses, was particularly livid, and insisted that I come to her house and meet with her face-to-face. Only then, she said, would she reveal an "interesting tidbit" that might explain Gabe's disappearance.

Normally, I would not agree to meet Lyudmila anywhere, except for a well-lit church that was packed to the gills with my friends and family. Lyudmila would be in the choir loft, and I would be positioned by the front door, with my brogans securely tied, just in case I needed to make a run for it.

To make a long story short, Lyudmila hates my guts. She's hated my poor innards since the tenth grade when I wouldn't let her copy my answers to an American history exam. After school that day, she called me "Goody Two-Brogans," and started spreading the rumor that I had a crush on Danny Culp. That wouldn't have been so bad had it not been the truth. The next day, to get back at her, I did what every Hernia

High kid did as the ultimate act of humiliation: I sat on Lyudmila's lunch sack.

I had no way of knowing that Lyudmila packed her own lunch, giving herself only Hostess Twinkies injected with booze. Needless to say, I thoroughly mashed the little crème-filled cakes, but in the process inadvertently invented a dessert the British refer to as trifle. Sadly, to date, I have not been accorded the recognition I deserve from our good friends across the pond. Inventing such a venerable institution is no trifling matter, and, at the very least, I think a title would be in order. Her Ladyship, Magdalena Yoder-Rosen, Countess of Hernia, practically rolls off the tongue, don't you think?

At any rate, I was feeling only mild trepidation as I rang Lyudmila's doorbell. Agnes and Ida were still in the car, happily trading insults. If I called for their help, they most likely wouldn't hear me. On the other hand, if I plumb disappeared, they'd eventually get around to investigating. After all, I had the car keys.

Lyudmila snorted a greeting as she opened the storm door. It sounded to me like, "Hello, Goody Two-Brogans," but, then again, I might have been listening for it. Be assured, I said something quite pleasant in return. I had no choice if I wanted to locate the Babester as soon as possible.

"Well, do you like it?" she demanded, before another second had passed.

"Like what?"

"This!" She gestured rapidly around the room, like a museum docent who'd worked a double shift, and was facing her final visitors of the day — ones that had shown up just before closing time.

I couldn't help but gape as my mind was hurled back into the 1970s. The Prendergast home was a shrine to the days of bell bottoms and a bloated Elvis. Velvet paintings of the King of Rock, toward the end of his reign, adorned those walls not dedicated to velvet portraits of the King of Kings. Pots of half-dead pathos, cradled in macramé slings, hung from the ceiling at meaningless intervals. Although the coffee table was merely a laminated slice of redwood held above the shag carpet by cypress knees, it made quite a statement.

"Well?" she demanded again. "Do you like it?"

I flashed her a practiced smile. "It's definitely something."

"I did it all myself, you know; I don't believe in decorators."

"I hear you, sister. Decorators, shmecorators, I always say. They'd just tell you that you were caught in a time warp. Imagine anyone not liking velvet art? They're just the kind of people who wouldn't appreciate Captain and Tennille either."

" 'Muskrat Love' is my favorite song! Would you like to hear it?"

"I'd sooner hang from one of your macramé pot holders," I mumbled.

"What did you say?"

As you can see, I was forced to lie. I said, "Tell me that interesting tidbit about my husband that you promised."

She pointed to a crushed velvet sofa, the color of overripe concord grapes. "Sit."

I did as bidden.

"First," she hissed, "I want an apology."

"Okay, I confess. I lied. But muskrats are nothing more than destructive rodents that ruin the banks of ponds and streams, and besides, they stink — that's why they call them *musk*rats. The rat part isn't very romantic either. Muskrat love, indeed."

She looked stunned. "Huh?"

"Call the county agricultural agent if you don't believe me."

"Magdalena, are you daft? Are your braids pulled too tight? None of what you just said has anything to do with the apology that I want."

"Oh, *that!* Yes, it really was me who told our homeroom teacher, Mrs. Wilson, that your lunch sack smelled remarkably like her husband's breath, but at the time I didn't know anything about alcohol, so you see, I didn't try to get you in trouble on purpose."

"Not that either, you idiot — although, I did become rather popular for a while. Even Brian Melke asked me out. But the apology I want is for the twelve bucks I donated to your stupid Holstein competition. You said it would put Hernia on the map. Did you know that a reporter from the *Pittsburgh Post-Gazette* was there?"

"He made it after all? Terrific."

"Ha. You won't say that tomorrow when you read his article. Thanks to you, he thinks we're a bunch of losers. He said at first that he thought your husband's performance was a joke. Then, when he realized it was for real, it really ticked him off, having come all this way just to waste his time. Let alone gas. Do you know what he said he was going to title his article?"

"Nope."

" 'Hernia: Even Surgery Couldn't Save This Dump.' He said it was going to go out on AP wires everywhere."

"No way!"

"You better believe it. We're going to be

the laughingstock of the country."

"I suppose one must gather one's accolades whatever they may be."

"You're crazy, Magdalena. Now apologize."

"Share your tidbit first."

"Like heck."

"I bet it's really juicy." I made slurping noises. It was disgusting and childish of me, and I should be thoroughly ashamed. No Mennonite woman in her right mind would even think of doing such a thing; but since I was ipso facto nutso, it was totally in keeping with my character.

What mattered is that my comment primed Lyudmila's pump — so to speak. She let her gaze wander around the room, as if making eye contact with others who had convened to hear her spiel.

"He kept glancing at his watch, and then at one of the contestants — well, not one of the cows, but you know what I mean."

"*Which* contestant?"

29

"I don't know."

"But you just said —"

"Really, Magdalena, use that oversized head of yours. They were all standing in a bunch, in a roped-off area. I guess that was so they wouldn't interfere with the judging. Anyway, there must have been at least fifty of them. How could I tell which one he was flirting with? But I guess you can't blame him, can you? I mean, a handsome doctor married to an older woman; it would be only natural for him to have second thoughts."

"Sixty-two."

"Yet we were in the same grade! You must have flunked more years than I thought."

"Sixty-two *contestants,* dear. And not that it's any of your business, but I'm forty-eight and holding, which, I believe, makes me a year younger than you. My husband, by the way, is six weeks older than I."

"Harrumph."

"If you couldn't tell which woman he was flirting with, how do you even know it was a woman?"

"I smelled her perfume."

"What? You're not making sense, dear — even for you."

"For your information, Miss Smarty-Pants, I made a point of saying hello to him, just before he started acting crazy. After all, if he decides to divorce you, there's no point in letting all that manly goodness go to waste."

"So *you're* that woman?"

"Honestly, Magdalena, I don't know what possessed me to try to copy off your history exam. I smelled the other woman on him. That's how I knew."

I prayed for a Christian tongue while I thought this over. Gabe is fastidious about his grooming, and showers every morning. Therefore, it certainly wasn't me she'd smelled. And since I trust the Babester with my life, I trust his fidelity as well.

"All the cows are women. It was probably just Eau de Holstein you got a whiff of. It's supposed to be all the rage down on the farm."

"I know what cows smell like, Magdalena. This was Shalimar."

"Is she a friend of Dr. Rashid? Because any friend of Faya's is a friend of mine."

"Shalimar is the name of a perfume, you ignoramus."

"No need to be rude, dear." Since she hadn't asked me to sit, I didn't have to haul my patooty out of a chair before making a beeline for the door. Before turning the knob, I turned and looked her right in her bloodshot eyes, but when I opened my mouth to spit out a pithy zinger, none was forthcoming. Zilch. Nothing. Nada. "Oh Lord," I moaned, "why did you have to answer my prayers now?"

Lyudmila Prendergast beamed happily. "The rumors are true, Magdalena; not only have you lost your mind, but you've completely lost your edge."

Words more hurtful than that have seldom been spoken to me. One must understand, then, why my face might have been damp when I returned to my car.

"So now this one cries," my mother-in-law said, as if I wasn't even present.

Agnes, who'd been forced to sit in the backseat, set her considerable bulk into motion by leaning forward and patting the back of my shoulder. Although she meant well, I felt as if I were a piece of origami, and she was — well, King Kong. Not that I watch films about giant apes, mind you, since such things can't possibly exist. After all, Noah took at least a pair of every sort of creature into the ark, and from the movie posters I've seen of this ape, just one of its kind would have sunk that wooden tub.

As long as I'm on that subject — the ark, that is — I may as well let it all hang out, as my sister, Susannah, used to say. So here goes: Noah's boat was big, but was it large enough to accommodate the five million species of insects that still exist in the world today? How about the ten thousand different kinds of birds? And even though there are only four thousand different mammal species, a lot of them are quite large.

For instance, there are two kinds of elephants, the African and the Indian. It simply does not suffice to say that Noah took just one species of elephant into the ark, and that the other species evolved from it *after* the flood, since we know that evolution doesn't exist. Besides, the two elephant species are so different that they belong to different genera, and with one notable exception in 1978, cannot interbreed. Now throw in mastodons (said to be the ancestors of elephants) and mammoths, of which there are numerous skeletons to be seen in museums, add one full-grown brontosaurus, and the ark would have sunk.

I know about these things — and I am ashamed to say it — because I check books out of the Bedford County Library that would not be approved of by my fellow church elders. I can't seem to help it. If I am to sign off on a particular way of thinking, I need to at least familiarize myself with the other side's point of view. This makes me a fence-sitter on many issues, and believe you me, the tops of most fences are not comfy places to sit — especially if they're picket fences.

One might legitimately ask why I just don't pick a side, jump off, and get on with my life. The answer is: I'm a coward. I find it easier to agonize amongst the familiar symbols and rhythms of everyday life in Hernia, than to have to make a choice. Whether I stayed in the conservative Mennonite vein or left, I'd be giving up an important part of myself. Paradoxically, as long as I remain perched atop an eight-foot fence, I remain a whole woman.

Is it any wonder, then, why my poor brain is so befuddled that at times I seem a mite disconnected? But as for the tears that streaked my face — well, there was no good explanation. I'd been on the verge of crying for the last two weeks. So far, Freni had been the only one to notice it. Now, when I arrived at the inn accompanied by Mutt and Jeff, she found a way to discreetly dry my face with a corner of her apron.

"There was a telephone call for you," she whispered. "They said you should call back."

"Who?"

"Barbara Westheimer."

"Oops, did our dear, sweet Alison get in trouble?"

"I did not ask; the call was for you."

The master suite is downstairs, behind the parlor. To get to it, I had to go through the dining room. Even so, I was on my private landline in a matter of seconds. Just how Freni prevented the twin shadows from following remains a mystery, but I like to think that she did her famous rendition of a turkey on Thanksgiving Wednesday. Whatever it was, I finally had a moment of privacy.

"Uh — hello?" Barbara Westheimer sounds surprised every time she successfully answers the telephone in her home. This convenience — an absolute necessity if you ask me — is one of the modern compromises her family has chosen to make. Although they've used the community phone their entire lives, the Westheimers (or so Alison says) stare at the ringing device in their kitchen as if it were a bomb about to go off.

"Be careful, Barb. If you let it ring more than four times, the Devil listens in on this special gizmo, and records everything you say."

"Ach!" She either dropped the phone, or hung up. Whatever the case may be, the second time around, she picked up after the first ring. "Is this Magdalena?"

"As big as life and twice as ugly, although I've been told that I'm not so hideous after all, and that I've been suffering from body dysmorphic syndrome all these years, but even if I am as ravishing as my husband says, my cheery, though somewhat enigmatic response, would still not be appropriate, given that you can't see me, hence I do not appear as big as anything."

"This must be Magdalena Yoder, young Alison's mother."

"Right as rain — another quite senseless rejoinder, since whether or not rain is right or wrong is a purely subjective observation."

"May I please hang up, Magdalena? I am afraid that you are giving me a headache."

"Sorry, dear. I'll get to the point. May Alison stay with you a couple more days? She can continue to ride the bus with Mary Ruth, and I insist on chipping in for groceries."

During the silence that ensued, my hair grew an inch. "Uh," Barbara finally said, "are you still there, Magdalena?"

"Yes, dear, and now it's your turn to speak. May she stay over?"

"But she is not here."

"Gone out to the barn, have they? I'm not saying I approve of it, mind you, but girls will be girls. Frankly, there's no stopping them once they start. I was addicted to it once, you know. It's all I could think about for months on end."

"Ach!"

"Oh, yes. But then Mama *made* me crochet booties for our neighbors' baby girl, and that took all the fun out of it. I went from loving to crochet, to the point where just looking at a skein of yarn made me sick to my stomach."

"Alison is not in our barn, Magdalena, because she did not come to stay for the weekend."

"You're mistaken, dear."

"I am afraid that it is *you* who are mistaken."

"But I happen to know that she is there, and since we both can't be right — well,

267

just do me a favor and count your children."

"Magdalena, if you continue in this foolishness, then I ask your permission to hang up the telephone."

Then it hit me with the force of a runaway train. I felt my knees grow weak.

30

Honey Ice Cream Recipe

Ingredients:
5 egg yolks
1/2 cup honey

1 pint (500 ml) milk

1/2 pint (250 ml) double/heavy cream
1 teaspoon vanilla extract

Beat together the egg yolks and honey in mixing bowl. Heat the milk in a saucepan until it reaches boiling point, then simmer. Whilst it's simmering, stir in the egg yolk–honey mixture. Continue to stir until it thickens.

Remove from the heat, strain, and leave to cool.

Stir in the cream and the vanilla extract,

and then transfer the whole mixture into an ice cream maker. Freeze according to the manufacturer's instructions.

31

The fact that Alison Miller is not a perfect girl was what gave me hope. It was quite possible she'd hitched a ride into Bedford (she's done that before) and was having the time of her life hanging out with "the bad girls." I didn't, however, for one second believe that she was staying at some boy's house. Quite frankly, for better or for worse, I trust her too much for that.

The so-called bad girls — it's Alison's term, not mine — are cousins of Levina Nichols, herself not such a good girl. Their mother, bless her heart, is a single mom and holds down three jobs just to put day-old bread on the table. Mrs. Nichols has neither the time nor energy required to raise three teenagers, and thus, it appears, has opted for the comfort of pretending that all is as it should be. The fact that her daughters habitually skip school, acquire clothes and cosmetics via the ten-finger discount, and sneak out of their window almost every night to roam the streets escapes Mrs. Nichols. Or does it?

I wrested my crew from the pleasant warmth of Freni's kitchen, and back into the car. Of course, I didn't say anything about Alison having gone missing; Freni and my foster daughter are as thick as thieves. Two halves of an apple, as it were — just not the same variety. Freni is a Granny Smith apple, and Alison a Golden Delicious, although both can be crab apples upon occasion.

"Nu," Ida demanded, "vhere do vee look now?"

"Bedford."

"Vhat? Vee are yust going to drive around looking for my Gabeleh *mit*out a plan?"

"Actually, at the moment, we're looking for Alison."

Ida gasped, and clapped her pudgy hands to her cheeks. "You mean your sheudo-shtepdaughter?"

"Yes, I'm sorry to say."

"Pray tell," Agnes wheezed, "what is a strudel-shtup-daughter?"

"Oy," Ida moaned, "dis von is a potty mouse."

"She is not a potty mouth," I said. I turned and addressed Agnes. "That would

272

be pseudo-stepdaughter, dear."

I filled them in on the Alison saga as I shtepped on the gas. In times of stress — perhaps a few other times as well — I have been known to press the pedal to the metal. It is an evil vice that I knowingly engage in. Speed kills, especially on our winding roads, which are heavily trafficked by slow-moving Amish buggies.

But we made it to the Nicholses' house without a major incident, and everyone, including myself, managed to keep her lunch down. When Ida saw the sort of house the bad girls called home, she feigned a hip problem. Agnes, ever the caring woman that she is, volunteered to stay in the car with my mother-in-law, leaving me to face alone whatever lay behind the sagging porch and peeling front door.

The bell was missing, so I used my infamous knuckles. When, after I'd worn off several layers of skin, they failed to elicit a response, I tried the knob. The door was unlocked which, at least in my book, is tantamount to a formal invitation to come right on in and make oneself at home. This code of behavior, however, does not apply to my house.

"Yoo-hoo," I hollered pleasantly. "Is anyone here?"

There was no response, but just when I was about to back out gracefully, I noticed what appeared to be a jumble of hastily discarded clothes in front of the swayback sofa. These days, it's hard to tell which gender wears what, but it looked to me like these items represented both sexes.

"Is everyone decent?" I called. "Because I'm coming in, whether you like it or not. I am, after all, a semi-official deputy of the Hernia Police Department, and I'm here on a missing person's case. If the person in question can hear me, then I suggest she hie her hiney in a hurry to my car, which is waiting outside, or face the wrath of an overly distraught mother — one who has enough energy to make her daughter's life miserable for decades to come."

Like a jack-in-the-box — make that a Jack and a Jill — from behind the sofa popped two teenagers. They were as naked as baby jaybirds.

The girl spoke first. "We wasn't doin' nothin'. Honest. Please don't tell my mama."

"It ain't what it looks like," the boy muttered.

Still recovering from the shock of what I'd seen, I turned my back on the nude couple. "Is Alison Miller here?"

"No!" Now that the girl knew I wasn't gunning for her (to borrow a Presbyterian term), she'd traded in the vulnerable act for one of utter impudence.

"Are you sure she's not here?"

"Yes, I'm sure." She spit the words out like sunflower seeds.

"You might want to watch your tone, missy. I'm not above butting in and letting your mama know what you've been up to. In fact, I think I will. Kids your age have no business doing the shag carpet shag without the benefit of clergy. Even then — Just how old are you, anyway?"

"Eighteen."

"When were you born?"

"Uh — that ain't none of your business."

"Guess again, dear. From the glimpse I caught of your boyfriend, he's been able to vote for several years. That could make him eligible for statutory rape charges. In that case, I, as a concerned citizen, would feel obligated to issue a citizen's arrest."

"Jimmy," she whispered, "when was eighteen years ago?"

"It don't matter," Jimmy said. "I'm only fifteen."

"You *are?* Why Jimmy Cantrell, you lied to me! You telling me I almost did it with a baby?"

"I ain't no baby!"

"Kids," I bellowed, "shut up and put your clothes back on."

Yes, those were harsh words, coming as they were from the mouth of a gentle Mennonite woman, but desperate times call for desperate measures. What counts is that they were effective words, and, a few seconds later, the teenagers informed me that they were dressed, and it was all right for me to turn around.

"You ain't gonna go blind looking at a naked kid," the girl said.

"That depends on whether or not I feel compelled to poke my eyes out."

"Good one," the boy said.

"Shut up," the girl said.

"Don't use that kind of language," I said.

"Why not? You did."

"I'm a grown-up; we have different rules." I flashed them a benevolent smile. "Now, kids, you said that Alison Miller isn't here, but do you know where she might be?"

The boy shook his head.

"Me neither," the girl said.

I was about to deliver a short but pithy parting lecture, when a second girl bounded down the stairs, stumbled, and landed at my feet. She gasped when she looked up and saw me.

"Miss Yoder!"

"Levina Nichols, as I live and breathe. Does your mother know you're here?"

"Of course she does; not that it's any of your business. I come here all the time. This is my aunt's house, you know."

"Indeed, I do. And that's why I'm here. I was hoping to find Alison. For some inexplicable reason, she seems to find you Nichols girls more entertaining than the fleshpots of Hernia."

"Man, this lady's nuts," Jimmy said.

I favored him with a frown. "Nuttier than a PayDay bar, so be careful how you speak to, or about, me. There's no telling what I'll do when I'm provoked."

"Weird," Jimmy's girlfriend said.

"Speaking of weird," Levina said, "you try looking for Alison at that weird Amish kid's house?"

"Mary Ruth Westheimer?"

"Yeah, that's the one."

"Alison isn't there. I called."

She shrugged casually. "Well, that's what she said on her cell phone when that guy was giving us a ride. I thought she was talking to you — But hey, it's not like she doesn't lie to me too. Alison's awfully smart."

I counted to three in order to properly

absorb the compliment to my stepdaughter, then I morphed into manic mom mode. How dare that child ask permission to stay with a nice Christian family for the weekend, when all along her goal was to hang out with the likes of the Nichols cousins? As I huffed and I puffed, possibly even pawed the carpet, the most salient point popped into my perennially alliterative mind.

"*What* guy? Who gave you the ride?"

"I dunno. Just some dude who was driving by."

My instinct, which I suppressed, was to grab Levina by the shoulders and shake the words out of her. "When?" I demanded. "Where? I want details!"

"You ain't gonna snitch to my mom, are you?"

"A snitch in time stops crime." I slapped my wisecracking mug lightly. "But these lips are sealed, dear."

"I ain't your dear, and you gotta swear that you won't say nothing to my mom. She thinks my aunt picked me up from school."

"In her spare time between the three jobs?"

"Is that, like, sarcasm, Miss Yoder?"

"Undoubtedly so. But you have my word, Levina. All I want to know is the whereabouts of Alison."

"Make her swear," the resident Nichols girl hissed. "Like on a Bible or something — only we don't got one of those."

"She can't *swear* swear," Levina said, much to my surprise. "She's one of them old-fashioned Mennonites. Kinda like being Diet Amish."

"Oh."

Levina turned back to me. "If you rat me out, Miss Yoder, you'll be sorry."

"Duly noted. Now spill."

Levina was a big girl; not just chunky, but tall and raw-boned. One could easily imagine her in a Viking helmet — the kind with horns — yet her voice was soft and reedy, more befitting a ten-year-old than a young woman. Every few words, she paused to lick the corners of her mouth.

"We was ditching school, you see, on account of my aunt really didn't have time to pick us up, and my mom — well, you don't want to ride with her once she starts drinking. So you see, Miss Yoder, we was being safe."

"Your logic is far better than your grammar. Continue, please."

"So we tell my mom that we're coming here after school, only we never show up at school — we ain't the only ones who sneak into the woods when the bus driver ain't looking."

"Isn't there supposed to be a teacher out front?"

"Yeah, there's two of them. But Miss Hanson and Mr. Sullivan got the hots for each other, and they don't never see what's going on. Anyway, me and Alison was gonna walk from Hernia all the way into Bedford, but this truck pulls up, see, and this guy offers us a ride. We say sure, because it's like ten or twenty miles into Bedford, so Alison gets in first, 'cause she says she knows this guy. I throw my backpack up on the seat beside Alison, but before I could climb in, he takes off." Her tone turned plaintive. "Miss Yoder, I had to walk all the way here, plus that dude's got my stuff, and it wasn't just junk neither. My Gaps were in there."

"What about Alison?"

"I ain't seen her since then."

"And you didn't call me?" I wanted to throttle her thick neck.

"Hey, I didn't think it was, like, any kind of emergency. Except for my Gaps being stolen. I mean, she knew this dude — at least she said she did."

"Did you hear his name?"

She shook her thick, dark blond mane. "Nah. But you could just tell them two

280

knew each other. She weren't afraid of him, if that's what you're thinking."

By now, my legs were wobbly, so I elected to sit on an overstuffed chair — one that bore the remains of someone's breakfast. Crushed Cheerios and sticky milk stains were suddenly meaningless.

"Levina, do you know what Alison's dad — uh, my husband — looks like?"

"Yeah, who doesn't? I mean, he's really good-looking for an old guy, Miss Yoder. At least that's what the other girls say. I wish my dad —"

"Was it him?"

Her locks got another workout. "Nah."

Denial is not just the name of an Egyptian river. Who knew that I could be so good at it? Ever since my wedding night, I'd been living with the fear of Melvin Stoltzfus resurfacing in Hernia, but up until this moment, I had not entertained the possibility that Alison's whereabouts might be linked to the murdering mantis. Neither had I considered this an explanation for Gabe's disappearance.

I exhaled deeply several times, all the while praying for strength. "Levina, did this man with the pickup truck have a huge head set on a spindly neck, and did his eyes bulge and look in separate directions?"

"You mean like that police chief we used to have?"

"Exactly!"

"Nah, it weren't him. This guy was more regular-looking."

"Regular-looking? What does that mean? Can't you remember anything else?"

She gave my questions a second or two of thought. "Honestly, Miss Yoder, I didn't look at him all that much. Him being old and all, there weren't no point. Then when he took off with my Gaps, I was so ticked I gave him the finger."

"A lady doesn't offer the finger, unless they're ladyfingers, and in which case they should be served with hot chocolate that's topped with whipped cream."

"Geesh! You're even crazier than I thought."

"Coming from you, that is indeed a compliment."

"And who the heck says *indeed* all the time? That's just plain weird. I mean, ain't that Spanish or something?"

"Definitely something. Now focus, dear. What color was the truck? Was it a pickup? What make? Did you see the license plate?"

Despite the fact that it was still April and cool outside, the big gal was wearing shorts, and a tank top that exposed a considerable portion of her midriff. But it was downright cold inside the Nichols apartment, and I could see the gooseflesh on her tummy and hefty biceps.

"It was a truck. That's all I know. A pickup, I guess — you know, like one of them trucks that's been hauling them cow trailers into town all week. It might have been white, or a light color like that. Oh yeah, and it smelled like cow manure." She actually used a less polite word, one Ida might have uttered, had she tried to say "sit."

Although mine is an unscientific poll, let it be known that it is easier to squeeze water from a stone than it is to extract facts from a fourteen-year-old on a subject about which she is uninterested. It was time to quit while Levina merely disdained my mental state. After all, I might need to put the screws to her again.

"Thank you, dear, you've been very helpful."

"Yeah, I guess I have. So, you gonna pay me?"

"*Pay* you? For what?"

"You know, like they pay them TV whatchamacallits."

"They're called interments," the cousin pronounced with utmost confidence. "It's a fancy word for tattletales."

Suddenly, the goose that had been puckering Levina's tummy pranced over my grave.

32

With Ida and Agnes to support me, I filed a missing person's report with the Bedford County sheriff and, of course, our own young Chris Ackerman. Sheriff Dewlapp explained that since there was no ransom note, Alison would be treated as a runaway, which meant that the FBI would not immediately be involved. He did, however, issue an all points bulletin for the county, and sent a photo and description of her to every sheriff's department in the state, as well as to several counties in Maryland. As for the Babester, because he was an adult, he would not be officially considered missing for another thirty-six hours.

Although I didn't like it, I understood the sheriff's position. What I couldn't understand was Gabe's position on his precious mother. Why had he agreed to have her live with him when he was single? And now with us? If it was to cut his meat for him — well,

I've heard that capuchin monkeys have been trained to do similar things for the blind.

"So maybe," Ida said, pointing a stubby finger at the sheriff's midsection, "my son has run away from his vife."

"Excuse me?"

"That would be me," I said. "I'm the vife."

"Such a bossy voman you heff never seen."

Sheriff Dewlapp stroked his neck. "Well, my wife can be pretty, uh, directive — but I would never consider skipping out on her. Not without at least leaving a note."

"Yah? But *mit* a note you vould?"

"I'm not saying that —"

"You might as well save your breath, sheriff. The elder Mrs. Rosen hates my innards. You see, I've committed the terrible crime of getting her son to love me. Plus, I refused to take her along on our honeymoon."

He smiled. "That bad, are you, Magdalena?"

"Even worse. Her precious baby boy and I danced the mattress mambo — if you get my drift. More than once, in fact. Not that it's anyone's business."

"Oy, such a mouse on dis von. Eez it any vonder my Gabeleh's gone back to New York?"

"New York?" The sheriff seemed to pay

286

close attention to Ida for the first time.

"Yah, dat eez vhere vee leef."

"Dat eez vhere *you* leef," I snapped. "Gabe leefs here."

"Ladies, please, I don't speak Jewish."

"It's not Jewish, sheriff. It's English with an accent — one that seems to get worse by the minute. And if you believe her preposterous story that my husband ran out on me, then don't think for one minute that I'm going to continue to contribute to your reelection fund."

"Why, Magdalena Yoder, is that a threat?"

"Don't be silly, dear. We still have freedom of speech in this country, and I'm simply exercising that right. Besides, I didn't say that I *wouldn't* continue my support, I merely told you not to think it."

"Miss Yoder — uh, Rosen — for someone who disapproves of dancing — with the notable exception of the bossa nova — you have mighty fine footwork."

"You really think so?"

"Absolutely. You ever consider being a lawyer?"

"What? And lie?"

"With your record of stretching the truth, they might even waive law school. All you'd have to do is take the bar exam."

"That is really not fair to lawyers," Agnes

said stoutly. "Many of them are more ethical than Magdalena."

"Et tu, Brute?"

"I told youse to stop speaking Jewish," the sheriff snapped. "Now ladies, I've done all I can do for the moment. Go get yourselves a bite of supper or something."

We chose the bite.

Agnes was the only one who was hungry, but since the Sausage Barn is as good a place as any to collect one's thoughts and put together a plan, I acquiesced to dropping by. In a similar vein, Ida needs no special venue in which to vent her intense dislike of yours truly.

Only Wanda Hemphopple seemed to disapprove of our plan. "What are you doing here, Magdalena?" she demanded. "We only serve breakfast, and it's almost suppertime."

"Too true, dear. But the breakfast you do serve is available until ten p.m."

"Humph."

"That's *harrumph,* dear."

"I beg your pardon?"

"Look it up in Webster's, if you don't believe me."

"As it so happens, I *did* look it up. They're both in there, and 'humph' is exactly what I mean in this context."

Agnes, ever the friend, stepped in to rescue me. "Can we please dispense with the semantics before I starve to death?"

Ida stepped back in alarm. "Oy, and now dis von is anti-semantic. Vhen vill it ever shtop?"

I extended a rakelike arm, and pulled the little woman back into the conversation. "Wanda, what will it be? A big fat tip for some mediocre food and bad service, or no coins for your coffer, which, by the way, seems to be mighty hungry tonight as well?"

Wanda glanced around at her practically empty restaurant, and then zeroed in on me with a glare. "Okay, I'll seat youse, but just so youse know, the Fat's Where It's At Platter is unavailable this evening on account of the new fry cook threw up in the grease catcher, so there's nothing with which to adequately grease the griddle."

"Grease the griddle, wear a girdle," I said gamely, in an attempt to patch things over. Just because Wanda hates my guts, is no reason that I shouldn't be concerned that our relationship might deteriorate to the point where she despises me.

"Was that supposed to be a joke?" she snarled. "Because if it was, I don't get it."

"Magdalena, Magdalena," Agnes chided.

"Fat jokes are so not in."

"But it wasn't a joke; it was merely a witticism, and not aimed at anyone in particular. Honestly, Wanda, you're almost as touchy as that Pearlmutter woman."

"Jane Pearlmutter? The one whose Holstein took first place in the competition?"

"The very one. It makes you wonder what that very handsome husband sees in her. By the way, how do you know who won? I mean, the competition has only been over for a couple of hours. Were you there when the prize was presented?"

"Humph. Some of us have to work, Magdalena. Besides, this is Hernia we're talking about. I bet you a dozen people either called with the news, or stopped in before the guilty party itself showed up."

"The Pearlmutters were *here?*"

"You sound surprised. You think them New York types are too highfalutin for my establishment?"

I glanced at Ida. "I certainly wouldn't say that; I'd be more likely to say that the word 'establishment' is a bit highfalutin for a place like the Sausage Barn."

"Oh yeah? They must have liked my food, because they weren't gone more than twenty minutes when they came back for more. You should have seen what they carried out with them."

"Wanda, dear, asking for a doggie bag is not the same as endorsing one's cuisine. Maybe they just didn't want to offend you by leaving it on their plates."

She rolled her eyes — and I'm not exaggerating when I say that the left one almost got stuck in the "up" position. "These were orders to go, you idiot."

"When did you start offering carryout service?"

"Only for the last eight years. I'm sure it's skipped your notice because you're too busy licking the last speck of my terrible food off of your plate."

"Well, I must say that no restaurant in the tri-county area can cook bacon like your guys. Nice and crisp on both ends, with just a little play in the middle."

She grinned happily. "Just the way you like it. Now these people — the Pearlmutters — how many children do they have?"

"None, as far as I know."

"Humph. Well, when they came in the first time, they ordered regular meals: eggs, bacon, toast, juice, coffee. But the second time around, when they did the takeout order, they asked for three orders of pancakes — one buttermilk regular, one buttermilk silver dollar style, the third one buckwheat — regular toast, cinnamon toast, French toast — both plain and stuffed, like them fancy places like IHOP make — scrambled eggs, and four orders of sausage links. Oh, and two large milks. Two juices as well. I just assumed they had kids with them this time, and they were waiting in the car."

"Buckwheat?" Agnes asked. "I didn't realize you still offered those. I haven't had a buckwheat pancake in ages."

"They're by request only." Wanda tipped her beehive hairdo at some invisible spies and lowered her voice. "They're from a mix. I keep some on hand because every now and then some relic from the past shows up and asks for them. 'We Aim to Pleez.' That's our motto. Says so right on the menus."

In the interest of saving both time and energy, I bit my tongue so hard that I felt it all the way to my toes. How will kids these days learn to spell if their computers automatically correct them, and if they are constantly subjected to what I call bizspell? The clever names that companies think up for themselves are, in fact, signposts on the road to literary perdition. And to what end? Puns? I eschew puns, viewing them as nothing more than intellectual laziness!

But I digress. Something Wanda had said

was percolating through my brain. Buckwheat pancakes — particularly the ones the Sausage Barn served — were Gabe's favorite. As for Alison, she could never make up her mind, so I always ordered both kinds of French toast for her, knowing that the Babester would happily polish off what she couldn't finish. After all, my sweet pseudo-stepdaughter was in the middle of a growth spurt, and invariably started her breakfasts at the Sausage Barn with silver-dollar pancakes, followed by a small stack of buttermilk flapjacks.

Both of them loved Wanda's link sausage, and commonly ordered double helpings. Milk and juice were also staples of a visit to the Hemphopple Temple of Icky Stickiness (as Alison calls it, in reference to all the maple syrup she spills, which never gets cleaned up). That left just the scrambled eggs and plain toast unaccounted for, but on the days when Gabe is particularly stressed, or decides to work out, his appetite soars.

The thought that was beginning to make my blood run cold was simply this: what were the odds that the Pearlmutters would eat breakfast at the Barn, and return twenty minutes later and order the same meal my sweet patooties habitually consumed? It just didn't seem like a coincidence. And if it wasn't a coincidence, then the Pearlmutters had to know the whereabouts of my darlings. But beyond that, it could also be that the half-dashing duo from the Garden State were holding Gabe and Alison against their will. But why?

A poke in the arm from Agnes brought me back to my surroundings. "You in there somewhere, Magdalena? If I wasn't a practicing Methodist, especially one of Mennonite extraction, I'd say you've been abducted by aliens, and this is only a shell I'm looking at."

"Humph," Wanda said, just to spite me, and then turned her venom on Agnes. "I thought you Methodists believed in the possibility of extratesticles — or whatever they're called."

"I don't think we have an official position. Personally, I find it hard to reconcile the gift of salvation through Jesus with alien life forms. It doesn't say anywhere in the Bible that Christ died for them as well."

"That's because they don't exist. Frankly, Agnes, you wouldn't have this crisis of faith if you'd remained a good Mennonite."

"I'm not having a crisis of faith! And as long as we're being frank, Wanda —"

My shell sprang into action. "Ladies! I

294

have reason to believe that there's been a real abduction. Those people, the Pearlmutters, for whatever reason, have taken Alison and Gabe hostage."

"*Hostage?* My Gabeleh? My only son?" It was as if Ida, who had been behaving herself up until then, had stuck her finger into a light socket.

"Ida dear, that's not for sure. I'm just jumping to conclusions like I usually do. Who knows, maybe they're off playing peewee golf somewhere."

"*Oy veys meer,*" Ida said. She looked ready to faint.

There was no reason to tell the Babester's mother the rest of my theory. Her eagle-eyed son, the famous heart surgeon, had detected something unkosher — if I may be pardoned the incorrect usage of this term — about the Pearlmutters' entry. As Jane was a plastic surgeon, and udder enhancement was *the* most common way to cheat in dairy cow competitions, it followed that my husband had spotted a suture line in the bovine's feminine expression — so to speak.

It had also occurred to me that Alison was the first to be abducted, and that they'd used her as a pawn to get Gabe to move the competition along at lightning speed, just as fast as a dog wants out of a roomful of mother cats. It was possible that Gabe might have been able to save his own handsome neck at any point along the way by calling the police, but as long as the welfare of his pseudo-stepdaughter was at stake, he would have cooperated with Satan himself. My heart glowed with love.

"Magdalena," Agnes said, "are you in there someplace?"

"*What?* Of course I'm in here! I don't believe in astral projection; I barely know the word."

"Well, you said they could be playing pee-wee golf, right? But what if they're really tied up in an abandoned lumberyard somewhere. A giant table saw with two-inch teeth is spinning just in front of them. Suddenly, two hooded men in black grab Gabriel and push him in the direction of the blade —"

"Agnes!" I barked. "This is not your creative writing class. What you just said could be really happening."

"Sorry, Magdalena. I guess I got carried away. What would you like me to do?"

"Call Sheriff Dewlapp, and tell him that I have a hunch that the Pearlmutters have my missing husband and foster daughter. If he refuses to take it seriously, tell him I said that a hunch from a woman is as good as two facts from a man, and remind him of all the times I've been right." I turned to Wanda. "In the meantime, I'm going to stock up on provisions, because I feel a trip to Maryland coming on. Wanda, dear, lead the way to your pantry."

Wanda's ominous do teetered and tottered as she shook her head. "I don't even think so. This is isn't a grocery store, you know."

I patted my pocketbook. "Have you forgotten that I am a very wealthy woman?"

"Okay, but I'm going to Maryland with you."

33

"Who is this Mary Lynn?" Ida demanded. "Eez she my Gabeleh's girlfriend?"

"No, Ida," Agnes said. "Maryland is the state directly to the south of us. For some reason that only she can fathom, Magdalena thinks it's akin to the wild and wooly west."

"*Mit* Indians and vagon trains, yah?"

"Not exactly."

"Den how is it?"

"It's very much like here, except that it's thirty miles south."

"It's across a *border*," I hissed.

"Do we need passports?" Wanda asked.

Believe me, I was so tempted to lie that I would have given one of my silver-filled molars for the opportunity to do so, and without guilt. Alas, those opportunities seldom come my way. Besides, my cell phone was ringing and the caller was Chris Ackerman.

"Wanda, may I take this in your office?"

"No. Take it outside."

I put young Chris on hold. "If you expect posse privileges, Wanda, you'd better pony up."

Ida looked crestfallen. "But I dunt ride horses."

"I wasn't speaking to you, dear," I said kindly. "Never mind that a nag on a nag would be quite redundant." I smiled pleasantly. "So, how about it, Wanda?"

"You won't like my office; it's just a hole in the wall."

"I've survived many a hole."

"Not like this one."

As it was not an altogether unpleasant day, I was prepared to capitulate and take the call outside. However, today, more than on any prior occasion, I sensed that Wanda was hiding something in her hole, and I aimed to see it. I realize now that it was utterly selfish of me to concern myself with something so petty when two of my most cherished family members were missing and quite possibly in peril, but I couldn't help myself.

You see, for years everyone in Hernia has observed Wanda slip in and out of a small white door directly behind the checkout counter of her restaurant. She is not a large woman by any means, but the door perpetually scrapes against her bosom as her buttocks are pushed flat against the doorjamb.

Everyone has their own theory. Colleen Fitzgerald believes that Wanda keeps a pot of gold back there, one she stole from a leprechaun. Jimmy Hildebrand swears he heard an infant's cry once when the door was cracked. By the way, Jimmy and his wife, Gloria, lost a three-week-old daughter on the New York subway — literally lost her. Although the child was soon found unharmed, ever since then, Jimmy has never been quite right in the head.

My personal theory is that Wanda has secretly converted to Melvinism. This is an abhorrent and patently pagan religion, seeing as how it is based on a revelation not in the Bible, a book which every thinking person knows is true, if only because it says so right in it. Melvinism, on the other hand, was invented by Zelda Root, who just happens to be my half sister and a former policewoman.

Zelda was in love with her boss, the infamous Melvin Stoltzfus, and, although lacking any proof, came to the conclusion that the mantis is divine. One might suppose that such lunacy would be unique, but the cult of Melvin has inexplicably spread, and now there are hundreds of lost souls who claim to believe this word-of-mouth faith and its preposterous tenets.

"I know what you're hiding," I said, "and disgusted as I might be, I'm not shocked. You're a Melvinite, aren't you? You have an altar in there dedicated to Melvin — possibly even with a goat's head on it."

"That's disgusting. But, since you're such a smarty-pants, be my guest."

Wanda may be small, but she's also very quick. Before I could think through her change of heart, she'd opened the mysterious white door and pushed me through. The space was indeed not much more than a hole, but it was well lit. Still, it took me several seconds to comprehend what I was seeing.

"Ack! Get me out of here."

"Seen enough?"

"Almost. Give me another minute, so that I can commit it all to memory. I'll need details for my lawsuit."

Wanda grabbed the collar of my dress, and yanked me out so fast that I left my dandruff behind. In one fluid motion, she kicked the door shut behind me, and secured it with a padlock.

"You sue me," she hissed, "and I'll sue you."

Agnes draped a large, heavy arm across my bony shoulders. "Magdalena, what is it? What did you see?"

"Yah, vhat?" Ida tugged at my sleeve, like a street urchin begging for alms. "Vhat? Vhat?"

I could feel Wanda's beady black eyes boring through my back. Slap a three-inch scar across her left cheek, and she'd be an archetype — just not the type to mess with. Not now, at least.

"She has male pinups on the walls," I lisped, as I lied through my teeth.

"Vhat?"

"Pictures of half-naked men."

"Yah? Vich half?"

"Diagonally, from top right to bottom left."

"Magdalena," Agnes whispered, "you're dissembling, aren't you?"

"Maybe." I shrugged free. "Wanda, dear, I'm not so sure you should come along."

"Because of what you saw in there? That's no fair! You practically forced me to show you."

"It's not that. You see, I read somewhere that it can be confusing to have multiple characters take part in the same conversation."

"Not if there are ample tags," Agnes said.

"Maybe you have a point," I said.

"It's a very good point," Wanda said.

"Vhat are you talking about?" Ida said.

"Never mind," I said gently. "Any other questions, ladies?"

"Duh," Wanda said. "Why are we taking Route 96 down into Maryland, instead of the turnpike in either direction, or any of the other million roads that lead out of the commonwealth?"

If patience is a virtue, then I am most definitely a woman without merit. I sighed, I tapped my toes, I even rolled my eyes a wee bit.

"*Because,* dear, if you really must know —"

"Which I must. I am, after all, supplying the food."

"And I'm driving," said my best friend, Agnes Judas Mishler.

"*Und* I am geefing da moral supports."

"That's not necessary, dear; you already gave at the office."

"I *did?*"

"Oodles of it. Just remember come March that it's tax deductible."

"Tanks."

"Mags, you're awful," Agnes said.

"Tanks," I said. "Look, gals, it's like this: unlike some of the other contestants — and

I hereby exercise a great deal of Christian charity — the Pearlmutters are both bright people. She's a surgeon, and he's a stockbroker. They're going to stay clear of any major roads. At the same time, they're going to be checking a map, looking for the quickest way across the state line. And guess what?"

"Vhat?" Ida said.

"That was a rhetorical question, dear."

"That means it wasn't meant to be answered," Wanda said.

"Like most of Magdalena's qvestions, yah?"

Give credit where credit is due, I always say, so I gave Ida an air point. After all, the woman is merely annoying, not dense. Who knows, if we both weren't in love with the same man, in another time, in another place, she might even grow to like me.

"Anyway," I said, "Route 96 is torture if you're pulling a trailer, which is exactly why Gabe and Alison, if given the chance, would urge the Pearlmutters not to take it."

"Because den dey vould for sure take it, yah?"

"You bet your bippy. And once you start down that road with a trailer, there's no turning around."

"Oy, but it's getting dark outside!"

"Exactly! You see, there is a little pullover — where there used to be a kind of primitive rest area — and the odds are that, if they have indeed taken this route, they will avail themselves of this place until morning."

"Hmm," Wanda said, pretending to write on a pad, "now let me see, we have an order of kidnappers, and an order of rest area, and if we add an order of deputies — I'm sorry, to say, Magdalena, but they don't add up. If this couple is as bright as you say they are, they're not going to park a cow carrier alongside a highway."

"O ye of little faith," I said, quoting the latter part of Matthew 6:30. "I said there *used* to be a rest area. Now it's just a dent in the trees where folks in the know park to get to know each other in the Biblical sense. Not that *I* know whereof I speak, of course, at least not from personal experience — okay, so maybe once, or twice, six at the most, but we were already married, and how else were we going to get away from the prying eyes of you-know-who, and anyway, whether or not I did the backseat bossa nova is nobody's business but mine, and —"

"Such a slut, I tell you."

I prayed for patience, and for once it was granted. "Since it was with your son, I will choose to take that as a compliment, dear. But listen up everyone, there is one other very important reason I think that the Pearlmutters are on Route 96 headed for the Maryland state line, and that is because once they reach it, there is another state line just five miles farther south."

"West Virginia," Wanda said knowingly. "Their motto is 'the Mountain State.' It's supposed to be even wilder and woollier than Maryland. If you don't get captured by a mountain man and taken back to his cabin to be his sex slave, you could hide for the rest of your life in those hills, and even the feds couldn't find you. I get this from my customers, by the way."

"Do you think any of those mountain men like their sex slaves on the plump side?"

"Agnes!" I cried. I was shocked from the top of my cap-covered bun to the tips of stocking-clad toes. I was also somewhat pleased by her gumption, misplaced as it was.

"Actually, they don't," Wanda said. "They prefer gaunt women. But don't worry; I get plenty of unmarried male customers who much prefer the curvier sort. Would you like me to fix you up?"

"Yes," she said shyly.

"*Und* do you get unmarried Jewish vomen

customers?"

"I don't think so. Why?"

"She's just being silly."

"Speaking of being silly," turncoat Agnes said, "Magdalena, you take the cake. This is the computer age. States share their information. It's not like you can hide anymore, not in this age of Big Brother."

"Yes, but computer systems break down — so do power grids — and sometimes even the local jurisdictions engage in disputes. Tell me, Agnes, if you were on the run, where would you rather hide out, in the mountains of West Virginia, or in the Commonwealth of Pennsylvania?"

"Touché."

I clapped my hands. "Ladies, attend to your assignments. Agnes, call the sheriff as previously instructed, while I talk to the chief — if he's still on the line. Wanda, pack us up a box of nonperishable food sufficient for three days. As for you, Ida, just stay out of trouble."

I have sturdy Christian underwear older than Police Chief Ackerman, yet he had the gall to forbid me from undertaking my trek south to Maryland. Not only was it too dangerous, he said, but somewhat silly. Since none of my guests had arrived from that direction, none were likely to return by that route. People were creatures of habit, he informed me, as if I were a first-year psychology student inquiring about the workings of human nature. Besides, he went on to say (somewhat carelessly, I might add) that my assumption that my loved ones had been abducted by Holstein aficionados was absurd. What could possibly be the motive? To make an unwarranted trip to the wilds of Maryland was to behave foolishly.

When I trotted out my "two facts from a man" theory, he countered by claiming that gay men were the exception to the rule. "One hunch from a gay man is worth two hunches from a straight woman," he said.

"What if I were a lesbian?"

"Then my hunch would be worth one and a half of yours."

"You're just kidding, aren't you?"

"Weren't you?"

I'd been mentoring young Chris ever since his arrival a year ago as a fresh-faced assistant to our late chief, who met her untimely demise at the hands of one of Hernia's homegrown killers. Chief Ackerman had originally come across as both shy and eager to please. Clearly, he now had found his stride, which, although somewhat out of sync with mine, was a good thing.

No longer did I have to hold his hand. This freed me up considerably, allowing me a lot of time to behave foolishly. And that is exactly what I intended to do.

34

My team was on the ball. Agnes successfully relayed my message to the sheriff, who,
like Chief Ackerman, openly scoffed at the
idea of cow owners rustling humans. His
APB, he said, was effectively cancelled, due
to the fact that one of his deputies had just
returned from a hunting trip to Maryland
via Route 12, and no cars had been encoun-
tered coming the other way. He'd keep a
watch on the interstates, but I shouldn't
expect any dramatic news. Alison, he assured Agnes, was a runaway who would
surface safe and sound at the time and location of her choosing. Ever a faithful friend,
Agnes wished a pox upon his house and his
descendants down to the fifth generation.
(Fortunately, although the sheriff is married, his wife, like me, is past the breeding
age.)

Wanda came through with boxes of dried
cereal, bags of dried fruit, ultraviolet-treated

milk, a couple dozen sticks of beef jerky, and oodles of bottled water. She also produced AAA maps of Pennsylvania, Maryland, and West Virginia. Perhaps just as important, she thought to bring along several rolls of toilet paper from her supply room.

Ida, bless her heart, honored my request and managed to stay out of trouble. She even helped Wanda carry the supplies out to my car. Taking into consideration that her son was missing, I tried not to be critical. But if the road to you-know-where is paved with good intentions, then I am a first-class highway engineer.

"Ida, dear," I said sweetly, "why on earth are you carrying that cute little television?"

"You vant dat I should miss *Yeopardy?*"

"It's battery powered," Wanda said, "if that's your concern, Magdalena."

"My concern is that we don't get distracted from the task at hand."

"Nu," Ida said. "You vant dat I should drive?"

"No thanks, dear."

"Maybe you should let her," Agnes said. "That will free the rest of us up for sleuthing."

"She doesn't have a license," I said.

It wouldn't have mattered if she had. I'd

seen Ida drive. In order to reach the pedals, she has to slide so far down in the seat that she can't see over the dashboard. This doesn't stop her. Every so often she hurls herself into the air to get a quick look-see of the road.

So far, she's miraculously avoided hitting anyone or anything of consequence — although some of our more worldly Hernia teenagers have taken to mimicking her technique for fun. "Doing the American Ida," they call it. Since the craze began, there have been three serious wrecks, one involving an Amish buggy, which sent three children to the hospital, and which resulted in the horse having to be put down. At any rate, on the plus side, the day Mattie Taylor saw a "driverless" car barreling down Hertzler Road is the day she gave up drinking.

At last, the four of us piled into my Ford and set off on our rescue mission. Once we passed the blinking lights of Hernia, the road quickly grew dark and even more winding. If my vertically challenged mother-in-law had been at the wheel, at the first sharp turn, we would undoubtedly have sailed right off the road, perhaps even landing in the trees. In the autumn, some unlucky deer hunters would discover four skeletons — one clutching a pint-size TV.

We would become the stuff of urban legend: the four ghosts of Route 96 that lay in wait for teenagers on weekend nights.

"Earth to Magdalena," Agnes said through cupped hands. "Come in, Magdalena."

"What?" I snapped, although not altogether unpleasantly.

"You almost drove off the road at that last curve."

"I most certainly did not." Truth be told, I couldn't recall what the last curve looked like.

"Speaking of flying off the road, where is it that you had your accident?"

Wanda must have forgotten that I have the hearing of a bat. "Magdalena almost died in a tree," she whispered to Ida. "And she had to wear a tampon on her forehead."

"Is she meshugah, or vhat?"

"Or what," I said.

"My point," Wanda said, "is that you drive way too fast. I, for one, am not ready to meet my maker."

"Why, Wanda Hemphopple," Agnes said, "and you're always getting after me for no longer being a Mennonite."

"I would be one, if it wasn't for Magdalena."

"What?" I said.

"What?" Agnes said.

"Vhat?" Ida said.

"Tag," Wanda said. "I guess I'm it. You see, ladies, Mrs. Rosen — née Yoder — and I have a long history."

"You vere lovers?" Ida said. She sounded hopeful.

"No," Wanda said, "but the possibility did cross my mind once. Anyway, we've been feuding since we were kids, and then —"

"Since *high* school," I said. "It wasn't like we were toddlers when it all began."

"Actually, we were," Wanda said. "According to my mother, we were playing together in a sandbox, and you hit me over the head with a bucket."

"You mean that I had discerning taste all the way back then?"

"Very funny."

"And what's this about you having a thing for me? Or were you just pulling my leg?"

"A very shapely leg, Magdalena — now stop trying to distract me. The senior Mrs. Rosen would like to know why I'm not ready to die just yet. Or, for that matter, to welcome the Second Coming."

"Vas dere a first?"

"Good one, Ida," Agnes said.

"She's not joking," I said.

"As I was about to say," Wanda growled, "before I was so rudely interrupted, I don't

314

want to die just yet because I'm not through hating Magdalena."

It was a cool evening, so I had the windows closed. When the three of us gasped, we literally depleted the car of oxygen. Perhaps that explains why I felt momentarily giddy.

"You *really* hate me that much?"

"I despise you. That's why I have all those life-size posters of you on my office walls."

"The ones on which you've drawn arrows going through my head and daggers into my heart. Don't you think that's a bit of overkill? Pun quite intended."

"This doesn't make any sense," Agnes said. "After all, you let Magdalena eat in your restaurant all the time."

"That's because I have to, or she'd call the police. She has them in her pocket, you know. Plus, her money is just as good as anyone else's."

"You know vhat surprised me vhen I moved to dis country," Ida said apropos nothing.

Agnes, always kind and considerate, took the bait. "What?"

"Dat dey use the same money here dat we used in New York."

"Wait a minute," Agnes said, "I must be confused. Which country uses the same currency as New York?"

"Oy, is dis von slow, or vhat?"

"The place she is referring to," I said, "is the Commonwealth of Pennsylvania. She thinks it's a foreign country."

Ida clucked like a hen being robbed of her eggs. "Von must get a new license to drive, yah? *Und* pay new taxes. In Europe, vee called dat another country."

"I see," Agnes said, although she clearly didn't. "Magdalena, you don't seem at all upset that Wanda hates you. Do you hate her back?"

"That wouldn't be Christian, dear. I will, however, admit to intensely disliking her. But don't get me wrong, I'm not proud of the way I feel, and I pray for a change of attitude." There was nothing to be served by adding that my prayers to feel better about Wanda are intermittent at best.

Agnes sighed loudly. "What a fine kettle of fish we are. I'm two hundred pounds overweight and so neurotic that my only friend is Magdalena; Ida believes we're in a foreign country; and you other two hate — or at least, intensely dislike — each other. What if there really are kidnappers, and we catch up with them? What are we supposed to do? Baffle them into submission?"

No one said anything for a long time.

"Vas dat a historical question?" Ida finally said.

"Yes," I said.

"*Gut.* Den I vill go to sleep."

One by one, all three of my passengers succumbed to the sandman. That was fine with me. Although I was tired, I wasn't a bit sleepy. Route 12 through southern Pennsylvania twists and turns like a stubborn garden hose, requiring one's full attention. As if the topography isn't enough to keep one occupied, there is the constant possibility — maybe even a probability — that a deer will leap into the roadway and be blinded by one's headlights. Throw in the good chance that my missing loved ones might be in grave danger, and I had all the adrenaline I needed to make sure that my peepers stayed wide open.

But to be absolutely honest, I was thinking more about Wanda Hemphopple than anything else. Her words stung my soul; I could feel the pain just as surely as if I'd been slapped in the face with a latex glove — not that I've had a lot of experience with such things. What had I ever done to her that was so awful that she would risk hellfire rather than forgive me? Okay, so maybe I did whack her on the bean with a bucket, dip her braids in my inkwell, put gum on her desk chair, sit on her paper-bag lunch, encourage her to copy the wrong answers from my paper during a math test, drop a hot dog into her beehive hairdo, spread a few rumors about her high school love life — but I was just a kid then, for crying out loud. Believe me, I have an even longer list of Wanda's sins against me, and I've managed to forgive her.

Perhaps it has little to do with what I've done, but a lot to do with who I am. Scientists have suggested that people have an inborn negative response to approximately one fifth of the general population. This response is visceral, and based on such cues as scent and physiognomy. It supposedly serves some evolutionary purpose — although, of course, there is no such thing as evolution.

I remember Mama saying that, in the 1930s, there was a woman living in Hernia named Barbara Peters, who always had it in for her. For as long as Mama could remember, Barbara Peters was mean to her. Mama never could figure out what she'd done to get on Barbara's bad side. One day, Mama could no longer stand it and wrote Miss Peters a note asking the woman to please explain what it was that she had done to deserve such treatment. Barbara's answer was cryptic to the extreme: "I've *never* liked you." Mama was actually so afraid that Miss Peters might have used poisoned ink in her reply that, after reading the note, Mama scrubbed her hands until they bled.

So preoccupied was I in pondering the enigma of Wanda's hatred toward me that I almost missed seeing the truck and trailer parked in a picnic area a few miles north of the border. Fortunately my passengers were buckled in. Nonetheless, there followed shrieks of genuine fear and enough blue language to color the Pacific Ocean. I waited patiently for the latter to end before addressing the woman with the mouth of a sailor.

"Really, dear," I said to my mother-in-law, "is that the same mouth with which you used to sing lullabies to your son?"

"Vhat? You tink I have another?"

"You could have warned us," Agnes panted.

"Magdalena," Wanda snarled, "if you'd peed back at the Sausage Barn, you wouldn't have to go so bad now."

"Ladies," I said, "if you're capable of it, turn your heads and look back up the highway about a hundred yards. Tell me what you see."

"*Oy vey!* I can't turn my head."

"Ida, darling," I said with utmost patience, "perhaps it would help if you unbuckled your seat belt."

"I can't turn my head either," Agnes said. "Do you think I have whiplash?"

With the help of the Good Lord, I avoided stating the obvious: Agnes was incapable of swiveling her noggin for the same reason she couldn't touch her toes.

"Wanda, what do you see?"

"Darkness. The highway. Maybe some trees."

"Look further to the left."

"It's a truck — with a trailer!"

"Bingo."

"Gabeleh!" In the blink of an eye, Ida had released her seat belt and was crawling over Agnes's lap.

I pushed the child safety lock button. "Oh no you don't, missy. Not until we have a plan."

"Plan, shman. My only son is in there."

"So is my only husband, and I say wait."

"Yah? Vell, who cares about your husband?"

"Your son and my husband are the same person, you — you — dummkopf."

"You see how dis von talks to me?"

"Catfight!" Wanda suddenly sounded happy.

"Vhere? I dunt see any cats."

"Fie on the felines," I bellowed. "There may be human lives at stake here."

The women were silent for all of two seconds. It was Agnes who spoke first.

"Get on your cell, Magdalena, and call for help."

That's exactly what I attempted to do, even though I already knew that we were out of range. That particular corner of the commonwealth is so remote that even Daylight Savings Time doesn't arrive until an hour later. Of course, the ladies had to try their own cellular phones, and with each confirmed lack of success, the panic level rose, like the waters of Slave Creek during the spring thaw. Something had to be done before the more volatile ones, like Ida, flipped their lids.

"Don't worry, ladies," I said, "I have an idea."

"Dis better be *gut,*" Ida said. "It vas your idea dat got us here in the first place!"

"And to think," Wanda said, "I could be back at the Sausage Barn watching *Jeopardy.*"

"Listen to Magdalena," Agnes said sharply. "The woman is a genius at getting out of impossible situations. Why, once she even brought down a giantess by using her bra as a weapon."

"Oy, such an imagination dis von has."

"She's telling the truth," I said. "I used my Maidenform as a sling. One well-placed stone, and that giantess was down on her knees. Just like David slew Goliath, only I didn't kill the giantess, and I certainly didn't cut off her head."

I could feel Ida's eyes roll in the dark. "*Nu,* so now you are David? Somehow I dunt tink so."

"I may not be David," I said, "but despite all this yammering, I've come up with a plan. Does anyone want to hear it?"

"I do," Agnes said.

"So do I," Wanda said.

I had to swallow my surprise before speaking again.

35

STRAWBERRY ICE CREAM RECIPE

Ingredients:
2 cups of strawberries
4 oz (100 g) sugar

3 egg yolks (beaten)
1/2 pint (250 ml) milk
1/4 teaspoon salt

1 pint (500 ml) double/heavy cream
1 teaspoon of vanilla extract

Take the strawberries, and mash them in with half the sugar in a bowl. Place in the refrigerator whilst making the rest of the recipe. In a separate saucepan, mix the egg yolks with the milk, salt, and the remaining sugar. Place over a medium heat *just* to boiling point, stirring all the time. *Do not let it boil.*

Transfer the mixture into a chilled bowl to

cool. When cool, place in the refrigerator for up to three hours, remembering to stir the mixture from time to time. When cool, stir into the mixture the cream and vanilla extract and then blend in the strawberry-sugar mixture.

Transfer the complete mixture into an ice cream maker, and follow the manufacturer's instructions.

36

My plan was simple: Agnes would stay with Ida, while Wanda and I reconnoitered the pickup and trailer. I chose to have my nemesis accompany me because she was in better physical shape than the other two, and frankly, because she hated me so much; if I were to die, Wanda would have the most to lose. I mean, with me gone, who could she possibly loathe so deeply? Absolutely no one. All the joy would drain from her life, and she'd be just another miserable, middle-aged woman with posters tacked to the walls of her office. Therefore, it was in her best interest to see that I survived whatever it was that lay ahead.

At any rate, we weren't more than ten feet from the car when we noticed — simultaneously, I might add — a flicker of light deep in the woods. I was the first to react.

"Look," I whispered. "A light."

"Jinx, you owe me a Coke."

"Diet or regular? Caffeine or no? Lime flavored or cherry? Really dear, you need to be more specific."

"You see how difficult you are?"

If you can't beat them — even after sticking a hot dog down her bun — you might as well join them. "Indeed, I do. I am an evil woman, the great-great-grandspawn of Attila the Hun. In fact, if I wasn't a Mennonite, I'd become an Anglican, just so I could call myself a Despicopalian."

"Now you're just mocking me."

"Not just now. Hey, look, the light is really a fire!"

"Are those people I see, or deer?"

"People. But they're all in silhouette. Anyway, we're too far away to make out their faces. Still, we better keep our voices down."

"Who said you could tell me what to do?"

"Scream and shout then, for all I care. What's the worst that can happen? Maybe they have a gun; maybe they'll shoot. I could get hit and die. Then whom will you hate? While you're trying to find a replacement Magdalena, I'll be flip-flopping about Heaven learning how to fly. I might even try rollerblading on those golden streets."

"Okay, you win. But you have to shut up as well."

"Agreed."

"And no fair dying until I tell you so."

"Yes, ma'am."

We crept along in silence — well, relative silence. I'd read *The Deerslayer* as a girl, and one of the things that I'd always remembered about that book was the description of Indians moving silently through the woods — so silently, in fact, that nary a twig snapped. By comparison, Wanda and I were a pair of pregnant rhinos. Nevertheless, when Wanda next spoke, even though it was in a whisper, I nearly jumped out of my brogans.

"But if you do kick the bucket," she said, "and assuming that Heaven even allows rollerblading — there are liability issues, you know — reserve a pair of skates for me. I wear size eight triple-A. You wouldn't believe what a burden it is to have such narrow feet."

"Issues?" I hissed irritably. "Who would sue God?"

"Plenty of people. After all, He is very rich. America is the most litigious society on earth, Magdalena. You ought to know that, seeing as how a woman fell down your impossibly steep stairs. As I recall, she died — didn't she?"

"Yes, but folks can't get hurt in Heaven."

"Maybe not, but I bet they still make you sign a waiver."

"Listen! I think that's my beloved's voice."

"Don't be stupid, Magdalena. The Lord doesn't mind if we joke about —"

"My *husband's* voice."

We listened; sure enough, it was the Babester. He sounded tired. Also extremely sad.

"By all means kill me," he said, "but let the child go."

"I'm not a child!"

"The kid's got spunk," a familiar male voice said.

"Which means that if we let her go, she'll turn us in. A normal kid you can threaten, but not this brat."

"Hey! I ain't no brat."

"You are so."

"Ain't!"

"You are. Now shut up, before I make you."

"Go ahead and try, you old witch."

"Now you're asking for it. How does a pair of cement boots sound? After I get you fitted, I'll toss you into a farm pond. Or better yet, I'll find a swimming pool and make you walk the diving board, like pirates make their captives walk the plank. Of course, with your cement boots on, you'll be hopping the plank, not walking."

She laughed cruelly. Suddenly I knew her identity — Plain Jane! I almost said the words aloud. Just wait until I got my mitts on that disagreeable woman; I'd think of something very un-Mennonite — possibly even Methodist — to do to her. The nerve of that woman, threatening my pseudo-offspring, my demi-daughter. And how dare the two of them threaten the Babester?

Wanda and I crawled on our bellies until we were so close to the campfire that we could feel its heat. I could scarcely believe what mine eyes beheld: my loved ones were trussed up like turkeys, their hands and feet bound with plastic clothesline. It was only by calling upon all my willpower, and of course, the help of the Lord, that I was able to refrain from charging at the Pearl-mutters right then and there. It was Wanda, bless her hating heart, who insisted that we retreat and sort things out a bit first. Who knew it was possible for a person you'd like to pinch to actually help out in a pinch?

"I've come up with a new plan," I said to Wanda.

"Does it involve knocking the stuffing out of that witch?" Unlike Alison, Wanda used the B-word.

"You bet your bippy," I said, trumping her

with two B-words of my own.

"I am supposed to do *vhat?*"

"We have to distract them," I said, "and the best way to do that is to get them to chase their prize-winning cow through the woods."

That was the essence of my plan. While the Pearlmutters beat the bushes for their buxom bovine, Agnes and Wanda would untie Alison and Gabe. If the situation called for it, both women were more than willing to physically engage the pair of kidnappers (alas, my strict Mennonite upbringing still held sway, and I was pretty much limited to pelting giantesses with pebbles). Wanda, on the other hand, wanted to extinguish the campfire by dragging Jane through it by her hair (although a liberal Mennonite, Wanda has a bit of Baptist blood coursing through her veins). Not to be outdone, Presbyterian Agnes expressed an eagerness to sit on Dick Pearlmutter while she pummeled him with her relatively tiny fists.

Ida had initially been enthusiastic about my plan, until she learned what her role was to be. Although my warriors had long since crept into place, Ida was still staring up at the cow. To be fair, it towered above her.

"You vant me to ride dis beast?"

"She's a cow. Just think of her as a well-endowed horse."

"I dunt ride horses neither."

"Then what are you waiting for? They say that senior citizens who try new things live sixty-point-three percent longer."

"Longer den vhat?" Despite her thick accent, my mother-in-law had not fallen off the turnip truck — at least not in recent times.

"Longer than fruit flies, dear."

"Den get da flies to ride da cow."

"Ida, dearest mother-in-law, we have to do this in order to rescue your son. This cow is worth a lot of money to the Pearlmutters. If it's lost, that's all they'll think about for the moment. You saw me try to push the cow off the trailer; she wouldn't budge. But if someone is sitting on her back, that might do the trick."

"Den vhy dunt you climb on?"

"Because I'm too heavy, and could damage her spine. Cows aren't meant to be ridden like horses. But a pint-size thing like you — that's a compliment, dear — well, she'd barely know you were there."

"Den vhat difference vould it make?"

"Trust me, you'd be just enough of an irritant to get her going."

331

"Oy, da tings I must do in dis life."

"So you'll do it? Please, pretty please? With sugar on top?"

She sighed deeply. "Vell, maybe, eef —"

There was no time for eefs, ands, and buts. Can I be blamed, then, for taking this as tacit agreement? I think not. After all, a mind half made up is like a cake half eaten: if one's come that far, one might as well commit to the rest. So, to save her the trouble of committing further, I scooped up the scrappy little New Yorker, and plopped her on the cow's broad back. Unfortunately — for Ida, that is, not the cow — I'd set her down facing the animal's patooty. I grabbed the startled cow's tail and thrust it at Ida.

"Hold tight to this with both hands."

"Help!" she yelped. "I vant off da cow now."

"This is no time to be rhyming, dear." I gave the animal a good swat on the rump, causing her to bolt from the trailer like Mrs. O'Leary's cow from a barn on fire. Within seconds, human and Holstein were crashing through the woods like some prehistoric creature (not that there ever really was such a thing, mind you).

I cupped my hands to my mouth. "There's a cow loose! Help, somebody! Help me catch this cow before she gets hit by a car

— or eaten by a bear."

For the record, the sound made by two greedy people crashing through a woods is almost equal to that made by a prize-winning cow. I listened happily to the noise, secure in the knowledge that my SWAT team — Scrawny Wanda and Agnes the Tremendous — were loosing my loved ones. Stupidly, I neglected to get my own keester out of harm's way while I had the chance.

37

"Well, well, look what we have here," Jane said.

Dick was less happy to see me. "Forget about her right now. We can't let the cow get away."

"We can't let her get away either," Jane snarled. Fortunately for her, she had a revolver to back up her attitude.

Unfortunately for me, I had only my mouth. "Oh, look, see spotted cow run. See Dick run. See Jane run. See Dick and Jane run after cow."

"Shut up!"

"Oh, oh, oh. See, see, see. See Jane get mad. See Jane puff."

"I said shut up. If you don't, I'll shoot."

"Darn it, Jane," Dick said (although to be sure, his language was a mite rougher than that), "we've got to catch that darn cow, or else we're really up stick creek without a paddle."

"Look, look, look. See Dick get mad at Jane. See Dick and Jane get mad at each other. See spotted cow run very, very far. Run, spotted cow, run, run. See Dick and Jane in jail for kidnapping."

Perhaps I'd gone too far, because by now Jane really was puffing. Even worse, she was holding her revolver at eye level.

"You think you're being funny, Miss Yoder, don't you?"

"Perhaps a wee bit."

"It's not funny," she grunted through clenched teeth.

"Come on, you must admit that the thought of you two serving twenty years in prison, thanks to my mother-in-law riding bareback on a cow, is worthy of a chuckle or two." I tried to illustrate my point by chuckling, but instead produced several cackles that would be the envy of hens everywhere. "But seriously, folks, I can already picture you two in your prison duds. You, Jane, should opt for orange instead of stripes — if you get the chance. I mean, with your somewhat dumpy figure and all — well, enough said. Unless, of course, you'd like a boyfriend named Baby Sally. You, Dick, on the other hand, are a very handsome man, and are sure to draw admirers no matter what your choice of prison clothes. How would you feel about a girl-friend named Thumper Bob? He has a six-inch scar across his face and only two fingers on his right hand, thanks to a game called chicken."

Jane's plain little eyes narrowed to slits, and her revolver began to shake. "I *will* shoot. Don't tempt me."

"Oh, oh, oh, see Jane shoot. Shoot, Jane, shoot. See Jane go to prison for the rest of her life."

"She's right," Dick said. "If we kill her, we don't stand a chance of seeing daylight for the rest of our lives."

"That's not true at all," I heard myself say. "I heard that they have a little courtyard that they let you wander around in for an hour a day. You have to share it with the other convicted killers, but that goes without saying. I mean, count your blessings, right? Because the rest of the time, you'll be working in a hot, steamy laundry room, or stamping out license plates. My point, dears, is that it won't be all drudgery — just mostly. Of course, to be fair, I must point out that Baby Sally and Thumper Bob will undoubtedly both be eager to offer you emotional, as well as physical, comfort."

Even though it was a moonless night, I could see Dick's fist resting on his hips. "It's

Jane's fault," he said, spitting out the words like they were bits of rhubarb.

The gun swayed widely while Jane struggled to keep her focus. "Oh yeah? You begged me to operate on that darn cow. It was your chance to make a name for yourself, you said. Failed stockbroker who can't make it in the big city finally becomes somebody."

Dick turned to me. "Don't listen to her. I was a big name on Wall Street. I had Fortune 500 clients."

"Had," Jane said, doing some spitting of her own. "That's the operative word — *had.*"

"Pun intended, dear?"

"What?"

"Never mind."

"Then shut up!"

Dick was still looking at me. "It really was Jane's idea."

Jane snorted. "At *first* it was my idea, but I was just joking. We could take a moderately good cow and turn her into a champion — that's all I said. Then he took the ball and ran with it. Got obsessed with it."

"Well, you're both nuttier than a bag of PayDay bars," I said. "Plastic surgery on cow udders is nothing new. That's one of the things judges are instructed to look for."

"Yes, but Jane is perhaps the most skilled plastic surgeon there is, aren't you, honey?"

"I was," she said matter-of-factly. "Then Dick insisted that I give up my practice and move out of the city. He said he'd always wanted to live on a farm — like Eddie Albert on *Green Acres*."

"*Green Acres*? I loved that show! It is the only thing that was ever worth watching on TV, as far as I'm concerned."

"It was hideous. And anyway, the show had nothing to do with Dick's reason for wanting to leave New York. You see, after he got fired, he didn't want to run into his old Wall Street colleagues."

"You can be so cruel, Jane." Dick's voice quavered, almost spanning the range of two octaves.

By then I'd lost all my patience. "And *you're* not cruel? What do you call kidnapping a child?"

"*Child?*" they cried in unison. "That's no child," Dick said quickly. "That girl is a holy terror on two tiny feet — uh, you must admit, Miss Yoder, that they are considerably smaller than yours."

"A monster," Jane agreed. "She called us naive and stupid. Said we were a pair of bumbling amateurs. Offered to teach us the proper way to kidnap someone — if we paid her a thousand dollars. It was like a page out of 'The Ransom of Red Chief.' "

"That's my girl," I said proudly.

"I can't believe my ears," Dick said. "You approve of her behavior?"

"Absolutely not!" I said. "But as long as she was going to charge you anyway, at least her fee structure was reasonable. I'd have been downright ashamed had she asked for any less. Tell me, did she offer an option package?"

"Come again?"

"You know, like RABBLE. Surely you've heard of Rob A Big Bank Lessons."

"Ha!" Jane barked. "You're not so smart after all. You forgot the E."

"I did not; I'm saving it for last."

"Then what does it stand for?"

"Eternity. That's what you'll spend in Hell if you shoot me."

I heard the safety click off as she stepped forward. She was so close, I could smell sausage on her breath. The gun was now aimed at my belly. Apparently, instant death was too good for me. Instead I would die from blood loss, my innards having been blasted to kingdom come.

Although my faith prevents me from acts of violence — a few of my ancestors have actually died on that account — it also requires that I be a loving parent and a faithful wife. How could I do either if I was pushing up daisies in Settlers' Cemetery up on Stucky Ridge? Clearly, then, I had no choice but to follow my God-given instincts.

In one seamless move — no pun intended — I whipped my generous skirt over the vicious woman and clamped her in a headlock. Taken off guard, she dropped the gun, but then immediately began pummeling me about the shoulders and across my back with her fists.

"Duck, duck," she squawked, her mouth filling with gabardine each time it opened. "Hup me, duck."

I was kind enough to translate for Dick. "She's talking to you, dear."

"Uh —"

"So what will it be, Duck? Are you going to add attempted murder to your rap sheet?"

"I haven't touched you." Indeed, he hadn't moved.

"But you did bludgeon an eighty-year-old man. Either you help me restrain your psychotic wife, or you're about to become an expert on laundry."

"Miss Yoder, I swear, I don't know what you're talking about."

"Au contraire. You were there when dear, sweet Dr. Shafor crawled to the front door of the inn, leaving a trail of blood that led to the barn. Did you know that he wrote a message with his blood?"

"Honestly, I swear on a stack of Bibles, I didn't do it."

"I wish you'd stop all this swearing. You may not have done it — personally — but your wife certainly did. I saw her coming from the barn that evening, around the time it happened."

"Yeh poo-fed idjet," Jane shouted in my ear. "I tound him at tay." Either she was getting tired, or my body was getting used to her pummeling, because her fists didn't hurt nearly as much anymore.

"What Jane's trying to say," Dick said, "is that she was in the barn checking on Clarabelle — that's our entry, as you know — when she found the old man lying there. He'd already been beaten."

My headlock tightened like a constricting noose. "You *left* him there? You left an old man bleeding to death? What kind of doctor are you?"

"Mags, stop it!"

Mr. Pearlmutter's familiarity enraged me. "Looky here, slick Dick," I bellowed, "how dare you call me Mags?"

"No, hon, it's me — Gabe."

"What?"

"Mom," I heard Alison say, "it's all right. You can let her go; Agnes has the gun."

"I sure the heck do," Agnes said. "If either of them tries any monkey business, they'll be minus some toes. I have no problem shooting feet."

Suddenly I was dizzy and weak in the knees, but for some reason I couldn't let go of Jane Pearlmutter's skirt-wrapped head. I seemed to be stuck to her, like Brer Rabbit to tar baby. Who knows how long I may have held her in my grip, had not Gabe's strong hands pried my arms loose.

"I've got you, babe," he said, as I inhaled his safe, manly scent.

A second or two later, I blacked out.

38

When I came to, my head was in Gabe's lap, and we were in a moving car. Surprisingly, I felt fine. As my dear, sweet husband hadn't seemed to notice my fluttering eyelids, I decided to fake unconsciousness — just for a few minutes, mind you!

"Not only is Magdalena my hero," Agnes said, her voice swelling with pride, "but she's my best friend."

"She's my hero too," Alison said.

"Gosh, but I love her," Gabe said, as he gently stroked my cheek.

How can I be blamed then, for faking it a mite longer? The odds were that the next time I heard accolades such as these, it would be at my funeral. And since then I'd be listening to them from all the way up in Heaven, they'd hardly count.

"Harrumph," Wanda said. "Before youse award her the Purple Heart, just remember that she put a ninety-year-old woman on the back of a bull and sent her off into the woods to be eaten by black bears."

"*What?* I'm only fifty-four!" Ida suddenly seemed to have lost twenty years along with her accent.

Gabe's hand stopped in midstroke. "But you're okay, Ma, right?"

"I'm better than okay. Riding the bull was the high point of my life. Such a thrill, I tell you. It sends shivers up my dingledorf just to think about it."

"Grandma Ida, do I have a dingledorf?"

I forced myself into a sitting position. Only then did I notice that I'd been lying across Wanda and Alison's laps. Ida was riding shotgun, as they say, and, thank heavens, the normally sane Agnes was driving.

"Hon," Gabe said, "you're awake!"

"Mom!" The relief in Alison's voice made me kvell with love.

I rubbed my eyes for show. "Whew, that was some nap."

"Mom, that weren't no nap; you was out like a cold fish. What did you call her, Grandma Ida? Oh yeah, like a lump of filter fish."

"Gefilte fish," my beloved said.

"Oy, so now the leetle von gets me in trouble. Mebbe I should have stayed in New York."

I managed to rein in my smile. "I won't argue with that, dear." I glanced outside, and could see a sprinkling of lights. "Hey guys, where are we?"

"Almost back to Hernia," Agnes said, always the cheerful servant. "After I drop off your mother-in-law and the little one — and Wanda, of course — the rest of us are headed straight up to Bedford Memorial."

Alison stamped her feet, and in the process all but obliterated the smallest piggy on my right foot. On the bright side, at least now I was as fully awake as I'd ever been. I could also now wear one of those skinny-toed shoes that Susannah refers to as "roach killers" (her friend Gina chases bugs into corners, then impales them on the toes of her designer shoes).

"I am *not* little," Alison said.

"Oops," Agnes said, and giggled. "I guess compared to me, everyone is little."

Alert or not, it was still a struggle to think. "Why are we going to the hospital?"

"Because, darling, you're not well. If I wouldn't have been there to catch you, you would have fallen to the ground. You might even have gotten a first-class concussion."

"Stuff and nonsense."

"You see?" Ida crowed triumphantly. "Already she dunt make no sense."

"That's because you don't read enough English novels, dear. I'm perfectly fine. Why don't you try saying this: how much wood could a woodchuck chuck, if a woodchuck could chuck wood?"

"Hon, that's just mean."

"No," Ida croaked, "I try it already. How much vood can a vood shuck huck — oy, such shtuff and nonsense, I never hoid."

Everyone laughed. And not *at* my mother-in-law either. So much for this hero's fifteen minutes of fame; the clock must have started while I was unconscious. It wasn't fair.

"Tone it down, Ida," I said, "will you, dear? All this hilarity is hurting my head."

"Mom, you're jealous, ain't ya?"

"*Moi?* Please, everyone, I'm feeling fine. Really, I am. I just have a chip off my block — I mean I'm a chip off the old block — whatever. Now, would somebody please tell me the whereabouts of Plain Jane and her handsome hubby. Did Chief Ackerman and the sheriff haul them off trussed like Thanksgiving turkeys?"

"Mags, hon, we couldn't get through to either of those men."

"I know, only the Devil's cell phone works in that corner of the state, but the Maryland border was just a whipstitch away. All one

346

has to do to get a police escort, is press the pedal to the metal and lay on the horn."

Agnes switched from high beams to low. "That's exactly what I did, Magdalena, and was it ever thrilling. It was my first speeding ticket, you know. Anyway, the patrolman who stopped me — well, let's just say that if all goes according to plan, you could be trying on a matron of honor dress real soon."

"And I get to be a bridesmaid," Alison said.

"But Agnes, you're engaged to one of the Dorf brothers!"

"That's Dorf*man,* Magdalena. Unlike you, I've never been married; I've never even come close. Now suddenly, the heavens are smiling on me, and all because of this silly Holstein competition. I want to keep my options open, just in case one of them falls through."

"What if neither of them falls through?"

"Then who knows? I might just commit bigamy." She tinkled like a wind chime.

"Auntie Agnes," Alison said, sounding a mite worried, "if you marry that fat farmer with the cow, do I still get to be a bridesmaid?"

"Of course, honey."

"Vhat about me?"

"Sure, Ida," dear, sweet Agnes hastened

347

to say, "you can be a bridesmaid as well."

"Nut dat," Ida said enigmatically. "I mean dee otter." At least that's what it sounded like to me.

"Oh yeah," Gabe said. "After we locked those two in the cattle carrier, and before we went off searching for a highway patrolman, we had to find Ma."

"And did you?" I asked pleasantly.

"Yah, dey find me — in a tree!"

"How utterly romantic, dear."

"You see, Gabeleh, how meshugah dis von is? Better you should marry da zaftig von. Wid dose hips, she's got to be foidle, and wid so many men chasing after her — vell, mebbe dey know someting, yah?"

"Ma, that's a terrible thing to say. And besides, I'm already married to the crazy one."

Honestly, my feelings were not hurt by this. At least not by the Babester's off-the-cuff comment (I'm sure he meant it lovingly). And even if I was offended, that was just too ding-dong bad, because, as I awoke from my fainting spell, it was with a clarity of vision that had thus far eluded me. Magdalena Portulaca Yoder Rosen (although officially still Yoder) had a serious crime to solve before she could take the time off to nurse hurt feelings.

Just before I'd gone under, I'd been utterly (please pardon my concussion-induced pun) convinced that the Pearlmutters were innocent of bludgeoning Doc. Now, suddenly, it hit me that Melvin's escape from prison, the assault on Doc, the men sighted running from our barn, and the break-in at Doc's place were all related. It all boiled down to one menacing mantis with wandering eyes and a brain the size of a baby pea: Melvin Stoltzfus.

Of course, I couldn't prove anything just yet. And since *real* law enforcers couldn't seem to bother themselves with my opinions, I would handle this one on my own, thank you very much. If I died in the process, then everyone would realize just how much they missed me. A grief-stricken Babester would kick his mama back to a New York curb (gently, and with the honor due a parent). Agnes would forget about marriage and devote herself to being my full-time friend (she was after all, very good at the task). Alison would rename herself Magdalena, and would strive to fill my brogans.

Perhaps even Hernia would be renamed Magdalenaville. Someone could compose a song, create a nonalcoholic drink . . . I shook myself. There would be time to daydream later. What I had to do now was play it cool, and respond to Ida's pointed remark that Agnes must be "foidle" because she had wide hips.

"And I'm *not* foidle?" I asked.

"Like da Goblin Desert, yah?"

"And *you*," I raged at Gabe, "you really think I'm crazy?"

"No — maybe — but in a delightful sort of way."

"That does it! Stop the car, Agnes."

"But Magdalena, we haven't gotten anywhere yet."

"We're on the outskirts of Hernia, for crying out loud; this most certainly is somewhere."

"Hernia's too small to have skirts," Gabe said. I think he was trying to be funny.

"Agnes! This is my car, and you are my friend, so — Oh my stars, I think I'm going to be sick."

"Sick?" My buddy may be large, but her feet are pretty darn quick. Had we not all been strapped in, one or more of us might have shot through the windshield.

"My hair," Wanda cried in dismay. "Look what you've done, Agnes. It's about to topple."

Sure enough, the infamous Hemphopple tower of vintage vermin was hanging by its last bobby pin. Even a small jolt would now send waves of filthy hair cascading in all directions, quite possibly killing us all with deadly toxins, which would then leak out the vent and spread like a plague across the nation. It wouldn't be the wrath of God that was ultimately responsible for the devastation, it would be some woman from the 1950s who had a rattail comb and a surfeit of hair spray lying around on a Saturday morning.

"Everybody out," I hollered. "I'm about to blow my cookies!"

Trust me, *that's* the fastest way to empty a vehicle. Everyone piled onto the shoulder of the road, including Agnes, who should have known better — everyone that is, except for me. My buddy even left the keys in the ignition, which is exactly what I had been hoping for.

I made a show of clambering from the backseat, but I slid into the front seat just as smoothly as a key into a greased lock. Then, just like a key is supposed to do, I locked the doors.

"Hey," Gabe yelled, "what are you doing?"

"Chocolate-covered corn and the man in the moon," I whispered, whilst moving my lips in an exaggerated manner.

"*What?* I can't hear you."

"Seventeen blue monkeys are running for president." I pointed to some vague spot behind him.

When he turned to look, I mashed the accelerator into the floorboard. The car lurched forward, leaving everyone in the lurch. This unfortunate fact was regrettable, but could not be helped.

Besides, it wasn't like I left them in a dangerous situation. Outside of murder, there is very little crime in Hernia. Our worst offender is probably Cynthia Higgins-bottom, who is fond of stroking ankles without their owners' permission. With the Pearlmutters under arrest, my friends and family were safe — except, perhaps, from each other. I, on the other hand, had several metaphorical miles to go before I could sleep.

Doc's front door was ajar, permitting a spear of light to bisect his porch. After pausing to pray for a second or two, I pushed it open the rest of the way. I thought I knew what to expect, but boy was I dead wrong. I stood staring, dumbfounded, until she spoke first.

"Close the door, please dear. It's getting cold in here."

"Yeah, Yoder," he said. "Were you raised

in a barn?"

"Fancy meeting you here," I said, having rejected a string of invectives unworthy of a Presbyterian, much less a Mennonite.

"I knew you'd be back," he said. "That's why I took the risk of returning to this dump."

"It's not a dump; it's quite cozy. You of all people shouldn't be one to complain."

"Skip the lecture and just bring your sister to me."

I glared at his mother. "How can you be okay with this? You can't possibly think you're somehow helping him."

"Shut up," he said, "and do as I say. That is, unless, you want someone to get hurt."

"Hurt? You'll be ruining her life if you convince her to go with you. You'll ruin your mother's life too."

"My mother's life is none of your business."

The Good Lord shut the lion's mouth for Daniel, but it was Mrs. Stoltzfus who shut mine. "It *is* her business, Melvin," she said.

"Mama." He managed to drag it out into an eight-syllable whine.

"Shut up, Melvin," she said. Her voice lacked invective, but not authority.

"Yes, Mama."

Elvina Stoltzfus turned her full attention

to me. "Please forgive my boy, Magdalena. It isn't his fault — the way he behaves, I mean."

"You mean because he was kicked in the head by a bull? One he was trying to milk?"

"I was only nineteen," the mantis said. Perhaps it was due to his mother's presence, or perhaps it was due to the lack of starch in his prison clothes, but he did seem almost boylike. He certainly appeared smaller than I remembered.

Elvina Stoltzfus was in her mid-eighties. Although she'd been flirting with the Grim Reaper for several years, she reacted now with surprising vigor.

"I have to face it, Magdalena: I'm responsible for the miserable way my son turned out."

Miserable? Were my ears deceiving me? For years, I'd been referring to the mantis as miserable, all the while believing I was being unkind. But if his mother thought this, then I'd merely been making an honest observation.

Melvin's eyes bulged more than usual, causing his head to wag to and fro like a bobble-head doll. It was a wonder he could maintain his balance.

"You didn't do anything wrong, Mama, because I turned out all right."

She dismissed her son with the wave of a shriveled hand. "I shut down emotionally after I gave you away, Magdalena. I felt as if my soul had been ripped out of my chest. I had no business marrying anyone then, much less your father."

"My *father?* Forgive me, Elvina, but did that bull kick you as well?"

She blinked. "You really *don't* know?"

"I know plenty. I know that you Stoltzfuses are as nutty as a pecan pie."

"I honestly thought you knew — that they'd told you — and that's why you treated your brother so bad."

"That would be 'badly,' dear, if it made any sense. I don't have a brother, and since my parents have both been dead for over a decade, it's probably safe to say that I never will have a male sibling."

The mantis couldn't seem to follow these bizarre babblings any better than I could. "Mama, tell her to call Susannah and make her come over so we can get out of here."

But Elvina was not in the mood to indulge her son. "Be quiet, Melvin, so I can talk to your sister."

That's when the Devil possessed me lock, stock, and barrel. "Crackers," I said, and made a circular motion whilst pointing to my head. "Polly wants a cracker."

355

If Elvina was offended by my rude behavior, she didn't show it. "I was only fifteen when I became pregnant with you. I was too young to get married, and, of course, having an abortion was out of the question. I was a good Mennonite girl; we didn't get pregnant, and if we did — well, I had no choice but to go away and visit the proverbial aunt in some faraway city. But you see, I couldn't bear never to see my baby, not to watch her grow up." She took a deep breath, setting in motion rivulets of tears that coursed down the creases of her face. "Then I remembered your parents, that they'd been married for years and never had children. Fortunately, I had a real aunt who was in on my secret, and she approached your mother, who then talked with your father."

"Please excuse me," I said, "while I wobble over to the couch and lie down." I arranged my lanky frame over Doc's much-used loveseat. "Go on, dear, with your utterly fascinating deconstruction of my life."

"I'm sorry, Magdalena. I really am — for breaking the news, I mean. I always thought you knew."

"Ha! If I'd even as much as suspected that there might be a ghost of a chance that your murdering son and I were more closely related than third cousins, I would have jumped from my silo onto a strategically placed pitchfork."

She had the temerity to feign shock. "Well! I must say I am surprised that your mother didn't raise you any better than that."

"But her mama wasn't her mama," Melvin mewed. "You are."

"Hush, boy," Elvina said sharply. "Magdalena, do you want to hear the rest of the story or not?"

"Fire away when ready!" I closed my eyes, and put my hands next to my ears, just in case I needed to block out reality at a second's notice.

She wasted no time. "You see, the trick was getting the rest of Hernia to believe that it was your mother who'd given birth, not me. For the first four months, we both wore loose clothing. Then about the middle of the fifth month, we left town — not together, of course; your mother and I never got along. At any rate, I returned first, still wearing loose clothes. About a month later she returned with you in her arms. I tell you, Magdalena, the day I first saw you in her arms, I almost died of jealousy."

I opened one very skeptical eye. "Let's say, for the sake of argument, that this story is true. Who is my papa?"

39

"Why, my husband of course! May poor Siegfried Stanislaus Stoltzfus rest in peace." She seemed not to remember that her husband had been anything but a peaceful man. In fact, he had such a short fuse that he was known throughout the county as Dynamite Stoltzfus.

"Ah, but you see, there's where your tale falls apart. If Dynamite Stoltzfus really was my father, then Melvin and I would be full siblings."

"Please don't call Siegfried by that ugly name. It wasn't his fault he found everyone else so irritating."

"Hmm. There are, in fact, those who might accuse me of having a short — Never mind that. Just look at your son and I; we look nothing alike."

"You take after my side of the family, while Melvin takes after your father's."

I sat up, feeling as sick to my stomach as

I'd ever felt. "Melvin, have you heard this bizarre story before? And if so, do you believe it?"

"Of course, Yoder. Do you think I'm an idiot?"

"I don't know that your being an idiot has anything to do with this. I just want to know if you've been privy to this bit of nonsense. If so, how could you marry your sister's sister?"

"You mean Susannah?"

"Are there more?" I wailed.

"Yes, she means Susannah," Elvina said, and shook her head. "That business with the bull was so unfortunate. Did you know that my side of the family — your family — are exceptionally gifted? Your cousin Marilyn has an IQ over 150."

"If all this is true," I said, "is there anyone who can back up your story?"

"Freni Hostetler."

"*My* Freni Hostetler?"

"And mine. As you know, she's my best friend. She was the only one who really knew why I was going away, and for so long. Even Siegfried wasn't in on it."

I remember sitting still for so long that I felt as if Doc's worn-out loveseat and I were melding. Together we'd become one fossil, causing curious archeologists to postulate

359

that . . .

"Earth to Yoder. Come in, Magdalena, before I have you declared legally dead."

"Melvin," Elvina said, and clucked like a pullet whose nest had just been raided. "This is your sister you're talking to, so be nice."

"Oh yeah, my sis. Mama, does this mean she's not any better than I am?"

"Go play with your toys, Melvin."

"But Mama, I don't have any toys; you took them all away last year when I married Susannah. Remember?"

"Then just sit there and be quiet."

"I have a better idea," I said. "Go out in back and chop some firewood; it's freezing in here."

"I ain't chopping nothing for you, Yoder."

"Then do it for Mama." The word felt dirty in my mouth.

"Mama, is that what you want?"

She hesitated briefly. "Why yes, son, it is. Your sister and I need some girl time."

"But can't you do that *after* we're some-place safe? At least after she's called Susannah."

"We want to talk about our periods," I said. "Maybe even our colons and semicolons. Some of these girl things can't wait."

This time Elvina jumped right in, proving

to me once and for all that we were indeed next of kin. "Not that it's any of your business, Melvin, but your sister's diagram has come loose. If I don't help her right now, it could result in a dangling modifier."

"Maybe even an elliptical clause," I said.

"You wouldn't want that on your conscience, would you, son?"

"No, Mama."

"Good boy."

"But before you go, *brother* dear," I said not too unpleasantly, "tell me how you escaped from prison and made it back to Hernia. And why you bludgeoned a sweet old man like Doc Shafor. The nutshell version, of course."

He snorted with derision. "I snuck out in the laundry, of course, like in the movies. You pay the right person, they don't always check on the outgoing stuff."

"But you're poorer than a church mouse, for heaven's sake. The only money you had was your pitiful municipal salary and the allowance I gave you."

"You see, Yoder, you don't know anything about prison life. Payment doesn't always have to be in cash."

"Skip right ahead, dear, and tell me how you managed to make it this far. I know you didn't walk. You once rented a dolly and had Susannah push you all over the state fair."

"You always exaggerate, Yoder; it was the county fair. I was wearing my white buckskin shoes. What would you have me do? Get them muddy? And to answer your stupid question, I just stopped in at a Food Mart and got some self-tanning lotion and dark hair dye, ducked into the men's room, and presto. Of course the tan took a couple of hours in all. How do you like it?"

"It ill-becomes you."

"I'm not sure what that means, but I'll take that as a compliment."

"I knew you would. What about the other guy?"

"He was a real Hispanic. An illegal. Scared out of his wits too. He did everything I said — well, as much as he understood."

"Where is he now?" I gasped. "You *didn't,* did you?"

"Of course I did. I'm not the fool you think I am; I told him to vamoose as soon as it occurred to me to come here to Doc's."

"So you didn't kill him?"

One of Melvin's eyes glared at me, while the other appeared to glance merrily around the room. "I don't kill people just for fun, Yoder. They have to really tick me off — you get what I mean?"

"Is that a threat, dear?"

Elvina slapped her shrunken cheeks in maternal distress. "Children, please!"

As distressed as I was, I wanted nothing more than to slap Melvin's cheeks until *they* were shrunken. Alas, that was neither the Christian, nor the practical, thing to do. I swallowed a piece of my tongue and got back to business.

"How did you hook up with this guy, and how did you get back here?"

"Fortune smiled on me, Yoder. It always does. José was standing outside the Food Mart, waiting for somebody — anybody — to come by who might need a worker. He said he'd done this lots of times. And sure enough, along comes this old biddy in a truck pulling a cow trailer. She hired us on the spot. She didn't ask us any questions, and I didn't ask her how she managed to get that Holstein up on the trailer by herself. Anyway, when she made that left turn on to Route 12, I nearly crapped my pants — sorry, Mama — and when she turned into your place, I really did."

"TMI!"

"Huh? You calling me names, Yoder?"

"It means 'too much information.' Please, move right along to Doc."

"Yeah, well, that man may have had a pet

dinosaur when he was a boy, but he's no man's fool. Even though I didn't speak a word to him, he spotted me right off. He froze all up and started walking backwards. So then I *did* start to say something — like I wasn't going to hurt him, or some such — and he ran. That's when I picked up the shovel, chased him down, and gave him a good crack. *Crack* — ha! That's actually what it sounded like."

"Why you miserable little mantis! If I had a shovel right now — Get behind me, Satan!"

"Are you blind, as well as stupid? I'm standing right in front of you."

"Indeed you are. As is the Devil, who, by the way, is urging me to do you bodily harm." I took a deep breath, one which hardly felt cleansing. "Back to your sordid story. Did you spend your first night in the woods behind my house?"

"Yeah. Yoder, you really should install a toilet in that fake outhouse of yours. Hey, how did you know?"

"You were spotted by an Amish girl."

Elvina wrung her hands in the anguish only an inadvertently inhospitable mother can know. "You should have come straight to me, son. I keep a pair of fresh jammies laid out on your side of the bed — just in case."

"Again with the TMI!"

Both of Melvin's eyes connected with mine for a split second. "Oh get off your high horse, Yoder. We don't do anything wrong; we only cuddle. There's nothing wrong with cuddling with your mama. After all, I did spend nine months inside her stomach."

"That would explain some things, dear; nine months of gastric juices are bound to have an effect."

"Yeah, Mama is pretty smart. Thanks for the compliment, Yoder. That's the second time you've ever said anything nice to me."

"You're welcome, I'm sure. Before you go out and chop wood for us poor, weak females, is there anything else you need to tell me tonight? Anything you might have left out? Any nocturnal omissions, as it were?"

"Nah. You sure I need to chop wood? Can't the three of us cuddle under a blanket or something?"

"The 'or something' is that you chop. Put your shoulder to the grindstone, your head on the block, and chop, chop, chop."

"Dang it," Melvin swore, and stomped off, slamming the door behind him.

The house had barely stopped vibrating when Elvina turned to me. "Now what is it you'd *really* like to talk about, dear?"

I jumped from the loveseat, a plan taking shape in my mind. "Let's talk in the kitchen, Mama. I really don't want him to hear some of the things I'm about to say, so I need to keep track of his whereabouts."

I picked a spot between the window and the stove. From where I stood, I could see my supposed brother grappling with an ax that was almost as large as he was. If he really applied himself to the task at hand, then I'd managed to borrow a chunk of valuable time. After all, the mantis I knew couldn't cut balsa wood with a chainsaw.

His mama seemed to have temporarily forgotten him. "Magdalena, sweetie, what is it?"

"Do you love me?"

"Of course I do!"

"You gave me away."

"Like I said earlier: I had no choice. Things were different back then."

"No doubt. But you've had forty-eight years to acknowledge me. Why now suddenly? Is it to save him?"

She had to get on her tiptoes in order to peer out the window. The object of her concern had managed to subdue the ax, and was now attempting to flail a stick of kindling into submission.

"Melvin called me from Doc's phone. He wanted me to run away with him and Susannah. Of course, I said no at first. Then he let it slip that he was meeting you here. I made him promise that he wouldn't hurt you, but I couldn't let it go at that. Magdalena, my little Melvin doesn't always know what he's doing."

"I'm sure the laundry room has a supervisor."

"Always so quick with the tongue, Magdalena. Just like me when I was your age."

"Stop saying how much we're alike! Do you honestly expect me to welcome you as my mother with open arms, while you're aiding and abetting a very wicked man?"

"But I explained —"

"You say that you love me? Then prove it!"

"I'll do anything! Oh, my baby, I can't tell you how much this means to me."

"If you want me to be your daughter — *Mama* — then you have to help me do what is best for my brother."

She dabbed at her eyes with a hanky pulled from her enormous bosom. (That was another thing I had *not* inherited from her.) "But he's really a dear boy. He just needs help."

"Exactly. And that's what I plan to do: help him. I'm a wealthy woman, you know. I can afford the best help in the world. After all, nothing is too good for my brother." Even just for saying those words, I felt like a professional harlot on the Devil's payroll.

"Does that mean prison, Magdalena?"

In for a penny, in for an Enron executive's fortune. "No, of course not. They have special programs for men who do away with their ministers. It's called CHUMPS," I added quickly. "It stands for Cretins Harming Unsuspecting Mennonite Pastors."

"What? I didn't quite catch that."

"It's not important, dear. What *is* important is that we get Melvin the best help available. Maybe someday he can rejoin society as a productive member. Then he and Susannah can live happily ever after."

Although the truth was that, despite my five hundred years' worth of pacifist genes (the Stoltzfuses were every bit as inbred as the Yoders), I would sooner break both of Susannah's kneecaps than have her run off with the husband from Hades. As for what I'd be willing to do to the mantis to stop this from happening — I shudder to think of it now.

At any rate, Elvina began to do some serious thinking of her own. While on one hand this sexagenarian seemed to have all the wisdom of a teenager, and not a speck more, on the other hand, one couldn't help but admire her capacity for unconditional love.

What might that be like? I wondered. My own mother — by that I mean the woman who raised me — threatened to disown me if I attended the University of Pennsylvania like I wanted to. She also threatened to disown me if I was ever divorced. Surely an annulment from a bigamist counts as the same thing. In that case, since I was already disowned — albeit somewhat posthumously — why not adopt Elvina as a mother? It would mean a great deal to her, and need not have anything to do with my relationship to Melvin. Who knows, someday Elvina might even prefer me over her son. Wouldn't that fix his wagon?

"Look, Mama, we have to decide on something fast; my brother's going to get tired of chopping wood pretty soon. Paul Bunyan he's not."

"I know, sweetie, but what can we do? Your brother will never agree to institutionalization."

"He doesn't have to," I said. I grabbed

her hand, which felt strangely familiar in the "flesh of my flesh" sappy sort of way. And yes, I was being manipulative. "We just need to find something to restrain him with. Maybe some clothesline or something."

"You're not going to hurt him, are you?"

"Whatever makes you say that, dear?" Then I spied what I needed — not to restrain the mantis, but to make him amenable to the idea. Pliable might even be a better word.

"Here's an apron," Elvina whispered. "It has long strings."

"Perfect." When everything was in order, I cracked open the window. "Yoo-hoo! Melvin!"

He immediately ceased pretending to cut wood. "What *is* it, Yoder?"

"Dear little brother, I need you to come in and kill a spider for me." Believe me, the B-word did not easily fall from my lips. I fully intended to wash my own mouth out with soap when this was all over. Antibacterial soap, of course.

"Kill it yourself," he yelled, but he was already headed for the house.

Despite Elvina's murmured protests, I met Melvin at the back door with a raised skillet — one which I did not hesitate to bring down soundly on his oversized noggin. My nemesis crumpled to the floor like a dropped marionette.

"I can forgive you for almost anything, Melvin," I said, feeling sick to my stomach, "but not for making me do this."

"What have you done to my son?" Elvina wailed, proving that we were indeed related.

"Better safe than sorry, dear," I said to my newfound mother. Then I selected a smaller pan from Doc's formidable collection of cookware, and gave Elvina her own personalized whack on the head.

40

CREAMY ORANGE ICE CREAM RECIPE

Ingredients:

1/2 pint (250 ml) double/heavy cream

1/2 pint (250 ml) single/light cream

2 oz (50 g) sugar (more if you prefer sweeter ice cream)

2 cups of fresh orange juice

Gently stir together the cream, sugar, and orange juice, and then beat until creamy.

Transfer the complete mixture into an ice cream maker, and mix/freeze according to the manufacturer's instructions.

41

I awoke to find Elvina Stoltzfus sitting by the head of my bed in Bedford County Memorial Hospital. She was reading me "The Three Little Pigs" out of a large and ragged volume of fairy tales.

"Then I'll huff, and I'll puff, and I'll blow your house down."

Up until that point, I'd had my eyes closed. I opened one warily just to confirm my circumstances. Satisfied, I shut it again.

"As you may recall, dear, my house is fairly new, seeing as how it was rebuilt after the tornado of 2004. If you puff that hard, you might give yourself a hernia."

"My baby!" she cried, and throwing aside the book, threw herself on me. Alas, after a lifetime of feasting on the three main Mennonite food groups — lard, sugar, and starch — Elvina is a well-rounded woman. It was like being hugged by a small whale

— one with exceptionally dexterous flippers.

"Argh, I can't breathe."

"Praise the good Lord! You've come back to me!"

"But I'll be leaving real soon if you don't get off of me." Each word was accompanied by a dying breath; about this I do not exaggerate.

"Always so quick with the wit," she said, but eventually redistributed most of her weight onto her flippers.

I gasped, filling my lungs with sweet oxygen. "Where exactly am I, and what am I doing here?"

She told me a whale of a tale — one as hard to swallow as that of the three little pigs. According to her, she found herself lying on the floor of Doc's kitchen, playing hostess to the mother of all headaches. In fact, her head was still throbbing, and the only thing making it bearable was the knowledge that I had merely passed out, and not, as she'd originally suspected, knocked on Heaven's door.

"Where's what's-his-name?" I said.

"You mean your brother, Melvin, right?"

"I mean the convicted murderer who goes by that name. Frankly, Elvina, I'd rather have a rattlesnake for a brother than Melvin.

374

At least a real snake can be defanged. I could put it in a terrarium, which I'd keep in the barn along with some other harmless critters. Maybe a one-eyed sheep, a lame horse, a two-headed calf — Magdalena's Menagerie, I'd call them, and charge tourists ten bucks a head to get a gander. Oh, not a real gander, of course; I meant a looksee. Real ganders, as you know, are ornery. Tell me, do you think ten bucks is too much? There'll be other animals as well; one of my chickens this year has just a hint of a third leg."

Elvina stood back to gaze at me lovingly, and that's when I noticed that we were not alone. Had Elvina's fairy tale been about Snow White, I might be inclined to comment that it was Grumpy I beheld lurking in the shadows.

"Why, Freni," I said happily, "step forward and announce yourself."

"Ach, just as crazy as ever! I am glad, Magdalena."

"So you heard what happened."

"Yah, I heard."

"Is it true that Elvina Stoltzfus gave birth to me?"

"Yah, I was there."

"You've known this my entire life, but never said a thing until now. Is it only because the jig is up?"

"Ach, I keep secrets, yah, but I do not dance."

"Freni, you've been like a — uh — mother to me. Why did you keep the truth from me?"

Although still unable to properly hang her head, she came pretty close this time. "I did not keep this matter *from* you, Magdalena, I kept this a secret *for* Elvina. You know that I cannot lie." Her chin came within a hair's breadth of touching her bobbling bosom. "Perhaps someday you can forgive me, Magdalena."

"Perhaps — Oh, what the helmet! Come here, Freni."

She shuffled to my bedside without making eye contact.

"Now throw yourself on me, like Elvina did."

She straightened, her eyes as wide as hens' eggs. "Ach," she squawked.

"I have every reason to be mad at you for the rest of your life, so either give me some love — English-style — or deal with the consequences." The consequences were, by the way, inconsequential; I could never deny forgiveness or friendship.

Poor Freni is too stubby to throw herself into my arms without first climbing onto the bed, like a mountaineer assaulting Everest. And like the mountaineer, the effort (and perhaps lack of oxygen) exhausted her, so that she was gasping by the time she was safely ensconced in my arms.

"I love you, Freni," I murmured.

"Ach!"

Aware that I'd already tested her limits, I did nothing more than give her a light squeeze and then gently pushed her off. She made it safely back to her feet, where she stood panting with excessive vigor. As long as she huffed and puffed, she didn't have to speak. This was fine with me, so long as she didn't blow my house down.

"Just so you know," I finally said, addressing the duplicitous duo, "although I've forgiven you both your lies, that doesn't mean I'm happy with you — either of you. Nonetheless, Elvina, I must admit that I admire you for turning in your son."

"But Magdalena, I didn't."

"A mother and her chrysalis — *What* did you say?"

"By the time I recovered consciousness, Melvin was already gone."

I stared into her eyes; it was like staring into a mirror, but perhaps sixteen years into the future. Her calm gaze said it all.

"Did you at least call the police?"

"Yes, dear, I told them about Melvin just as soon as I'd asked them to send an ambulance for you."

"Elvina has a huge bump on her head," Freni said. "Melvin almost killed his own mother, yah? Whoever heard of such a thing? Elvina, show Magdalena the bump your son gave you."

For the first time I noticed that she was sporting a large square of gauze on the back of her head. It covered a lump the size of a navel orange.

"It looks like *you* should be in bed."

"I am," she said. "Well, I was, until Freni told me that the coast was clear."

"What?"

"It is Nurse Latchkey," Freni said, her gentle, loving spirit sagging just a bit. "She has forbidden you to have visitors. I sit in the wait room all night, and only now she goes."

"*All night?* How long have I been here?"

"Hmm, it is now almost noon. You know I am not so good at the math."

"The nurse left only because Freni bribed her with her buns," Elvina said helpfully.

I stole a peek at Freni's rear end. It was safe to say that my cousin's caboose had not left the station in a long time — maybe even years. Elvina must have been referring to Freni's famous cinnamon rolls.

"Yah, forgive my pride," Freni said, "but others have said that my buns are very tasty. English men, especially, lust after them."

"And with good reason, dear." I wiggled back against my pillows until I'd pushed myself into a sitting position. "I feel fine. Where's the doctor? What's wrong with me?"

"We do not know. The doctor said she would not tell us this until you woke up and we were all together — the whole family, yah?"

Elvina shot me a pleading glance. "Okay, dear," I said, "you can hang around, but on the fringes. But until there's been a DNA test, you are still just a provisional birth mom. No offense intended."

Elvina lit up like a jack-o'-lantern with two candles inside. "None taken. And Magdalena, it's going to prove that we are mother and daughter, and we're going to be so happy —"

Fortunately for me, the door swung open, cutting Elvina off in mid-gush.

"Susannah," I cried. "Oh, Susannah, Susannah!"

"That's my name, Mags. Don't wear it out."

"It's just that I'm so happy to see you."

"And surprised?"

"Yes, as a matter of fact."

"Well, that bites."

"Susannah, don't be vulgar!"

"Yeah, but are you saying that you think I'd actually run away with that jerk?"

I waggled my brow in the direction of Elvina.

"So?" she said. "I see his mother; I'm not blind. But that creep had the nerve to wake me up in the middle of the night by throwing stones at my window — You know, the window of the room I'm staying in at Gabe's. He begged me to run away with him. We could go to Argentina, he said, if I did a little waitressing in Philadelphia — or something *else* — to earn the money."

"What else?" Freni and Elvina demanded simultaneously.

"Let me explain, dears," I said. "Ladies, you may recall that Genesis, chapter 38 — the entire chapter, as a matter of fact — is about a woman named Tamar. Anyway, she pretends to be something she's not, in order to seduce her father-in-law."

"Ach, a Protestant!" Freni's stubby hands were clamped to her chubby cheeks in a gesture of pure horror.

"The word is *prostitute,* dear. But yes, Elvina's son wanted his wife to sell herself on the street. Do you still think he's so sweet?"

As for Elvina, she looked so crestfallen that I almost felt sorry for her. "Well," she said at last, "at least I have a daughter."

"Huh?" Susannah grunted.

"Never mind, Sis, it's a long story."

"Sorry I missed it, but on my way into the building, I ran into Attila the Hunette. She was just getting off a double shift, and she looked meaner than, uh — no offense, Mags — but she looked crabbier than even you can look sometimes. When she recognized me as being your sister, she almost bit my head off. She said that you need your sleep, and that under no circumstances was I to set one foot into this room."

"How did you get past her?"

"I bribed her with the promise of a date."

I tried in vain to stifle a gasp. "But you don't shving — I mean, swing — that way. *Do* you?"

"Swing, swang, swung, whatever. Besides, we're only doing coffee. After what's-his-name, anything has got to be better."

"He's still my son," Elvina wailed.

"Funny," Susannah said, "but Elvina sounds remarkably like you when she wails —"

The door opened yet again, this time

admitting a mop of brown hair atop a body every bit as skinny as a mop handle. "Mom!" it squealed with happiness. "Mom!"

Alison needed no encouragement to throw herself into my open arms. She proceeded to hug me so hard that I made a mental note to ask the doctor for a full set of X-rays — *if* she were ever to show up.

"Are you all right, dear?" I asked.

"Mom, I'm fine as frog's hair, like you always say. What about you? You're the one in the hospital." She stiffened in my arms. "Hey, ya don't have cancer, do ya? Like Jenny's mom?"

"No, dear, I'm sure it's nothing worse than the flu."

She jumped off the bed. "Ya coulda warned me. What if I catch it now?"

"But if you catch it, you'll get to stay home from school."

"But that's the problem; I want to go to school!"

I leaned back against the pillows. "What is the world coming to? Alison wants to go to school? Alison, you hate school."

"Yeah, but that was then; this is now."

"What's changed?" I asked warily.

"I bet it's a boy," Susannah said.

Alison beamed. "His name is Rambo

Kauffman. Yesterday he smiled at me. Of course, I had to drop a pencil to make him do it."

"Did you say Rambo Kauffman? Is that his real name? You don't happen to know his parents' names, do you?"

"Mom, how the heckle should I know? Kids don't talk about that kind of stuff. But I think I heard him telling Mindy that his dad owned a gun store over in Bedford."

That was the missing puzzle piece. Twenty-odd years ago, Walter Kauffman broke his parents' hearts by opening the weapons store, and shortly afterwards moved from Hernia to Bedford. I hadn't heard a word about him since (no matter whom I asked), because Mennonites are not a gossiping people.

"Mom, he's, like, really hot. All the girls like him."

"Were you wearing a loose blouse?" Susannah asked. "Remember, the looser the better."

"Susannah!" I turned to face my young ward. "Boys only pretend to like the tramps. I was always as virtuous as a turnip, and just look at the handsome men I've attracted: your father, your pseudo-stepfather —"

"Ew! Gross, Mom. They ain't hot; they're

my dads."

"Point made. Say, dear, how did you manage to sneak into this room?"

"I already knew that Nurse Hatchet weren't gonna let me in, so I kinda borrowed one of Cindy's hamsters. I let him loose down the hall, and started yelling that I'd seen a rat."

I turned away before smiling proudly. When I looked back, my Dearly Beloved, and his beloved mama, had taken their places at my bedside.

Ida was not given to preambles. "Der's da voman who tried to kill me!"

"Moi?"

"De bull," she bellowed, wagging a finger in my face. "You make me ride dis vild bull into da voods mit bears."

"Sounds like a stock report," I said, keeping my cool. "And since you ended up still on the bull, I'd say you came out ahead. You did manage to hang on, didn't you?"

"Hon," Gabe said softly, and then leaned so close that I could tell he'd had Grape Nuts for breakfast. "You must admit that was going too far; poor Ma was scared out of her wits. Can you at least acknowledge her pain?"

Her pain? What about everything I'd gone through? There had to be some kind of way to shut her up, to turn her son's focus from her and onto me, the woman to whom he should be cleaving.

While I have been known to think fast on my very large feet, I must now, in all humility, confess that I'm also pretty good whilst doing naught but occupying a prone position. On second thought, my marital life is none of your business. Now where was I? Oh yes, the point I wanted to make is that just because I was bedridden didn't mean I was bereft of ideas.

"Oh, Ida," I gushed, "I almost forgot. As mayor of Hernia, it is my pleasure to inform you that you are going to be awarded our very first Medal of Honor."

There were several suitable gasps, but Ida's was not among them. "A medal?" she croaked. "For vhat?"

"For meddling, of course — well, that and riding that fearsome Holstein through the gloam and bracken while I just sat idly by and watched the kidnappers turn themselves in."

"Mags," Gabe hissed, "now you're mocking her."

I pretended to stare at the ceiling. "Is there any chance — any chance at all — that the gander will see that what's good for one goose is also good for the other? If not, perhaps this flock should disband while they all three seek counseling." As I waited for him to reply, I drummed on my tum-tum with my fingers.

"You guys, *please* stop fighting," Alison said.

The pain inflicted by her words was similar to that of being stabbed with a Teflon spatula. It hurt like the dickens, but I knew it wasn't fatal, just as I knew my marriage could be saved if Gabe and I both committed ourselves to working on it.

"We're not fighting, dear," I hastened to assure my chosen child. "Your dad and I are merely negotiating our priorities."

"Maybe *you* are," my love buckets said, "but I'm not." He grabbed his sainted mother's elbow. "Come on, Ma, let's go home and wait for Magdalena to call with her apology."

"He's only kidding," I said in a loud, unrecognizable voice. "Tell her that you're just joshing. Tell her how *you* managed to sneak past Nurse Ratched."

"I didn't sneak past anyone," Gabe said. "There was no one at the door."

As if on cue, the door burst open and a beaming Agnes billowed into the room. Hard on her heels was Dr. Rashid.

"You're not going to believe it, Magdalena," my buddy boomed.

"Believe what?" I said, as I watched my cuddle bunny slip from the room. He was holding his mother's hand.

"Magdalena, there is something I must tell you." Dr. Rashid's voice was like a wind chime that was being stroked by the softest of breezes.

"Talk away, dear; the stage is all yours."

"But first we must get your husband back into the room."

"Whatever it is, you can tell him later."

"Perhaps. But surely you want the others to leave."

"Oh no, they stay. Now out with it, because you're making me antsy. Is it the big C?"

On any given day, Dr. Faya Rashid was a spectacularly beautiful woman, but at the moment her normally symmetrical features were twisted like a gargoyle's. She cleared her throat three times before attempting to speak.

"I — Oh, my gracious, this is very difficult to explain."

"Give it the old college try, dear."

"Miss Yoder, there was an oversight at the lab; a serious mistake was — uh — made."

"*Quelle surprise.* But just so you know, I harbor no ill feelings. I will, of course, be buried in Settlers' Cemetery up on Stucky Ridge. That part is not negotiable. And the epitaph on my headstone is going to read GONE HOME. But outside of that, I'm quite flexible — by that I mean that if there is anything in my service that you think would offend a woman of your religious persuasion, I'm willing to consider revising my plans. Although I don't anticipate a problem, given as how I'm already stripping it of its essential Christian character in order to accommodate an ungrateful husband."

"No, Miss Yoder —"

I grabbed Alison's hand and squeezed tightly. "Don't you worry for a minute, dear. We won't stop praying for a miracle. All things are possible with God."

"You can say that again," Agnes blurted, and in the most inappropriate of tones.

I gave my friend an appropriately stern look and got back to business. "Where is the big C, Doc? I want to visualize the location when I pray."

"But you don't have cancer, Miss Yoder!"

"Don't be silly. Of course I do."

"Listen to me," she said, sounding impatient for the first time since we'd met over a year ago. "You don't have cancer; you are *pregnant.*"

"Very funny, Doc, but not very believable,

since I know it says right there on my chart that I'm forty-eight years old. Besides, I haven't had a period in — oh my gracious, oh my soul! Is it really *possible?*"

She nodded. "Because of your — uh — enhanced age, the lab did not bother to do the simple pregnancy test. For that, I deeply apologize."

"Me and my enhanced age accept your apology," I heard myself say. I'm sure I hadn't moved my lips, but what did I know for sure anymore?

"Magdalena," Dr. Rashid said, and took my other hand, "the fetus is very strong, just as you are a strong woman. I think it is possible for you to have this baby." She paused, while she squeezed my hand. "Now I will ask you a question, and you must be honest with your answer."

"Aren't I always?"

Alas, no one laughed. "Shoot, Doc."

"Shoot?"

"Spit it out!"

"But I have no gum."

"Your question. Ask me already."

"Ah yes, the American English. The question is: have you been eating properly?"

"Of course — well, that depends on one's definition of properly. But that would be a cultural one, right? We speakers of the

American English eat far too much."

Susannah thumped the mattress next to my pillow. "Just answer her question, Mags."

"Okay! You don't need to be rude about it. Look, Doc, I might not have been indulging in three squares lately on account of I haven't been feeling exactly shipshape. Actually, I kind of feel like I'm on a ship, and the sea's a bit choppy, but then what would I know what that feels like, given that I've never been on a ship? Well, not a proper one, at any rate. Once, when I visited Charleston, I took a harbor cruise. It lasted all of three very miserable hours."

"That means she ain't been eating," Alison said, "because her tummy's upset, and she wants to puke a lot."

"I see. This is a classic symptom of early pregnancy, but there are things we can try that might help."

"Wait a minute," Susannah said, "from what I heard, she fainted on her wedding night. That means she was already pregnant —"

"Way to go, Mom!"

I glared at the girl whose life I was in charge of molding. "Shame on you, dear. I was most certainly *not* pregnant then."

"But Auntie Susannah said you fainted," she whined.

"That was most probably stress," Dr. Rashid said softly. "I too fainted on my wedding night. I think maybe this fact contributed to my unfortunately delayed diagnosis. Again, I apologize."

My heart was pounding with excitement and indescribable joy. Perhaps two hearts were pounding.

"Doc, do you really think I can give birth to a healthy baby?"

"*Inshallah* — if it is God's will."

I looked wildly around the room, stupidly searching for the Babester. Of course he wasn't there. But I just knew — from the top of my bun, to the tips of my extraordinarily long toes — that he would get back on board just as soon as he heard the good news. If only he were here now! At any rate, I wasn't given much time to stew in my own juices.

"I'm finally going to be an aunt," Susannah said.

"And I'm going to have a baby sister," Alison said. "Hey, the little brat better not get into my stuff."

"Mazel tov," Freni said.

We hope you have enjoyed this Large Print book. Other Thorndike, Wheeler, and Chivers Press Large Print books are available at your library or directly from the publishers.

For information about current and upcoming titles, please call or write, without obligation, to:

Publisher
Thorndike Press
295 Kennedy Memorial Drive
Waterville, ME 04901
Tel. (800) 223-1244

or visit our Web site at:

http://gale.cengage.com/thorndike

OR

Chivers Large Print
published by BBC Audiobooks Ltd
St James House, The Square
Lower Bristol Road
Bath BA2 3SB
England
Tel. +44(0) 800 136919
email: bbcaudiobooks@bbc.co.uk
www.bbcaudiobooks.co.uk

All our Large Print titles are designed for easy reading, and all our books are made to last.

L β